# A Conundrum

# A Conundrum

P. J. PEACOCK

Library of Congress Control Number:     2016915332
ISBN:           Hardcover               978-1-5245-1754-0
                Softcover               978-1-5245-1753-3
                eBook                   978-1-5245-1752-6

Print information available on the last page.

Rev. date: 09/12/2016

**To order additional copies of this book, contact:**
Xlibris
1-800-455-039
www.Xlibris.com.au
Orders@Xlibris.com.au
748221

# Contents

## Prologue

# The Murder

He loved the early morning light, and today would be a perfect day for sailing. There was a gentle breeze, and although he knew Hera would not join him, his Savage Nautilus was small enough to sail on his own. At just under twenty feet, it was the perfect size for his use. He could and did on occasions put the boat on the trailer, and take the two girls out for a weekend trip down the coast, but mostly, he sailed 'Penelope' on their own inland lake.

The lake was a combination of nature and excavations over the years. There was a river that meandered down from the hills across the flats, through the waterhole the girls used as their own personal swimming hole, then dispersed itself into the lake. The river eventually made its way to the sea, but at this time of the year, the water levels were down. There was a tendency for the lake to flood during the wet, but that hadn't happened for years now. The lake was huge, almost like a small inland sea; and because it was fresh, water was used by all the properties around for irrigation.

There were other boats in the boathouse, but not many were out during the week; and today, being the first Monday of the month, most of the other owners were in town at the council meeting. He never did go to the meetings, and for years, when he was home, spend this day sailing regardless of the weather. He knew he would have the lake almost to himself to think, plan, and dream. A time to be alone with his thoughts, this was the time he allowed himself to think back, to experience again his beautiful wife Penelope's love. He often felt that he could feel her beside him when he sailed. He missed her with an ache around his heart and in his gut that would never leave.

It was three years now since her death. He knew the girls missed her also, but somehow, he couldn't talk about it. He could give them no comfort, perhaps because he could give himself no comfort. There was a hole inside that seemed to be growing.

Today, he had more mundane and pressing issues to consider. He was determined not to allow that bastard, George, to have any involvement in any way with his business; and he had to make sure he kept the girls away from him and his machinations. He couldn't understand how George even knew about the new contract, and why he would be interested—his forte was art fraud. But the bastard was a slippery sod, so there had to be an angle somewhere. Some within the family were still ambiguous about his involvement in that Turner fiasco all those years ago. James knew a few of the more conservative members of his family were still unsure of who or what to believe. George was the youngest of his grandfather's children, and in fact was only about five years older than James himself—just one of the problems of belonging to a family of prolific breeders.

George was on first acquaintance the perfect gentleman, charming, sophisticated with a fine sense of humour. He was tall, incredibly good looking, with dark hair, and a great body. But he was manipulative, totally self-centred, and with absolutely no discernible conscience.

George still blamed him for his inability to allow the fraud to progress, and for him calling the authorities in. There was no way James would ever become embroiled in any of George's schemes nor allow any one he knew to have anything to do with him. He was completely untrustworthy. Somehow, he had to put a stop to whatever George was planning; so first of all, he had to make contact with Justin of course. Justin would know how to deal with him.

James took his mobile from his pocket; an SMS would be the easiest for a first contact. But the day was fine, the wind just right, James felt himself relaxing. The sails were set, and with the wheel lightly clasped in his right hand, he took a deep breath of the clean clear air. He was looking forward to several hours of sailing to rejuvenate his spirits.

Relaxing in the cockpit with a beer in one hand, James thought about the immediate answer to his text message to Justin. It was disturbing, even more so than he had first envisaged, and Justin had advised caution and to remain alert. What did that mean?

He became aware of a boat with an outboard motor approaching from the shore, and someone waving to him. He brought the boat around and waited. Taking out the binoculars, he scanned the occupant of the boat. No one he knew, so he was not from around here. He was young and fit looking, but only the one man. Should not be a problem. It was strange, though, to be hailed by someone unless there was some problem at home.

James waited for the small boat to come alongside, and was reaching over to take the hand held out to him when he realised too late that the hand held a small pistol within the palm pointed at his midriff. He started to move away when the gun jerked, and he felt the pellet hit him in the chest then another and another. There had been no sound; the gun was silenced. James felt his limbs becoming heavy, his thinking becoming fuzzy; there was no pain, just his mind clouding. He had been tranquillised. Then he was falling and managed to gasp, 'Why?'

He was on his back peering up, as his assailant—he didn't recognise the young assassin—bending over him. 'It's nothing personal. You're just in the way, but don't worry, we'll look after the girls for you.' James struggled frantically against the horror of those words, as the darkness closed in around him.

## Prologue Two

# The Dream

They were running silently on the balls of their feet, trying desperately to outrun the darkness following. Somehow, she knew it was imperative to be as silent as possible. Fear filled her mind and her heart. Fear for Hera and herself. She knew they would die this day, and not easily, so they ran, they ran through the darkness, away from the awful fear generating being behind them. The rasping breath being dragged out of her straining lungs wasn't helping. Her heart was pounding, and perspiration was running down her face and into her eyes. This fear was real, the threat real, but impossible to understand. How had this happened? Bede looked to her left and saw again the dark stranger running beside them. He urged them on with whispered words of encouragement. Where had he come from? Who was he? How had he known they were in danger? What was this insanity that threatened them? And, where, where were they were running to?

He was running easily with an athlete's natural grace. His much longer legs kept pace with both of them. Why didn't he just leave them? He could probably outrun this danger, but was staying with her and her sister. His whispered words were encouraging; and somehow, the words were keeping anxiety at bay. It was like having a guardian running beside them, someone to protect and care for them, something she and Hera had fantasised about when they were younger and their father was away so much. But there was something more about this stranger, some other disturbing element flickering across the nape of her neck, and at the edges of her mind. Something familiar; she felt she should know this person.

Why had they accepted this insane challenge? What had made them think that it was a prank? This was so serious; it wasn't possible to let up. Her heart was pounding so hard, her breath rasping in her throat, and her legs starting to shake. Maybe it would be easier to just lie down and see what happened. Let the darkness envelope them all.

The dark stranger was not only keeping pace with them, he was encouraging them to keep going. Bede heard his whispered words and strengthened her legs to kept them moving. His strength reached across the distance like a physical stroking across her shoulders and down her arms. The warmth was visceral. But the anxiety and fear she felt was very real. Again, her legs started to shake. She stumbled and could not go on. The stranger running beside her, reached out; and to her amazement, swept her up into his arms, and continued to run with her. Clinging to shoulders more like steel than flesh, she wondered how he could do this? But at least her heart was slowing, and her legs had stopped shaking.

In the next instant, he murmured into her ear, 'I'm going to put you down again in a minute, so be prepared. You must continue to run. I can only help so much. You must take over again.' He pressed his lips to her temple, and then slowly moved them down to the corner of her mouth. Their lips clung for a timeless, breathless moment. His breath was warm on her skin, and his lips sent tingling sensations wherever they touched. She wanted to turn in his arms and cling, but he was already lowering her to the ground while still running, and then she too was running. He was no longer there beside them. Was she hallucinating, had he really been there? But she remembered his arms, his lips, his warm breath, and those strong shoulders. Surely he was real. She reached out and touched her sister's fingers for encouragement and reassurance. Hera managed a small chuckle. They were both running strongly now. They would reach safety this night, and later, they would discover what had really been behind the challenge issued to bring them to this underground tunnel.

# Chapter One

## Going Home

B ede rolled over in bed and slowly opened her eyes. It was very early morning. She turned to the window, and there was light just streaking the horizon. The dream had been so very real. She could still feel her heart pumping, and the fear coursing through her, her legs almost ached with remembered strain. There was something so familiar about the dark mysterious stranger. She was sure she would remember those dark mesmerising eyes and that body like steel. The feel of his arms around her and his lips on hers stirred a deep memory, or was it simply desire?

She lay quietly, still caught in the miasma of those moments. She could still feel his lips on hers and the fear running through him. She knew in the way of dreams that his fear had been for her and her sister, not for himself.

Over the last weeks, her dreams had become filled with threats of violence, and this one had been the most explicit. She thought about her young sister. Not that Hera was all that young. She was an adult with her own life, her own dreams, and desires. Still, she was the elder and had always been the decisive one, the one to solve problems.

It was time to make the journey home. The dream, or rather, the series of dreams, had become more urgent and very insistent. Swinging her legs over the side of the bed, she picked up the phone. It was not a simple matter now to leave, not since James's death. There were arrangements to be made for the office, her own apartment she could leave for a few days, and of course, her small staff.

She smiled when she thought of Mikael. He was totally reliable and had been like a rock since James was killed, providing support and compassion through that very difficult time. James had trusted him completely. She felt secure leaving the office in his capable hands.

He and James, together, had started the overseas section of the freight service. James organised the contracts, but Mikael was a wizard with computers, and his contacts in Europe and America were invaluable. His was the driving force behind that valuable aspect, the export of their native flowers. He made sure that orders arrived on time anywhere in the world. He and James had built that part of the business together. He was older and had never married, sometimes Bede felt a little guilty about the way they all took him for granted. But he never seemed to mind, and she was only ever a phone call away—thank heavens for mobile phones and laptop computers.

She never learned the details of how he and James had met. What series of events in their early lives contributed to the complete trust between them? She did know it had been somewhere in Europe, but neither of them had ever talked about it.

Mikael would organise for someone to come in to feed her cat and water the plants, or he would do it himself. He had keys to her apartment, and she didn't expect to be away for more than a couple of days—a week at the most.

Early the next morning, she was on the road, glorying in the freedom of a long and peaceful drive. The road beckoned straight northeast for the hills in the far distance. They loomed a deep purple, almost black on the horizon, haunting in their magnificence. She would drive until dusk, then eat the food she had prepared, roll out her sleeping bag, and sleep under the stars. This was her favourite time of the year; hot, but not blazing hot, the air dry with that desert dryness she loved so much. Christmas always seemed the worst, but now, January was advanced with the hint of cooler days to come. The stars at this time of the year were so clear and low on the horizon she felt she could almost touch them. There were no ambient lights anywhere to dim the brilliance, the air so clear, so free of smog and humidity, nothing to block the startling light display. She relaxed and looked forward to another long drive tomorrow.

Next morning, with her wonderful little 4WD purring, Bede allowed herself to relax. She shook her mop of glossy brown hair back from her face and gave a shout of joy. She settled to enjoy this second day on the road. There would be time enough along the way to analyse her precipitous flight.

She drove quietly with her mind drifting, remembering the last time she had been home for more than a few days. Her father had been alive then. James, her magnificent, handsome, and charismatic father with his wonderful mane of curling chestnut hair, it was always difficult to remember he was well into his 60's. It was a stupid and unexplained accident that caused his death. Sailing, he had been sailing since his earliest years, so what had caused the explosion? He did his own maintenance on the engine of the boat, and besides with the sails unfurled, the engine should not have been running. The police had never managed to make any sense of it, and even now, the case was listed as unsolved. It may have been murder, and then there had been the suggestion of suicide, which was ridiculous. Her father would never take his own life, but who would want to kill him? A simple accident didn't ring true either. He was far too careful and methodical with anything to do with his precious boat.

He had lived quietly on their property for over twenty-five years, his finances were in order, he didn't gamble or take drugs, but it was still unsolved. The unresolved case was a blot on the record of Chief Inspector Campbell, but the coroner, taking everything into account, had finally decided on an open verdict. Now, with the spate of strange and fearful dreams, it was obviously time to go back, see for herself that all was well at home.

She was in charge of the business side of the business, running the office from Perth with frequent trips to Sydney and overseas when needed, but it had been months since she had any quality time alone with Hera, well before the accident. Perhaps the threat she felt was not anything to do with the company they ran between them, but something personal Hera had become involved in. She didn't like to pry into her sister's personal life, but she needed to be reassured that there was no real danger lurking.

Suddenly, she saw again the face of the dark stranger. The image was so clear. His eyes were very dark with long lashes; he had thick unfashionably long chestnut hair tumbling across a very high forehead. His nose was straight, and his cheeks long and thin. The chin was firm and the mouth wide with thin mobile lips. She had only caught that one glimpse in the dream when he turned to her and smiled. Where had the light come from to be able to see so clearly? The flash of recognition was still with her, but she was positive she had never met this person before. There was something unworldly, almost fey, about him, but that smile had been reassuring and somehow supportive.

That last dream was still haunting her. She could still feel Hera's fingers where she had reached out to touch and to encourage. Still feel the tingle across her shoulders when her eyes met with the stranger's. Suddenly, she was anxious again; and putting her foot down, she increased the speed, ignoring the 110 kilometres limit on the road heading north. A helicopter would have been a quicker option, but the drive was one of her favourite things. To sit behind the wheel, heading into these long straight roads, the colours so strong, red soil, black hills, and the grey green of the eucalypts. Only in this environment did she feel really complete. The mystery of the mountains, the flat plains, and the blue of the sky contributed to the peace and tranquillity of the day. But the anxiety riding her wouldn't be denied.

———————◆•◆———————

As Bede swept into the driveway of the house, Hera was flying down the steps two at a time, her restless energy always driving her. She would have spotted the car half an hour ago. They met halfway across the circular drive and fell into each other's arms, laughing and talking. Neither seemed capable of completing a sentence.

Bede looked at her sister. She was so lovely, a slim 5'6", with honey blonde hair and huge soft blue eyes. Hera took after their wonderful mother, while Bede at 5'10" had her father's colouring, her hair a shiny chestnut brown with red highlights, and hazel eyes. They both had the athletic figures, which they were assured was part of their family heritage.

Bede smiled. Obviously, everything was fine, wasn't it? She determinedly put the latest dreams from her mind and turned to greet her aunt, her father's younger sister, now descending the steps in a much more sedate manner. Tall and elegant, Meredith smiled calmly at Bede in welcome. Laughing with an arm around each of these precious girls, she directed them back up the steps and into the house.

'Sorry I didn't ring, but it was a spur of the moment decision, which I will explain when I've had a drink. It was a long drive, and then I want to catch up on all the news from here.'

Later, they settled in the living room with Mrs Robinson, the housekeeper, or 'Robby' to everyone, bustling around with a tea tray and of course fresh scones. They relaxed and exchange all the latest local gossip and news.

Robby had been with the extended family forever, and had been housekeeper on the property for the last five years. With the intimacy of long standing, she smiled at Bede, 'Glad you're back for a few days, missy, you're looking a little peaked.'

Bede smiled up at her. It was really good to be home. With all three sitting quietly, Bede in her favourite armchair, Hera sitting cross-legged on the floor at her feet, and Meredith gazing pensively out the window, it was so peaceful. Bede finally felt the tension draining from her shoulders, and she relaxed. It was obvious to her now that she'd panicked for no reason.

They finally exhausted all the local gossip. Meredith looked up, drew in a long breath, and broke the companionable silence. 'Bede, I want to hear what's been happening with you, and why you have suddenly decided to visit. I suspect you have you been having disturbing dreams too? And if so, we all need to hear the details.' She fixed her with her piercing grey eyes and waited.

Bede was startled. Everything had seemed in its rightful place, and she had sensed no tension at all in the house.

Meredith continued gently, 'Hera and I have each other to discuss and analyse our dreams, but you on your own in the city, may be really disturbed by them, particularly if they're at all similar to ours.' She loved these two girls as if they were her own. Then she moved quietly across the room to close the door.

An hour later, still seated in her favourite armchair, Bede was now even more anxious and troubled. Her dreams were the most detailed, but neither her aunt nor her sister recognised her description of the stranger. Yet both had experienced similar dreams, dreams suggesting danger, of being chased, and running in fear. The fact that Bede's had become more intense and specific over the last five days was a worry.

They had learned over the years to take note and listen to the messages delivered in this way, but they had never been able to come up with a totally logical explanation. The scientist in Hera insisted that they were directly from the subconscious based on something that had not registered consciously at the time. Bede, more inclined to a more esoteric explanation, put a lot of belief in their gypsy heritage, as did Meredith. But they all agreed there was a threat of some sort on the way, and there was someone or something coming to help. The feeling of recognition and connection that Bede had experienced in her dreams was inexplicable. It had never happened before. She tried to convey her feelings about the stranger, but somehow, it was too personal to go into too many details, particularly of that brief sensual touching of lips and the laughter in those dark eyes.

This was no big brother or uncle, but that feeling of protection had been very strong.

Finally accepting there was nothing they could do about the dreams but be aware, they talked of other things until dinner.

It was a delightful meal with much laughter, good food, and much wine. Bede, feeling the weight of responsibility toward both her sister and aunt, knew it was necessary to analyse and plan. In the morning, they would address the looming problem. They would start, she thought, by making subtle enquires of all their friends and acquaintances, the workers on the property, and even perhaps head into the interior to their friends there. They all agreed on one thing: the threat, whatever it was, was something to do with the property, maybe James's death, and they needed to be very careful about what they said and did. It was preferable to divide up their enquiries, so she and Hera would drive into the township and then go to the club, see if there were any newcomers to the area. Meredith should get on the phone, talk to her buddies from the wider community, and all three would talk calmly to the workers on the property.

Meredith was a wise woman, an elder within the Family. This had been explained to her and Hera when they were too young to ask too many questions. And they grew up with the awareness that even in the twenty-first century, it was still necessary to keep the Family secrets.

The Family a name, a word, to be whispered, was very large, extended, and secretive, with branches scattered throughout Europe and the Americas. It was connected financially and emotionally with tentacles like an octopus infiltrating into every aspect of even this modern world, and there was no possibility to ever sever those connections.

This small, very small branch, crouched inland of this very large continent was just one aspect. Both Bede and Hera were aware and had always been aware that there was something puzzling, something inexplicable behind their lack of contact with that larger part of their family. They knew of its existence of course, they knew the mythology, had heard mentioned some names, some places, but they remembered no more than that. There had been one visit to Europe when they were younger, but no more. No representative had come to their father's funeral for instance, which mystified them all, and angered Meredith.

In previous centuries, they had been healers, herbalists, and mystics. But now, here in their own minor part of that world, they were flower growers on a commercial scale. They still grew herbs and produced their own cosmetics, but this was mainly for personal use. Now they exported fresh, native flowers to five countries as well as supplying the domestic market. They grew Australian natives, waratah, kangaroo paw, Christmas bush, flannel flower, and a wide variety of proteas. It was a huge business and employed over thirty people, most of whom lived and worked on the property itself. They had offices in both Sydney and Perth. They had drifted a long way from the herbalists of the past, but that knowledge and experience was still there and kept alive within the Family mythology.

The wide-ranging family had diversified over the last few centuries, and Meredith suspected that they were now the only ones to maintain any aspects of those original roots. But loyalty toward all the various members of their extended family could never be severed. This was the legacy passed down over the centuries, generation after generation.

# Chapter Two

## *Prague*

It was cold—really cold—the snow thick on the ground. Children had been making faces in the snow-covered cars parked on the side of the road. The snowploughs had been out, and now the footpaths were icy and dangerous from the salt. Martin and Gabriel picked their way carefully along the middle of the road. It was midnight, and they were tired, cold, and anxious. The meeting had not gone well, and they were both frustrated and unsure of the motives behind the strange directives. It was made clear to them how essential it was they find Justin as quickly as possible. With only the two of them looking for him, it would be assumed (by whom?) that it was a normal familial visit from his two favourite nephews. What happened after that depended on the message they must pass on!

Tracking him through the streets of Prague was not easy. He was tricky at the best of times, but now, he obviously didn't want to be found. He seemed to have developed an interest in antique books; or was certainly giving the impression of becoming an avid antique book collector. Part of the current mystery?

They had followed several leads, but hadn't managed to catch up with him. Now it was dark and freezing and there was only one last place to look tonight.

Gabriel led the way to Tretter's, a café cocktail bar they knew in the Jewish quarter. It was after midnight, but Prague rarely slept before dawn. They slogged through the streets, trying not to slip on the ice while remaining alert and watchful. Tretter's was on Cervena, just behind the Old New Synagogue, and had been a hangout for the two of them in the year they'd lived and studied there. Justin introduced them to the bar when they first arrived, and it fast became their home away from home. It was Justin's suggestion they spend a year in Prague, finishing their formal education. He convinced their parents it made sense for them to learn the language, difficult though it was, and that it would help them in their future careers. Prague was, after all, the original home of the Family.

Justin, brother to their father, had always been a mentor of sorts to them. Never marrying, he looked on his nephews in a purely paternal way, although Gabriel considered this more sophisticated identical twin to his father something of an enigma.

'I just hope Justin will eventually find his way here,' Gabriel stated. 'If this new interest in antique books is what I think it is, then he will have been following leads for days, and will expect both of us to turn up here sooner or later. Those complacent idiots in Australia are finally starting to sit up and take notice, and we had better be ready when the shit hits the fan.'

They turned their very cold faces toward Ceverna, and breathed a combined sigh of relief when the lights of the Kavarnas gleamed just ahead, welcoming them as of old. They pushed through the door into the warmth, and the sounds of the jazz trio playing quietly in the corner at the back beside the open fire. It wasn't too crowded yet, but would draw many more as the evening progressed. This was one of the more popular bars around, the music was always good, and they were open until 5 a.m. every morning.

Gabriel relaxed into the comforting ritual of pulling off the thick scarf, hat, gloves, and padded jacket to hang on the rack just inside the door. They then made their way slowly among the tables, scanning for Justin. He was not there, at least not yet. But if he were still in Prague, he would arrive at some point before dawn. Some things were a given, and Justin would always finish the night listening to jazz at Tretter's.

## Chapter Three

# Meredith

M eredith had been agitated since James's death. She was aware of
many of the secrets within the various factions of the family,
knew there were unresolved issues, anger, jealousies, and perhaps
even enemies from James's past. It was time to relook at her brother's
motivation behind buying this property so long ago, and why he had
retired from the successful business he ran in New York. It had been out
of character for him, but at the time, he had used his wife and child as
an excuse to 'retire from the rat race.'

Now, they needed to dissolve the veils he had lowered over this past
life. They needed as much information as possible to determine if this
'coming' was something to do with his death, or a totally new threat.
Their extended family was large with branches in many parts of the
world, but mostly, they had kept to themselves—their only contacts
being on a business level.

Seated around the breakfast table the next morning, Meredith
startled the girls saying quietly, 'I want you to think back to dinner on
that last night before you left to return to Perth, Bede. It was only a few
days before your father's dreadful accident.' Meredith looked across at
the two people most important to her in the world. She needed to keep
them safe, but it was no longer appropriate to keep information from

them. They were both adults now; they were intelligent, mature, and sensible. It could be dangerous to keep them in ignorance any longer.

'We all need to remember the discussion we were having at dinner that night.' There was complete silence as Bede and Hera exchanged puzzled glances. Meredith continued, 'We were talking about the latest contracts with France and Germany, and your father was a little worried. Do you remember?'

Again, there was silence. Hera frowned, 'I remember he wanted to renegotiate the whole contract. And at the time, I thought he was being a little paranoid.' There was silence for a few brief moments.

Then Bede interjected, 'I don't remember really. I was more concerned about the message from Mikael about the problem with the latest delivery to San Francisco.' She looked toward Hera and continued with a shrug, 'And I suppose because of the accident, and the contract not being signed, it was defaulted and everything fell through. We didn't ever hear anything more about it at the office.' She drew in a long breath and continued, 'By the time I arrived back here, with all of us trying to deal with the shock and the details of the accident and the police, no one thought anything more about it.' She paused, thinking carefully. 'It is strange though that we were never contacted again. I suppose they heard about Dad's death and just let it pass.'

The two girls looked to Meredith with puzzled expressions. 'What does that have to do with the strange dreams we've all been having, and what are you suggesting, Bede?'

Hera was more puzzled than ever. There was obviously something quite serious that she was missing, and it was making her nervous. She looked at Meredith, and with her usual forthright manner, blurted, 'You think Dad was murdered, don't you? You think whatever he was involved in is not finished? I think you should explain, and why do you think it had something to do with that contract?'

Meredith continued pensively, 'I've never completely understood why James left New York. I suspected that he had some ulterior motive. He said he wanted you, Bede, to grow up in Australia, somewhere safe and secure. It made a sort of sense at the time.' Meredith looked at the two of them then went on, 'I've been thinking lately that perhaps we should look at that time in our lives more closely. And yes, Hera, you're right. I think James was murdered.' She stopped briefly, contemplating their shocked expressions, then continued, 'And we need to try to work out if it had anything to do with what he was involved in before, or whether it's something about that contract he was so concerned about.'

Bede interrupted, 'Meredith, it's been over twenty years since we left the US. Surely if there was a problem from that time, James would have said something about it.'

Meredith continued ignoring Bede's interruption. 'It's been over four weeks since his death, the police have not been able to explain any of the anomalies. And the strangest thing is no representative of the family came to the funeral. That really is very odd, although we did receive messages of condolence from several. It's not really so far that someone couldn't have made the trip. In normal circumstances, someone should have. I expected Justin at least, but now it seems that he's disappeared. No one's heard from him in weeks and no one seems to know where he is.'

Meredith got up from the table and started to pace around the room, 'His nephews, Gabriel and Martin, are in Prague at the moment trying to find him. I had a phone call yesterday from their mother. She's anxious about them, of course, and hinted that there was something nasty going on that Justin is involved with.'

'Do we have any photos of Gabriel and Martin? Meredith, I'm wondering if the dark stranger in my dreams is one of them.'

Meredith looked thoughtful. 'We can always look them up on Google. I'm sure they will feature there somewhere.'

Bede and Hera both laughed, and Bede spoke with a gurgle, 'That side of the family are so precious about their achievements, they probably advertise on Google.'

'And', Hera added, 'they probably have shares as well.' Both girls collapsed laughing.

They sobered quickly, and Hera, looking thoughtful, was the first to recover. 'Thinking back to that dreadful afternoon, Chief Inspector Campbell gave me the impression he thought it was suicide, although he didn't actually come out and say that. He and Dad knew each other really well. He kept talking about the depression Dad sunk into after Mum died. We know he was depressed, but not to the extent of killing himself.'

Bede was thoughtful, 'Yes, he tried to suggest depression to me, but there was no evidence of that. Dad was still fully engaged in the business, and although he missed Mum, he was still really alive and vigorous. I suspect that's why, with the lack of evidence to the contrary, they left an open verdict.'

Hera moved restlessly in the chair. She was feeling caged and needed to move. She pushed back from the table and paced to the window, then turned back to Meredith. 'That evening at dinner, Dad was not talking about New York, but before, when both of you were growing up in Sydney. He talked about one of the uncles and some cousins and an uncle who still lived in Europe, but I can't remember his name.' She looked at Meredith. 'Can you remember who he was talking about? You should remember the name. It would have meant something to you. He was angry, and it seemed to have something to do with the new contract.'

Meredith looked worried. 'Do you know, I really can't remember, it's as if that whole period is a blank. Maybe it has something to do with shock, but I really have no memory. I do remember dinner, and the fact that James was angry about something, but it's all blurred in my mind, dreamlike, there are no details at all.'

Bede no longer had any appetite. She stood and wandered into the office and called out. 'That old contract will still be here somewhere, and Meredith, please try to remember which uncle he meant.'

Hera continued to pace around the room, frowning, and trying to reconstruct details of that last evening.

'I don't remember much about that night, but I do remember the afternoon before. Dad had a phone call at around two. I remember because I was trying to write an essay. The mobile network was down, and only the landline was working, so he took the call in the office. He became quite agitated. In fact, at one point, he shouted at whoever was on the phone, saying no, no, no over and over again. He finally slammed the receiver down, and stalked out of the office. I had forgotten about it, I should have paid more attention.'

Meredith looked up. 'Hera, was it an overseas call, do you know?'

'No idea, but it did seem as if he was expecting the call because he stalked in and answered on the second ring. But that may have been because he knew I wouldn't answer it.' She grimaced.

Bede came back into the room. 'That contract is nowhere in here, did you move it, Hera?'

Meredith surged to her feet. 'We must find that contract immediately. Come on, Hera, we'll help Bede search.'

Hera narrowed her eyes while following Meredith into the office. 'I haven't seen it since that night at dinner. Meredith, you must tell us about these obscure relations of ours. I suspect it might be important. Was there someone in particular James would not have been happy dealing with?'

Meredith looked up from the desk where she was helping Bede search again through the many drawers. She frowned. 'I must think about it, and decide how much I can tell you.'

Both Hera and Bede turned toward her. 'No way, we need to know all of it, and now,' they spoke in unison.

They stood shoulder to shoulder the way they had when children. Bede taking the lead as always, glared, 'We've had enough secrecy Aunt Meredith, we are both mature adults and need to be told all the history, all the mythology, and even all the gossip about all the various branches. It seems to me that there are our relatives, and then there is a darker more threatening side of the family. And we need to know what it all mean. And if you won't tell us, then I'll start searching myself online.' She stood with her hands on her hips and glared at her aunt. Bede continued, 'I suspect there's a lot you don't know either, and we need to stick together with this. For a start, who is Justin? And if he's so important, why have we never met him?'

Meredith looked at the two girls, and seemed to collapse in on herself—she looked older and very tired suddenly. She realised she had made a tactical error with her automatic response to keep the girls in ignorance. In fact, she mused. They were adults and needed to know everything she knew about their extended family. It was obvious they would need that information. The world was shrinking, and Australia was no longer cut off, isolated, or 'too far away'. James had tried to keep them invisible, but the world had come to them and James was now dead.

'Okay, I will tell you all I know and all I suspect, but it will take some time, so we'll stick to your father's accident and what I suspect about that.' She dropped into an armchair angled beside the desk, and the two girls perched on the arms beside her. 'Back to that night, I think he was probably talking about George, a great-uncle on your mother's side, your grandfather's disreputable brother. He is the proverbial black sheep of that side of the family, and yes, if James discovered that George was involved in that last contract, he would have been furious. But what I can't see is why. We're talking about exporting native flowers for goodness sake. I would have thought flowers would be a bit beneath George.'

Bede frowned. 'But he would be really old now. Why would James be worried about him?'

Meredith smiled slightly. 'Well, the truth is that George was the last of the children born in that family. He was a very late, late mistake if you like. In fact, he's only a few years older than James.'

Bede and Hera started pacing, passing each other, going in opposite directions. Meredith threw her hands in the air. 'Stop moving you two, you're making my head spin.'

Bede asked, 'This Uncle George, is he Mafia or something? How does he get to be the black sheep? What did he do? And why would Dad not want to deal with him? That's a few questions that need answers. And how does my incredible dream fit into all of this? Come on, we need details.'

'Also, is Justin from Mother's family or from yours?' Hera asked.

Bede snorted, 'She already said he's a great-uncle from Mother's side of the family. Pay attention Hera.'

Hera snarled. 'She was talking about George, Bede, not Justin. You pay attention.'

'Girls, squabbling isn't helping.' Meredith sank further into the chair, leaned her head against the back of the seat, and closed her eyes. Taking several deep breaths, she calmed her agitated nerves and started talking almost to herself in a quiet, serene voice. 'Twenty odd years ago, we were all living in New York. Bede, you were only a few months old. George is a thief. He steals art works mostly, and he's extremely good at it obviously, as he's never been caught or, rather, has never actually been charged. He stole a painting, a Turner, had it copied, and then sold the copy back to the original owners. Or, rather, he ransomed the copy back to the original owners. Somehow, he implicated James when the switch was discovered, but it took quite a while to sort out exactly who did what. The police finally cleared James of any involvement, but I think that was the catalyst for him to make the move back here. He wanted a clean start completely away from anything to do with George or the Family. Your parents, as you know, were distantly related. There are the common great, great-grandparents.' She paused, looking into the distance. 'For quite some time, your mother's side of the family believed the lies George was spreading about James. He and your mother were furious, and as you know, James doesn't forgive easily. After the police finally sorted it all out and cleared his name, he declared he wanted nothing to do with any of them. George, smarmy character that he is, disappeared for a few years, but then came back like the proverbial prodigal son and took up his life as if nothing had happened.

'Both sides of the family were involved at one time with ostracising him for his criminal ways. But what they were mostly angry about was the potential for the family name to be cited in the newspapers. That, of all things, is the worst crime. At that point, all the forged documents implicated James. It really did take quite a few months to sort out the false trails George had laid down. And by that time, James and Penelope had had enough of the innuendos directed at James. They couldn't actually prove anything in the early days. It was Justin who finally managed to sort out exactly what George had done, and by that time, the original of the Turner had completely disappeared. It was a mess, the Family compensated the original owners of the Turner, but to this day, no one knows where it is. The copy is on display at the

Louvre, but of course, no one is talking about it. The authorities were furious, the original owner was furious, the potential buyer was furious, and James and Penelope left New York with you, Bede, and refused to return ever. They did take you to a few family gatherings in Europe, particularly after Hera was born. But basically, they had very little to do with Penelope's side of the family again.'

Both Bede and Hera, by this time, were looking intrigued. Hera spoke first, 'Dad must have been furious. He has had such a strong sense of ethics in all his dealings whether business or personal.'

Meredith looked thoughtful. 'George is such a slimy character. Nothing could ever be proved conclusively about his involvement, so James hoped never to have anything more to do with him.'

'If James had learned that George was involved with that contract in any way, he would have been ropeable. As for Justin', Meredith continued, 'he is a cousin of your father and mine, twice removed. Really girls, the family is very complicated, and you almost need a degree in mathematics to work it out.' The two girls glared at her and she continued, 'Justin is an extremely clever man, sits on a few boards, but mostly, he's a sort of trouble-shooter for the Family.' She frowned. 'Although I've heard that he's retired now, and Gabriel and Martin, his two nephews, have stepped into that role. They now keep various business aspects of the Family functioning and are the official trouble-shooters, I think, but I'm not sure about that either. Justin and his brother, Dominik, are identical twins. Gabriel and Martin are also twins, but they're fraternal twins.'

Bede, glancing now at Meredith, thought she was looking sheepish or embarrassed. There's something she's not telling us again, she mused.

'What exactly do you mean by various business aspects of the Family? And do they have anything to do with us now?' Hera paused for a moment, and then continued, 'If the original owners of the Turner were compensated, that involves a huge amount of money! There are two questions there, Aunt Meredith.'

'Well', Meredith temporised, 'in answer to the first implied question, the Family as an entity, are fabulously wealthy. And in fact, yes, you both derive some benefits, as do I. Every member, no matter how distant, receives some benefits, in fact, quite a lot sometimes. The money you both inherited recently from a distant Aunt was actually a proportion of the sale of one of the Family companies.'

That statement was greeted with a stunned silence.

Hera erupted, 'That means that both you and Dad colluded in keeping us in the dark about something that is obviously really important, and something we should have been told about at the time.' She shouted, 'What were you both thinking?' She paused to take a deep breath, then went on more quietly, 'And where does the herbalist aspect come in? Are we talking drugs here?'

Bede moved over, putting her arm around Hera's shoulders, 'Hey, calm down, getting into a temper will not solve anything.' Hera glared at her, but turned back to Meredith.

Meredith looked stunned and outraged. 'Of course not, as if James would ever allow his business to be used in that way. Whatever made you think of such a thing?'

'What about this awful great-uncle named George?' Bede demanded. 'Would he be involved with drugs?'

'No,' Meredith laughed. 'He's too much of a snob. He deals only with artworks of various sorts. I believe he's dabbled in jewellery, but he much prefers to keep with the two dimensional stuff.' Meredith continued, 'As to the answer of the second implied question, yes, the Family holding is fabulously wealthy. I have no idea of the details, and I don't know who does.' Meredith was looking very pale and drawn. She waved her hand at the two girls. 'James would have dealt with all of this if he hadn't died, and I do think it was murder. I'm sorry girls.' She dropped her head into her hands. Bede looked across at Hera briefly, shrugged, and without another word, both turned immediately and put their arms around her.

Bede contemplated Meredith thoughtfully. 'I think the most productive way forward at this point, Meredith, is for you to make some sort of list of the family members. Detailed notes, gossip and innuendo even, and no editing.' Meredith looked into Bede's blazing eyes, and with a sinking feeling in her stomach, realised Bede no longer trusted her unconditionally. 'And in the meantime, I've had enough. It was a long drive yesterday, I'm angry, and not entirely sure why. I suggest Hera and I take off for a bit, and leave you to sort out the list, which is important.' She paused briefly, and with a sigh, continued, 'Then you can come clean finally, and we will have no more secrets in this branch of this mysterious family that we seem to belong to. But be assured we love you, and I am not furious at you. At least I don't think I am.'

Meredith smiled gently and got up from the chair. 'You're right, my pet. I'll put my mind to the list, but we do need to find that missing contract.'

# Chapter Four

## Gabriel

G abriel indicated a table just vacated along the wall opposite the band where they could keep an eye on the door. It was early yet, but this was their best option for finding Justin tonight. It was frustrating when they were so desperately short of time and needed the information he obviously had, but traipsing all over Prague on a night like tonight was counterproductive. They sat quietly with every expectation of a few quiet moments to enjoy the music and collect their thoughts.

Martin looked across at Gabriel. 'I don't like anything about this, Gabe. I have the distinct impression no one is being honest. We don't have all the relevant details. And there is a hidden agenda to all of this. There is something other than the book and Justin that we're expected to find.'

'I agree there's something's definitely not right about this bloody assignment.'

Gabriel let his thoughts drift back to their arrival at the airport. Neither of them had come prepared for the icy weather—Martin less so than Gabriel. They were dressed for the office, which in fact was where they had been. Trendy suits and leather-soled shoes were not the attire needed to wander around the freezing streets, but there had only been time to grab passports, various reports, and head for their respective airports. The summons had been explicit and startling enough to have them rushing from different parts of the world to meet, incredibly enough almost simultaneously at Ruzyne Airport.

They had greeted each other with laughter, hugs, and much backslapping. There was a major problem looming, but the thought of spending a few days together was a bonus.

It had been over twelve months since they'd managed to catch up in person. E-mails were fine, but they didn't quite convey the intimacy of their usual communication. Fraternal twins were not as close as identical twins according to medical reports, but he and Martin had always had an awareness of the other's state, especially any injury or excessive anxiety experienced by either.

Gabriel grabbed Martin's arm and dragged him laughing toward the nearest trendy clothing store. 'You, my friend, are not dressed for this weather. You look suitably debonair, but decidedly chilly.'

They bought heavy padded jackets, gloves, scarfs, and woolly hats. The boots had been a little more difficult to purchase. While indulging in a spot of shopping, they exchanged lurid details of their latest 'conquests' and were delighted to be in their favourite city if only for a few days.

'We can get a drink, something to eat, and exchange a bit of gossip before heading to the first meet,' Gabriel had declared. 'Do you have any idea what this is really about?'

'Not a clue, old sod, but it's a welcome change to what I have been doing for the last two years. Istanbul is exciting, but it's not Prague.'

Gabriel pulled himself back to the present as Martin spoke softly, 'I'm looking forward to some snow for a change. Let's try to spin this out when we're finished. I missed the family gathering at Christmas, as did you. We're entitled to some R & R. I would love to spend some free time here just indulging in a bit of nostalgia. We could catch up with old friends, get roaring drunk, and pretend we're still in our early twenties, instead of heading fast towards the big thirty.'

Martin signalled to the waitress. 'We may as well have a beer and nostalgia dictates a Pilsner.' Laughing, they settled into the recently vacated table in a secluded corner.

'All jokes aside Martin, do you have any idea what this is about?' Gabriel took a small sip of his beer. 'The directive that came through was idiotic. Find Justin, but first meet up with Uncle Stefan at the office. What the hell does that mean, and why can't Uncle Stefan find Justin? Were you given anything more explicit?'

'Not much, but I did overhear something between Marina and Josephine. Something to do with the Family archives, I think, or maybe family history, but they slammed the door on me. They may be getting old, but they still have minds like steel traps. It doesn't make sense. If we are supposed to solve some problem, we need more detailed information. Unless Uncle Stefan knows more than he's telling, in which case, we just have to wait a little longer. It's a mystery, but it does mean we're here. All expenses paid for a few days at least, so let's find Justin, sort out the book, whatever it is, and get down to some serious socialising.' He grinned.

The band continued to play quietly as Gabriel continued his musing. They had a very frustrating meeting with Stefan, who alluded to difficulty contacting Justin, but didn't say why, stated the missing 'book' Justin was tracking down had to be found, as it was extremely important to the Family archives, smiled benignly at both of them, and showed them out of the office. Gabriel almost expected to be patted on the head.

After leaving the office, they had tried all Justin's old haunts, bookshops they knew he should have visited if he'd really been looking for an antique book, but he had not been seen at any of these in the last few weeks, let alone days. He obviously didn't want to be found easily.

Gabriel brought his thoughts back to the present, and looked across at this brother, a slow smiled dawned. 'You would think in this day of immediate communication that Justin would at least answer an SMS, but the bastard hasn't changed one bit. I've been trying since I left London to get an answer from him.'

Martin grinned in return. 'I'm looking forward to catching up with the old reprobate. He will probably be pissed as usual, but that has never affected that razor sharp mind of his.'

Gabriel pulled himself from his reverie with a suggestion of food. Neither of them had eaten since leaving the airport that morning. They had been moving too fast, so now they contemplated the dubious menu chalked up on the board. There was always the possibility that the standard had improved over the intervening years, but looking around at the few actually dining, it didn't look hopeful.

Martin grinned at him again. 'Maybe we could get a sandwich at least.' He signalled to the waitress then the two of them settled down to wait.

## Chapter Five

# The Waterhole

The two girls wandered outside. It was a beautiful morning, clear and cool, but the day would heat up very quickly. Bede headed for the shed, running. 'Let's go for a ride. Now!'

Suddenly, she was anxious to be away from the homestead, away from Meredith and her fears and anxieties, into the open spaces that she loved so much.

Hera called, 'Wait for me!' And they were both running, laughing joyously toward the open shed where their old battered trail bikes lived. This had been their escape from the time they were big enough to manage the controls.

Bede sat for a moment looking toward the hills in the distance. This was the wheat belt. It was flat and beautiful, and the colours had always fascinated her. The air so clear and clean, not a lot of bird sounds at this time of the day, but the horizon shone in the distance. It was possible to look from horizon to horizon. It was so flat, so clear one could see the curve of the earth. The hills in the distance were almost purple with the reflection from the brilliant blue sky. Bede drew a deep breath and allowed herself to relax at last.

No matter what Meredith feared, or thought she feared, she was at home on her trusty steed, heading toward the horizon fast on a straight line. This was the equivalent for her of following the reflection of the moon straight out to sea.

Hera shouted and whooped. She had her companion and best friend back. They could explore, laugh, drive fast and dangerously, and recapture some of the exuberance of carefree youth. Hera had missed Bede dreadfully. It had been essential that Bede take over the offices in Perth and Sydney. She had the best head for figures and business, while Hera's strength lay in the propagation of the various plants, but they had always been very close. Meredith needed help running the business here, and keeping all the staff on track. So now, Hera spent most of her time on the property, while trying to finish her master's degree online from Curtin University in Perth.

They both missed their wonderful father. He had been the one with enormous reserves of energy and drive, never too tired to help with a word of encouragement when needed. Now, they seemed to be on their own, struggling to find an anchor point from which to function effectively. Not able really to reconnect with that solid reality of family. Perhaps, it was the lack of a strong male to balance out the three strong females. Whatever, it was great to have Bede back home if only for a few days.

Today, they would leave the anxiety behind and head out to the hills, swim in their favourite waterhole, build a fire, and sit and talk, as they had always done in the past. Some of Hera's dreams had been really disturbing, and she hadn't shared all of them with Meredith. There was a strange sensual element to them, but definitely not sexual in content. It was more an awareness of the sensual elements of colour and texture, heat and cold, open spaces, and strange plants—species she had never seen before—but the details were engraved on her mind. She could still see some of them, and even knew somehow within herself the possible medicinal properties of each new plant. Talking to Bede would help her sort out whether these dreams were an extension of her research, or something else entirely.

Hera felt they had to protect Meredith from the other-worldly elements suggested in both hers and Bede's dreams. There had to be an explanation for the alien elements of her thought processes lately, and she didn't think it was the 'Dr Who' complex Meredith accused her of. There were no other world monsters in her dream world, not even other world places. It was always so familiar. It was difficult to convey this in words, but whether it was really communication from another sphere, nudges from their subconscious of something observed but not processed, or just weird longings buried for too long. Hera knew she and Bede needed to talk, to discuss impressions, and basically look at it objectively, then probably just let it go because what could they do with the strangeness of the thoughts and images until, and if, they became concrete?

This other element of the Family Meredith had introduced into the mix just added more confusion and seemed to muddy her thoughts. At the moment, the day was perfect, the air clear, they could strip, swim, and relax knowing there was no one nearer than the farm and that was many kilometres west.

They swam and talked not about the dreams, but about the past, the fun and challenge of their early school days, the trips they had made overseas with their parents in the long summer breaks. They talked about their gap years overseas, and their various romances when they were young, putting the anxiety about the last few weeks behind them.

Relaxing in the shade of her favourite River Red Gum, and watching the bees busily working away, Bede thought she could lie there forever. It was so peaceful. She allowed her thoughts to drift back to those early trips; there hadn't actually been many white Christmases. There had been skiing for Hera and herself, clumsy on their first slope, and only one year with the family with many cousins speaking French, German, and Czech.

The family was the reason given their schooling had to encompass languages, but for them, it needed only be French and German. Bede remembered their mother laughing at their inability to pronounce the incomprehensible Czech. Then suddenly, they had stopped going overseas, but French and German had still been an essential part of their education. At home, for as long as she could remember, there had been the 'French days' and the 'German days' when they were only allowed to speak in the respective language.

Hera lazily turned on her side. 'Do you think the strange guy in your dreams could have been one of those obnoxious cousins we met that one time we spent in Paris with seemingly endless relatives? I can't remember how old I was.' She rolled back onto her back. 'They stayed with Aunt Helena and were scathing about our accents. Do you remember what they looked like?'

'No, I remember one was darkish and one had fair hair, I think, but they were so snooty. They were a fair bit older than us, both at high school, and were the most arrogant of all the cousins there. There was something arrogant about the guy in my dreams that's all, the same sort of arrogance.'

Hera surged suddenly to her feet. 'Time for another swim, last one in's a rotten egg,' and shrieking wildly, she ran for the water.

## Chapter Six

*Tretters*

G abriel glanced up quickly as Justin walked through the door. He was a handsome devil, this uncle of theirs, with his lean frame, silver hair, and patrician features. He exuded a refined elegance. Amber and gold rings gleamed on his long tapered fingers. One had to look hard to see the dangerous edge beneath the surface. There was magnetism about him that women found irresistible, Gabriel thought, even now.

Justin saw them immediately, waved, and headed for their table. His thoughts were running chaotically through his mind. He took a long breath to remain calm, and fixing a smile of welcome on his face, moved across to join them. They had been summoned immediately, Stefan lost track of him. Justin knew they had been looking for him—his brother's only children. He loved them both, as if they were his own. He really didn't want to involve them in this—the latest of the Family's folly.

The Family, he fumed. It was so huge, scattered, and corrupt with more tentacles than an octopus. There was no continent where it could be said there was no representative, no major multinational company without a senior member of the Family high in administration or sitting on the board. The Family, so secretive and deadly, the name still spoken in whispers, was like a combination of European monarchy and the Sicilian Mafia. They kept the bloodlines pure and encouraged hubris in all, particularly the males. All were instructed early in secrecy and concealment. They kept the mystery of whom and what they were from all outsiders. They managed to keep a low profile, nothing in the newspapers, or the underground press; and mostly, they drew a line at murder, mostly. But there had been that time recently in Berlin when they had killed one of their own, and now, there was a question about what had really happened to James on his boat.

James was too good a sailor to have been careless with the maintenance on his beloved 'Penelope'. He still had nightmares about the Berlin execution even though it had obviously been necessary. Fabien was a homicidal maniac. He had been totally out of control and had endangered several family members before being finally tracked down and eliminated.

Fabien was a cousin, and there had been many who had advocated a private sanatorium, but that had already been tried and he had escaped. A more permanent solution was needed. The maniac had killed three young girls, but was far too clever to leave any clues, and the police were useless. Besides, the Family would never have countenanced his arrested. The Family took care of their own 'dirty laundry', and this was not the time to appear weak or vacillating. It had been done quickly, but now, he was not happy. There were rumblings within the Family, and he worried about the repercussions. There had always been an assassin in each generation, but now, in the twenty-first century, that knowledge was strictly need-to-know. The patriarch or the executive were the only ones to issue the directives.

The training was secret, extensive, and no one knew exactly who was chosen. He thought that at the moment, there could be as many as three fully trained. They were a fit healthy lot, and the Patriarch was only seventy. So there could well be someone from that generation, plus two more, with the youngest being in his early twenties. It was a little chilling to meditate on. He wondered if they compared notes, or had some sort of support group going, it would make a sort of macabre sense.

He drew a long breath. He must be totally out of his mind with worry to be speculating on that aspect of the family business. He was 'the fixer', or rather, he had been the fixer. Anything that came to the notice of the patriarch likely to cause a scandal of any sort, any negative aspect that might get into the newspapers, or even any family squabble that was getting out of hand, Justin was called in to mediate or to send in the heavies if necessary. Lately, though, he was aware that his nephews were called in first. He was near retirement, if one could ever retire from the Family. This latest problem didn't fit into any of his normal areas of expertise. Not something he could smooth over with charm.

A book had surfaced, an antique book that apparently had information about the origin of the Family in Europe in the early seventeenth century. He speculated that there were references to current members that could be dangerous. They had been a ruthless lot, and in truth, if you scratched the surface, not much had changed. But their historians had always made sure they acquired everything that even mentioned the Family, so where had this book come from? And who had it now?

He was tracking rumours, and he realised he'd made a mistake not keeping the patriarch in the loop, so now, the two boys had been called in. Stupid, short-sighted, and arrogant of him, both Gabriel and Martin were too intelligent and knew him too well not to start asking questions as soon as they found him. He had known they would be at Tretter's, drinking beer, and waiting for him to arrive. There was nothing he could do to prevent their involvement now, but perhaps he could keep it minimal. He needed to tell them enough to assuage their curiosity, but not enough for them to grasp the disastrous implications. He did need their help. They both had contacts from their time at university that could be extremely useful.

It was late and cold, and he was hungry and tired. Now, he looked at the two of them sitting there across the room with grins on their faces. He felt a surge of pure possessive pride when he saw them. They were his brother's sons, but they could easily have been his own. He too had loved their mother, but she had rightly chosen Dominik, much more stable, honourable and reliable. He had never managed to find a permanent replacement for her though; she still occupied a very special place in his heart.

They were tall and lean, a family trait, Gabriel with the dark chestnut hair so prevalent in the family, and Martin with the fine fair classic features and the soft blonde hair of his mother.

Gabriel was the first to spot him, and his harsh dark face lit with a smile of pure mischief. Gabriel looked across at their father's identical twin. He was, in many ways, the complete opposite of his brother. He was grinning at them, his eyes sparkling. There was something of the gypsy in him, a family trait, thought Justin sourly.

He felt his heart lurch. He knew they both possessed the same strength and stubborn determination that ran like a fever through all the members of their impossible extended family. He feared for them. He plastered a welcoming smile on his face and moved toward their table with the effortless grace of a younger man. He schooled his features into one of open delight to see them. He would keep them safe at all costs, and that meant that for tonight, he would wait. He was very good at waiting, waiting to see what they would reveal about what they knew. He hadn't seen the boys, men, he corrected himself, for two years and was not sure exactly what role they played now. He had a sudden premonition that it would turn out to be more than he would like or even approve of.

Martin grabbed his outstretched hand, pulled him into a bear hug, while Gabriel was slapping him on the back. They were delighted to catch up with him finally.

'Where the devil have you been you, old reprobate,' Martin asked, while grasping his shoulder and almost shaking him.

'Hands off you two, and let's sit down.' Justin looked closely into their eyes and had a moment of intense fear. They had changed in the last two years. There was hardness about the two of them now that hadn't been there two years ago.

He drew a long, slow breath and kept his features relaxed and smiling. He would have to be very careful; they would not appreciate his trying to muddy the investigation. Gabriel, in particular, was looking at him with those piercing eyes of his. He had always been the more sensitive of the two of them, and was also the more perceptive. He used his intuition as well as his powerful intellect in most situations. This was probably a legacy of being so badly devastated all those years ago by Kamila. Still, it had been a lesson well learned. He took nothing for granted now, and his speculations were always tempered with facts.

Justin allowed himself to be pressed into the vacant chair at the table. He grinned at them, but avoided eye contact and demanded a beer immediately. 'Well, I have to say you both seem larger than the last time I saw you. Have they put growth hormones into the beer in London and Istanbul?'

'No, Uncle Justin, we just appear to be larger because of the anxiety and frustration building within caused by a recalcitrant uncle who seems to be not only trying to avoid us, but now seems to be trying to obfuscate the investigation of whatever it is we are investigating,' he paused and raised one eyebrow.

Justin looked at Martin. 'Ahh, I see. Now I become Uncle Justin. Martin, I apologise, let's start again. All right, I admit I have been avoiding you both. I was hoping to find the bloody book before you two were called in or at least actually arrived. I strongly advised against it to both the committee and to the patriarch. I wanted you kept out of it.'

'Explain the bloody book, Justin. And also, what exactly are we to be kept out of? We have been given a lot of guff, told nothing that makes any sense, told to find you. "It's a matter of the utmost urgency, Justin will explain." Now explain!' Gabriel growled in frustration.

'A please would be nice,' Justin glanced at the two of them, sighed, and accepted the inevitable. 'Okay, the bloody book is apparently an embarrassment, or a possible embarrassment to the Family. It's very old, dating from around the early seventeenth century, hence, my sudden interest in antique books. It's supposedly a record of the Family beginnings written by the first patriarch. I don't believe in either the supposed age or the provenance of the book. But there is a mystery, and it is potentially dangerous. It's a particularly sensitive time at the moment, given the disaster of both Australia and Berlin. I take it you both know what happened? Do you have any idea of the potential disaster it would be if either of those two girls in Australia realised their father had been murdered? And by whom?'

Gabriel growled, 'That was the most arrogant and unnecessary piece of mismanagement I have ever heard of. James was not a threat, and the patriarch knew that, so did most of the executive, so who actually sanctioned the assassination?'

Justin sighed. So they both knew, which meant they were deeply entrenched in the administration; he damned whoever had arranged that. 'I don't know, I have been making discrete enquiries, but it's a dangerous exercise. I am worried. Those girls are extremely intelligent, but have been kept separate from the family and have been told almost nothing of their heritage, at James's specifically expressed orders. He wanted them kept away from the convoluted machinations. He wanted them safe, which is why they've been brought up in Australia. He thought that was far enough away. I personally think he should have cut all connections if that's what he wanted instead of allowing them to take part in a couple of the family gatherings when they were young. But there was never any hope of influencing James when he had decided on a course of action.'

Justin thought carefully before he continued. 'He obviously knew something that someone considered dangerous. But I cannot conceive of what. I have been making enquiries, discretely of course, in Oz, and have made contacted with the assassin. He, of course, has no idea who sanctioned the hit, which is of course normal procedure, but he did give me all the details including the message he was to give James before the end.'

Gabriel and Martin growled almost in unison and regarded him in anger and awe. Gabriel was the first to speak, growl really, 'You spoke to the assassin? How did you acquire that little piece of information, and how the hell did you get him to talk about it? I think you had better come clean with everything you know, or think you know about what's going on.'

Martin suddenly leaned forward, lowered his voice, and reminded both Gabriel and Justin of where they were.

'You're right, Martin, this is neither the time nor the place. I need a beer and a sandwich then I suggest you both come back to my place for the night. I take it neither of you have booked into a hotel yet?' He looked at them, nodded his head, and signalled the waitress.

# Chapter Seven

# Justin's Apartment in Prague

Justin strolled with them to his new apartment, which he explained was still in the process of renovation. It was walking distance from Tretters, a convenience that was not to be taken lightly, he stated.

The apartment was on the top floor of an old, early eighteenth century building on Śiroka. It was typical of the beautiful buildings from that era. Its façade was ornate, and the proportions of the rooms in the classical mode. There was no lift. They cheerfully walked up the seven flights of stairs, laughing and joking. Gabriel knew these old buildings and most had been allowed to deteriorate, but some, like this one, was experiencing a new lease of life. The fundamental structure was solid and the position to be envied.

As soon as the door was opened, they were hit by the smell of new paint and fresh sawdust. It was a strangely clean aroma, reminding Gabriel of the time when he and Martin were young, creating 'masterpieces' in their father's workshop. He looked around with curious eyes, as they all moved into the hallway and wandered through into what had obviously been a drawing room in former times. Justin switched on lights as they moved through, then with a flourish, threw open the double doors leading onto a wide balcony with the lights and sounds of Praha spread out before them.

'Welcome my young friends. I apologise for the state of the place, but it will be beautiful when it's finished. This apartment takes up the whole of this floor, so I have complete privacy and solitude when I need it.'

He took them on a tour of his new home, while explaining the changes he was making. As well as the former drawing room, there was a study, library, music room, and four bedrooms all with en suite. It was beautifully restored, and not even the smell of paint and new carpentry detracted. It was mostly unfurnished, but the stacked cardboard boxes in every room did not detract from the ambience of understated luxury. Justin excused himself, pleading a need to refresh just a little, so Gabriel and Martin wandered back into the drawing room; and moving some of the packing cases, made themselves comfortable while waiting for Justin to return.

'There must be a stash of grog here somewhere, Martin. You look while I make a call and let Stefan know we've found Justin.'

Martin poured three snifters of the fine French brandy he had found, and then settled down to wait. It was useless, they both knew, putting any pressure on Justin. He would talk when he was ready, and not before as the two boys knew from past experience. They also knew that what he told them would not be the complete story. They were used to Justin and his barely disguised machinations to keep them away from the 'dark side' of the Family. They knew he was unaware of their true role within the family business now, but suspected he was starting to be wary of them both.

Martin glanced across at Gabriel and raised his eyebrows in question. Gabriel grinned and nodded his head. He poured them each another small brandy and mouthed the word 'wait'. At this rate, they could well be pissed by the time they got any information out of Justin. He wandered back from gazing out the window to accept the glass Martin handed him, and spoke quietly. 'It's no good, Martin, he will take his own sweet time deciding how much to tell us, so the best option is to wait until he's ready. In the meantime, we need to decide how much we should tell him, firstly, about the meeting with Stefan and then about our directives.' He looked up as Justin came back into the room and said quietly, 'Keep on your toes, little brother.'

Justin smiled as he walked back into the room. He thought about what he knew as fact, and wondered how much he need tell them, and how much he could keep hidden. Accepting the drink Gabriel handed him, he raised it in a silent toast. 'It's great to see you both, and I know you expect explanations, but can we leave them for tonight. You must both be very tired, it's late, and I think we should sleep. I need time to recoup my resources. Not as young as I used to be.' He indicated one of the unpacked boxes. 'There are sleeping bags and pillows in there, so I'll just leave you to it. Make yourselves at home, goodnight.' And he sauntered from the room, cradling his snifter carefully.

Gabriel laughed. 'I though he did that very well, a complete piss off. We may as well sleep. I'm buggered. It's been a long day.'

---

Gabriel pulled himself slowly awake. The grey light of predawn was filtering through the half-drawn blinds. He had slept heavily and well, but now, he needed to let his mind free to analyse the information Justin had grudgingly imparted while walking to his apartment.

It was rumours and shadows, this book that supposedly cast a less than salubrious light on the origins of the Family, and why did it matter now. It was more than 300 years ago, if the rumours were true. There was more to this story than Justin, or anyone for that matter, was saying. But was that because Justin didn't know any more, or because the need-to-know directive had been implemented? If the latter, then they would get no more details from him, but if the former, then the implications more dire than he and Martin had first thought. Did it have anything to do with James's murder? What could possibly be in the book to have caused this amount of anxiety on so many levels, or was the 'bloody book', as Justin insisted on calling it, a red herring to take the heat off the assassination of James? Only someone in the executive council could have organised both events. They really needed to talk to Justin and in a way that backed him into a corner, so the truth could emerge.

Was Justin just trying to protect him and Martin again, or was it something he was involved in? The two of them had been the 'fixers' for the Family for the last two years. Surely, Justin knew that, or had he been sidelined so effectively that he wasn't aware of it? There were too many questions, no answers, and Gabriel was confused and slightly angry.

It was time for total honesty, but total honesty with Justin was a contradiction in terms, so he and Martin would have to lead him carefully along the path they needed him to go. The need-to-know directive would have to go hang. There was obviously a 'snake in the woodpile', as James would so colourfully have put it.

Martin and he speculated about a personal vendetta with this book as misdirection. If this latest problem hadn't surfaced now, they would both be on their way to Australia to investigate James's death. The fact that the committee had changed their initial directive about an immediate investigation was strange and extremely suspicious.

Then there was Justin's statement that he had spoken to the assassin—that in itself was astounding. That had to have been a slip on Justin's part, an indication that he was rattled and off balance. He'd quickly tried to gloss over his slip, obviously hoping that the two of them wouldn't notice what he'd said.

Justin had given them massive details of where he'd been and the number of antique bookshops he'd visited and why. He had talked about the people running, or owning the respective establishments, but in fact, he had told them almost nothing of any substance or significance. It was obvious he was not being completely honest, and Gabriel was beginning to think they would have to go around him to get answers quickly. They couldn't wait much longer before heading to Australia. Too much time had elapsed already. Gabriel knew enough about the two girls from James and his informants to realise exactly how smart they both were, and their Aunt Meredith would not be able to keep them contained forever. Besides, he owed it to James to sort out what was going on.

Before James's death, he and Martin had already talked about making a trip to Australia that was now. They needed all the details of James's activities over the last twelve months. There was a mystery that needed to be sorted. Gabriel considered the current committee members. Their thinking was hidebound with outdated morals and ethics, if any at all.

This was the twenty-first century, and there was no longer any need for that medieval secrecy. In fact, secrecy was almost impossible, given the current communication networks. But one could mostly manage to be discreet. Gabriel knew in detail what the family business had entailed in previous centuries, but now, most of those enterprises had been modified and homogenised. They were legitimate multinational companies mostly. So where to start looking?

He took his thought process right back to the beginning. Step by step, he thought, I have missed something. The belated and extraordinary information about James's death had put himself and Martin put on notice to investigate. All straightforward as far as it went, then redirected to a supposed threat in Prague. What threat? Justin was no threat, or should he be perceived as one? How could an antique book be a threat to anyone?

James died weeks ago, but the details had only recently filtered through, yet Justin had spoken to the assassin? Meredith would have notified the patriarch immediately, yet the details had only just been released in the family blog! Who had gone to the funeral for God's sake?

Then that ridiculous meeting with his supervisor in London, double talk, innuendo, and no hard details, yet there had been an urgency about the directive: find out what had happened in Australia. Martin reported the same, and then to be sidelined into this fiasco didn't make sense. They had been confused about the strange directives from Uncle Stefan, but he was the CEO for their Prague holdings. He sighed in frustration.

Then there had been that odd moment when he and Martin had first entered Tretters. A stirring on the back of his neck, but he had surveyed the room carefully knowing Martin would do the same. There was nothing obvious other than their vague sense of something not being quite right.

He raised his arms behind his head and settled more comfortably in the warmth of the sleeping bag, letting his mind drift. He thought back to his year studying languages in Prague, and his chaotic relationship with the beautiful, demanding, and unprincipled Kamila. They had always finished the night at Tretters, dreamily listening to the current jazz band before wandering home to her studio apartment. It had, of course, not lasted out the year, and he admitted now that it would have been a disaster of a marriage. But young, idealistic, and naïve, he had proposed with all the passion and romance in his soul, and she had laughed. It had felt like a death blow. He couldn't understand how she could spend all her days and nights with him, making passionate love, and not want to marry him.

He had been a naïve romantic idiot, but he had learned his lesson well—not that he had become a complete cynic. He had thrown himself into his studies afterwards, and it had paid off. He really did have a facility for languages, and his German and Czech were now as fluent as his Italian, French, and Spanish. The discipline required in his philosophy lectures had helped with his unfortunate tendency toward romance. Altogether in retrospect, he was grateful to Kamila for the pain inflicted at the time.

He had often wondered if it had been the huge bunch of flowers or falling to his knee to propose that had caused her spontaneous laughter. Whichever, it was in the past, but being there tonight and listening to the very excellent trio playing an old Dave Brubeck number had brought it all back.

There hadn't been many in the bar when he and Martin had arrived. Two couples, one old guy sitting quietly in the corner, and two students drinking at the bar. He reviewed the two couples. The first, just inside the door sitting, huddled close together at a table opposite the long mirror behind the bar. The guy was large with very dark curly hair cut short; the girl had short spiky red hair. She was turned away from the door and leaning against her companion's chest with her face buried in it. It could have been Kamila, but surely, she would have spoken! He had been hyper alert, and knew he had missed something at that point. The other couple had been further into the bar, gazing into each other's eyes, and holding hands; both very young, barely out of their teens, probably students.

The two, sitting at the bar, both university types from their clothing, and they were talking quietly. The older man looking to be in his late fifties was drinking beer and talking on his phone. They had all turned and looked up when he and Martin had noisily entered, laughing and chatting. Of course, he thought, except the couple opposite the mirror. Bloody hell he must have been tired and distracted. So why would Kamila not have spoken?

## Chapter Eight

# Kamila

Kamila shook her spiky, red head and glanced across the bar. She and Jakub, her tall, handsome husband had been at Tretters for an hour. Their instructions for the night were to watch and report anything or anyone they saw who could be of significance to Lucien. Lucien, their nemesis, was a charming but deadly elderly gentleman. No other way to describe him, with his silver grey hair, bushy eyebrows, and slightly rotund figure, his features were pleasant; and on first meeting, he would always be taken for a kindly older gentleman. Nothing could be further from the truth.

They knew him as the head of an international group of 'facilitators'—the only way to describe the work they had done for him over the years. It paid extraordinarily well, but was dangerous, and sometimes, they had real concerns. It was not just illegal, but perhaps treasonous as well.

Both she and Jakub planned to retire from the work. They had enough contacts and skills between them now to be able to work anywhere in the world, start a new life, one with less potential to end up in goal or worse. Admittedly, they would probably miss the danger and the adrenalin rush, but since their marriage, they wanted something else, somewhere outside the Czech Republic, they thought perhaps France.

This was their last assignment with Lucien, just a watching brief for the evening, but Kamila was not pleased to be in this part of Prague again, particularly in this bar. Her memories were not good ones from all those years ago. She had behaved badly with Gabriel, she knew that, but Lucien had been adamant, move out now, and so she did, but it had been brutal. They had both been very young, and she had been embarrassed at his proposal. Hadn't handled it well. To be back here now was unsettling, and this bar had been their favourite hangout. She had a bad feeling about tonight.

Jakub put his arm around her shoulders and pulled her against his chest. 'You're scowling, my pet, everyone will think we're fighting. Just relax.'

'I don't have a good feeling about this, Jakub. I feel as if there's ice water running down my back. Lucien was more enigmatic than usual.'

'Yes, my pet, but if we want out, we agreed to do this last job. I suspect it has something to do with the time you were stationed here years ago.'

'That's what's worrying me.'

'Just stay alert and all will be well.'

They leaned back in the booth, glancing toward the back of the bar where the tables were set up around the band. A jazz trio was playing quietly in the corner, old Dave Brubeck numbers, with the piano player improvising beautifully. Kamila felt herself relaxing finally. They had checked out all the patrons earlier, and there were no new arrivals, there was no one here of any significance.

It was after midnight when she was brought out of her reverie by the sudden opening of the door, sounds of laughter, and much stamping of feet to dislodge the snow. She and Jakub both looked toward the mirror behind the bar and saw reflected two tall, fit-looking men enter. As they pulled off their hats and padded jackets, Jakub said, 'One dark, one fair. They look innocent enough.'

Their backs were toward them, so it wasn't possible to see the faces, but Kamila knew there was something familiar about the shape of the dark head. And as they turned around, she caught her breath. 'Shit. I knew this was going to be tricky. It's Gabriel and his brother, Martin.' She turned away swiftly and leaned into Jakub

'They're fraternal twins. Gabriel is the dark one,' and murmuring into his ear. 'I think those two are the ones we are supposed to watch for. I told you Lucien thought him potentially dangerous all those years ago, and insisted I sever the connection immediately.'

Jakub murmured, 'He doesn't look dangerous. More like a tourist.'

'Don't let yourself be fooled. There's a razor sharp brain behind those intense eyes, and he speaks at least five languages fluently. He's not to be taken lightly, and his brother is some sort of scary mathematician. They have some connection to Justin, which is probably why Lucien is interested. This is just a watching brief, so we watch and do nothing else.'

She covertly watched their reflections in the mirror as they moved to a table close to the band and sat down. They ordered drinks from the waitress and seemed to be waiting for someone.

'They're probably here on holidays. They did go to Charles University for a year, so they're probably catching up with old friends.'

'No, I tell you, Jakub, there's something behind this. Gabriel was never interested in any of the political demonstrations, never attended any meetings. But Lucien thought him dangerous although he spent most of his time with his books and tapes.'

'When he wasn't screwing you, you mean,' Jakub snarled.

'It was nearly eight years ago. Pull yourself together, this is a ridiculous time to become jealous of someone I knew before I even met you, idiot.' Kamila smiled into his eyes, and kissed him gently. 'Go get some more beers,' she said.

He stood, and turning, looked straight into Justin's eyes. 'Ah, Justin, well met.'

'My young friends, life is a constant challenge, my two favourite people,' he said and they exchanged glances, as he hung his coat on the rack. 'I'm looking for my nephews.' He turned and looked around the room. 'Ahh, I see them at the back. Did you introduce Jakub to Gabriel, Kamila?' he chuckled. 'Or are you here on Lucien's orders?'

Kamila was stunned, 'Your nephews? Gabriel and his brother?'

'Yes, I thought you knew. It was my suggestion they study in Prague for that year. Lucien didn't like it when he realised who he was. I suppose it was Lucien's suggestion to end your relationship? I have always wondered.'

Jakub scowled up at the older man. 'You're playing a dangerous game with Lucien.'

'I suggest you ring him', Justin interrupted, 'and tell him I've arrived, he'll be beside himself with joy.' He strolled calmly away, raising his hands, palms outward, and called a greeting to his elder brother's sons.

Kamila watched Jakub's face as he made the call. He scowled for a moment then his face broke into a grin, and he cut the connection. 'That's it, my pet, we get to go home now and we're free.' He kissed her swiftly on the cheek. 'Lucien was furious that Justin had arrived, and was cursing beautifully when I hung up. Let's leave now before he wants anything else. We are done.'

# Chapter Nine

## Meredith . . . Still

After the girls left for some R&R, Meredith sat staring out of the window. She saw nothing of the beauty, nothing of the clear sky, the wonderful vista of colours before her eyes. She was looking backwards in time to another era when she was just 16 and James 19 years old. They had always been very close, and when their parents died in that dreadful train disaster, James had taken on the mantle of protector and head of their small family. They were devastated by the death of their parents, and finally agreed, after discussions with various distant family members, to move to Europe. The only near relatives were there, and there were plenty of them, including grandparents on both sides, uncles, aunts, and cousins. It had seemed a sensible thing to do.

They moved to France, and she had loved it. She loved being close to Paris, to the Louvre, and to the other galleries, museums, and historic sites. James started university, and she had finished her secondary education.

The family had been welcoming and supportive. She and James lived for a time with their paternal grandparents, but when James had decided on the Sorbonne, they had relocated to Paris. There were never any problems about money. They had been left extremely wealthy in their own right. She enrolled at École Massillon in the Marais, but found the structure tiresome. The French education system was quite arduous compared to her private school in Sydney, but she had coped.

It was only after George had started to take notice of her that the trouble had started. James was very intuitive and had recognised very quickly what George was up too. He told her he had recognised George for what he was as soon as they met. Their father had discussed various members of their extended family with James just months before his death. James knew about George's propensities even then, which was why he didn't wait, but tackled him immediately.

George arrogantly told him to his face that he would seduce his sister within a few months, and there was nothing he, 'the little shit from Australia', could do about it. George hadn't been prepared for James's flash of temper and incredible strength, or for the fact that James had recorded the entire episode including the beating he had inflicted. George, begging for mercy, came through crystal clear on the tape, and James had sent a copy to the hospital with his compliments.

That had been the end of it, or so they thought, but George bided his time. It was almost ten years later that George had become embroiled in the Turner fiasco, and there was no doubt in her mind that it had been deliberate on George's part to implicate James. By that time, both she and James were aware of George's penchant for inflicting revenge on anyone who crossed him.

James and Penelope were wed, and Bede was just a few months old. Meredith still had the tape, now on CD, but still as clear as the day it had been recorded. Perhaps it was time to use it. James had always been reluctant to go that far. It would devastate the former patriarch who loved his youngest son and would tolerate no criticism of him. Their parents had early rebelled against the restrictions imposed by the Family, and left to raise their children in an environment more conducive to the true meaning of '*liberté, égalité, fraternité*'.

She and James were strong, very independent persons, imbued with the strength and clear-sighted determination of the land that had reared them. She was certain in her own mind that James had been murdered and that George was behind it. She felt that George was behind the current troubles heading their way, and that it originated with that time James had stepped in to protect her.

George was a sod, had always been a sod, a lecherous, and sadistic bastard, but mostly, he kept his 'pursuits' away from family. He had always managed to stay outside his father's radar, his charm and manipulative tendencies had never diminished; and even now, most of the family still believed him to be 'whiter than snow'.

James had been arrogant in those days, as they all were if she was honest, and had refused to take George seriously. It was only years later when George had set him up to take the fall for the Turner substitution that he acknowledged George would not stop until he had avenged himself. As soon as James realised what George had been about and the narrow escape he had had, he had moved his wife, his daughter, and herself back to Australia.

James hoped following in their parent's footsteps would be far enough away from George's machinations for them to remain safe. It had taken George almost twenty-five years to finally wreak his vengeance. She would have to tell the girls the whole story, and as soon as possible. After dinner tonight would be best, or perhaps as soon as they returned from their swim, they would be cool and relaxed. She continued to think long and hard for another thirty minutes. She had two phone calls to make. Then getting to her feet, she picked up the phone and dialled.

## Chapter Ten

# The Intruder

Gabriel woke suddenly with his inner defences alert and adrenalin coursing through his bloodstream. He didn't know what had wakened him. He was a light sleeper, so any disturbance would register. He listened to Martin's even breathing beside him and took a moment to reorientate himself. They were in Justin's new apartment, on the floor, in sleeping bags amongst the cardboard boxes in what would eventually be the dining room. It was the farthest room from the street, away from the traffic noise, and close to the study.

Quietly, he slipped out of the sleeping bag and stood calmly for another moment then moved catlike across the room. His night vision was excellent; he needed no light to guide him. He eased open the door into the hall, and moved quietly toward the slight sounds he now heard more distinctly coming from the study. Justin would not be there at four in the morning without the lights blazing. His eyesight needed a little help these days.

He eased the door of the study, opened a crack, listened, and then peered in. The moon was full, the light illuminating the room with a soft white glow. He could see clearly, and there was someone bending over the desk standing in the middle of the room. The intruder had his back to the door and was easing open the top drawer. Not too bright was his first thought, and definitely arrogant was the second. The intruder, tallish and very slim, was dressed entirely in black with a black hat pulled low over the ears. There was something familiar about the figure, and he paused with the memory of himself and Martin taking off their coats at Tretters. And turning with a shiver shooting across his shoulders, the girl with the spiky red hair!

He moved silently across the room on bare feet, being careful to keep his breathing shallow. He knew this intruder well. Moving with the speed and grace, for which he was renowned, he swept her legs out from under her with a strange sweeping movement of his right leg, causing her to fall forward, hitting her forehead on the desk with a crash. She was immediately up twisting around and coming at him with a knife. But he had already leaped back away from the swing that would have sliced across his chest. He held both hands out in a dampening gesture, 'Cool it, Kamila, what are you looking for?'

Then the lights of the room snapped on, Martin and Justin stood in the doorway, Justin holding a revolver loosely in his right hand. They were both alert and ready for action, and Martin as naked as himself.

Justin calmly walked into the room, smiling slightly. 'I should make a habit of having you boys over. You do have your uses, but I think we'd be more comfortable if you both put some clothes on.' He looked across at Gabriel. 'Tie him up and we'll see what he's after.' He peered at the figure now crouching in front of Gabriel and then amended, 'Or rather, tie her up.'

Gabriel reached across, and taking the knife from her, swung her roughly around to face Martin still standing in the doorway. He pulled her arms viciously behind her back and held them together with one hand, while looking around for something to tie her with.

Martin, lounging just inside the door, straightened quickly and swore, 'Jesus, you bitch, what are you after now?'

Kamila snarled at him, and twisting her head back toward Gabriel, hissed, 'Let go of me, you bully, and put some clothes on. I don't talk to naked men.' He released her arms and shoved her away, as if he had been burned. 'I don't think you can make any demands in this circumstance. Just explain yourself as Martin suggested. What exactly are you after?'

Martin threw Gabriel's trousers across the room. 'Well, this is old home week isn't it, Justin? I take it you too know the not so lovely Kamila?' He turned to Gabriel. 'I think I will have to do the interrogation. By the look on your face, you would probably strangle the lady.'

Gabriel felt unaccustomed rage surge through his body. He wasn't sure where the emotion came from. He thought he had dealt with the pain, hurt, and betrayal years ago. Taking a deep breath, he turned away, pulled on his trousers, and zipped them with a quick jerk. 'No, I'm fine, Martin. Just a bit surprised, really.' He turned to Justin. 'Perhaps it would be best if we all sit down. Kamila, you first.' He indicated the straight-backed chair at the side of the desk.

Justin, still keeping his gun levelled on Kamila, said, 'I do know our intruder. She's tricky, so don't take your eyes off her. We need to secure her, and then we'll talk. From past experience, she moves very quickly.'

Martin raised his eyebrows. 'This seems to be a slightly different Kamila from the one you knew, Gabe. I'll get something to tie her with.'

Kamila hissed, 'You three great big strong men, do you think I will tell you anything?'

'That's okay.' Gabriel said calmly. He looked her over with loathing. 'We'll just call the police and explain that I caught you breaking in and you attacked me with a knife. That should keep you locked up for some time.' He watched her face carefully and saw her eyes flicker and lips tighten slightly. Smiling now, he asked, 'Is there someone we should call on your behalf? Or should we leave that to the police?' He raised his eyebrows and smiled coldly. His emotions were now under control. He was his usual icy self.

Martin walked back in with some packing tape he had found in the kitchen and indicated the chair for her to sit. He proceeded to bind first her hands behind her back, and then her ankles to the legs of the chair. 'Now, who is to do the interrogating? Justin, you first I think, as it's your home.' He grinned at the furious, struggling girl. 'Or should we be making that phone call?' He raised his eyebrows and looked across at Gabriel.

Justin pulled an armchair across the floor, placed his gun carefully on the desk, then sat facing Kamila. 'I will assume that Lucien is behind this invasion, my dear. I suggest you tell me what you were looking for. I will find out sooner or later, and it may be in your interest to deal with me now.'

'Call the police, I will tell you nothing,' she said coldly. She was watching Gabriel through slitted eyes her body tense.

Gabriel picked up the phone and started dialling. 'Police, I wish to report a break in.' He waited, looked briefly at Kamila, then shrugged and continued, 'We've caught the intruder and have her here tied to a chair.' He laughed into the receiver. 'Yes, I said her . . . of course, delighted . . . take your time, she's not going anywhere...' He hung up.

Kamila snarled cursed, swore, then softening her face, looked directly at Gabriel with tears pouring down her cheeks. 'Please, you can't do this to me. I will go to prison,' she moaned softly. 'Please.'

He looked at her coldly, 'Kamila, I remember how easily you weep. You told me once it was your one skill, so you have about ten, maybe twenty minutes, I think, then I'm afraid it will be too late.'

Scowling again, she thought for a few moments then looked across at Justin, 'Okay, I will tell you what I know, but you have to let me go before the police get here.' She drew in a long breath. 'You're right of course, you know I work mostly for Lucien. He's heard rumours that you're looking for an antique book relating to your family's past. He's not sure whether to believe the rumours. You know he and George have had a lot of dealings, but there has been a falling out, quite dramatic I think. Lucien believes George is planning something, and is really behind all the rumours about the book as a sort of diversion. He asked me look for any documents indicating what the book is, and why it's important. Obviously, I've failed miserably, and you know Lucien doesn't like failure. That's really all I know, now let me go.' She looked angrily around at the three of them.

Just as Justin was about to speak, there was a loud banging on the front door of the apartment. She became desperate, twisting and turning against the bonds. 'You have to let me go. I have told you all I know.' She looked pleadingly around at them all.

Justin considered her, and then turning to Gabriel, 'What do you think?'

Gabriel listened to the noise coming from the front door, then looked back quickly to catch a fleeting half smile on her lips. 'Nah, I think she knows a lot more than she's telling, I suggest we keep her for a while longer.'

Kamila snarled at him, but he ignored her and turned to Martin, 'Go and invite our friends in, see if you can keep them entertained for a few moments. We might still need them.'

He smiled at Kamila, 'Okay, the rest of the story, my pet, or I turn you over to our comrades in the next room.'

She scowled again, 'I may be better off with the police.'

Justin cut in, 'Of course, my dear, by all means, but I suggest you tell us a little more about this feud between Lucien and George. Also, I would like to know where to contact Lucien. We may be able to come to some sort of arrangement.' He looked at her very thoughtfully for a moment, and then smiled coldly. An unpleasant smile that very few people ever saw. Kamila's eyes narrowed in rage.

# Chapter Eleven

## Lunch

The table was set for lunch with Bede and Hera sitting quietly, neither of them making any attempt to consume any of the delicious dishes set before them. Meredith had left them moments before having been called to the telephone. Both had been stunned by Meredith's confessions, and both were shockingly aware there was obviously more to come.

Bede was the first to speak, 'I don't know about you, but I'm still dazed. The idea of Dad beating someone and putting him in hospital is something of a shock.' She drew in a deep breath and looked across at her sister. 'We have to believe it all, just retelling the story caused Meredith pain, that was obvious, so I will say it again. I have to believe it.' She got up from the table and wandered to the window, lifted the curtain, and looked across to the hills in the distance. 'It sounds so far-fetched, but when you add the dreams we have both been having, James's death and the memories I have of the family celebrations when we were young, it does fit together rather nicely.' She turned back to Hera, still sitting quietly at the table.

'Yes, but what, if anything, can we do about it?' Hera ever practical asked. She was leaning back in her chair and staring unseeing at the plaster ceiling rose.

'Nothing at the moment,' Meredith interrupted them, coming back into the room. 'I am waiting to hear back from Justin. I sent him a message yesterday and tried to ring him. He seems to have switched his phone off. Very suspicious for Justin.' She sat calmly at the table. 'Come on girls, we all need to eat, and Mrs Robinson has prepared a beautiful lunch with home-made bread, which must not go to waste.'

Bede grinned and sat back down at the table. 'Of course, you're right, but I think another conference is definitely called for, Aunt Meredith.' She helped herself to salad. 'Immediately after lunch, I think. There are a few gaps I need filled.' She looked at Hera briefly, then turned back to Meredith. 'And I will not be put off with vague mutterings from you.'

Meredith grimaced, but calmly continued eating. 'Pass the wine, Hera', she looked at her younger niece, 'and stop scowling.'

Hera spoke suddenly, 'Meredith, what I understand from what you said this morning is that our family, yours and mine, are all crooks of some sort and have been for generations, right?'

'Yes, dear, but mostly now, all the companies are legitimate, and although James, Penelope, and I tried to remain at a distance from the entity, the Family, we are still connected financially to some extent. James does have, or rather, did have business dealings with Justin and various other members. I think he has some connection to Gabriel as well.' She frowned and looked at the two girls. 'He's a cousin of sorts, but not really. The relationships within the family are almost impossible to work out, which is why it's become important that we have no more intermarriage.' She looked at the startled expressions on both the girls' faces then continued, 'So do not become emotionally involved with anyone with any connection to the family.' She dropped her head into her hands and sighed.

'So who did you become emotionally involved with, Meredith? Not George obviously, but perhaps Justin?' Bede allowed sarcasm into her voice. 'You are still concealing something, Meredith, so stop it and be completely honest with us for once in your life.'

Hera murmured, 'Stow it Bede, she's only trying to help.'

'No she's not, are you, Meredith? You have told us a lot but not enough. You have told us as much as you think necessary to stop us from investigating further. We need to know everything that could have a bearing, however remote, on the murder of our father, your brother. We need to know how much you suspect and who you suspect, if anyone.'

She was feeling anxious and confused. Pushing back slightly from the table, she looked down at the beautiful rug at her feet. The muted colours against the rich polished Jarrah boards took her back to when James had bought it back from Turkey on one of his trips overseas. She missed him dreadfully. Getting up from the table, she suddenly started pacing again. 'James was murdered, that's now beyond question.' She looked at Meredith again. 'Isn't it, Meredith?'

'I don't think you can make that sort of statement, Bede.' Hera was agitated, and she turned to look carefully at Meredith, then drew a deep breath and sighed. 'Okay, your face tells the story, Meredith, you had better come completely clean.'

'I don't have any proof. It's just a feeling, intuition if you like. Justin is avoiding me. And yes, Justin is, was, the love of my life.' She sighed. 'I may as well continue with all the sordid details you're certainly old enough to understand.' She looked around the table. 'If you're both finished, we should move into the office. It's comfortable there and Robby can clear the table.'

Meredith felt drained. Just remembering caused her heart to beat faster, and she felt a fine sweat break out briefly on her hands. She calmed herself and started baldly, 'Obviously, it was a long time ago, Justin and I were engaged to be married until he walked out on me to try to seduce Mette, Dominik's wife. Admittedly, it was before they were married, but you can imagine the fallout. James was furious on my behalf, to say nothing of how I felt. Dominik was furious, Mette was shocked, as he had tried to pass himself off as Dominik and had almost managed to get her into bed.' Glancing quickly at the startled expressions facing her, she continued quickly, 'It was years before the scandal was forgotten, or Dominik and Mette would forgive him. He admitted that it was a complete betrayal of his brother and his brother's fiancée, to say nothing of me. He insisted it was some sort of weird aberration and spent many years trying desperately to make it up to them. I don't know if they ever really trusted him again, but he eventually became a sort of mentor for the twins. He never married. I think personally that he did genuinely feel something for Mette, certainly more than he felt for me obviously, although there was always that competitive thing between him and Dominik.

'He tried to resurrect our relationship years later, but of course, I wasn't interested by then. I would never trust him again in that respect, but I think that he really does care to some degree, and he genuinely admired James. He would never now do anything to hurt James or myself or either of you.' She got up from the chair and walked across to Bede standing by the window. She put her hand on her shoulder. 'Bede, please, you must believe me. I was only trying to protect you and Hera from the worst aspects of the family. I trust Justin to look after our interests now that James is dead.' She frowned. 'But there is something that's not right about all of this. I just wish I could contact him.'

Bede smiled gently, and said quietly, 'Aunt Meredith, everything you have just told us argues against trusting Justin. He proved in the past to be completely untrustworthy and ruthless if he wanted something badly enough. What he did all those years ago is as shocking as anything I've heard so far, and how you can calmly say you trust him now? I don't understand. I know it was a long time ago, but I don't think I would ever be so forgiving.' Bede caught Hera's eye, and a look of understanding passed between them. 'We need to find that contract, and we need to speak to Inspector Campbell. I'm going to ring him now.'

Meredith was very pale. 'I don't, for a moment, believe you are right about Justin, but I've already rung Campbell. He's due here soon. I'll go through the accounts and all the contracts in the study, you two search James's bedroom and the library.' She left quietly.

Hera raised her eyebrows at Bede. 'It needed to be said, I know, but I think she is much more fragile than we ever realised. We need to go gently. I've always wondered why she never married. She must have been absolutely beautiful when she was young. I have a bad feeling about everything we've heard so far about this Justin person. Bede, it's all starting to look and feel very ugly.'

Bede was looking pale and tired. 'Yes, it's starting to feel really nasty. You take the bedroom, I'll start in the library.'

Bede wandered across to the library and looked around. She hadn't wanted to come in here since her father's death over a month ago; it was so essentially him. It was clean and ordered, she could still faintly smell his particular brand of cigarettes and thought of all the times she and Hera had nagged him to stop smoking. They could have saved their breath and not put such heavy guilt trips on him. Life seemed to be a confirmation to take each day as a bonus and make the most of it.

She drew a deep breath and moved to the large desk. Going through the drawers here seemed a useless exercise. The solicitor had been through everything, looking for the will, which he had found; all straightforward, no surprises there. Still, he wouldn't have taken any notice of a contract that should have been in the study, would he? She continued to open drawers while thinking.

Her father had been a secretive man in some ways. He had never hinted at any problems from the past, and although he had talked about both Justin and George, he had never even hinted at any involvement between Meredith and Justin. Would he have kept any references to the past? Meredith had the CD as a deterrent to George, but perhaps there was something else. She looked thoughtfully at the bookcase taking up two thirds of the wall space. It was an impressive collection, quite a few first editions, and some antiques—really quite valuable.

———◆———

Bede had been in Sydney on that dreadful day and had caught a flight immediately. She had been shocked, tired, and stressed when she arrived. Thinking back, Inspector Campbell had been saying something about the library being in something of a mess with books all over the desk, and some on the floor. She'd not thought anything about it at the time. James quite often had books all over the floor when he was engaged on one of his projects, but it was strange for him to go sailing in the middle of it.

'The library had been searched,' she said aloud, and astonished that she hadn't thought of it before. 'Hera', she yelled, 'get in here now, and you too, Aunt Meredith.' Seeing their startled faces, she explained. 'We need to look very carefully through all the books. I think someone searched the library the day Dad was killed.' She recounted her conversation with Inspector Campbell, but she had been too tired and shocked to respond in any rational manner. Now, her mind clear, she looked at her sister and aunt. 'This is going to be a long process I think, but we need to look at every book, make sure it's where it should be on the shelves, and there is nothing stuck between the pages.'

Meredith looked slightly startled and very tired. 'Do you really think that's necessary, dear? Don't you think you're making too much of this? Inspector Campbell will be here later. Why not wait and discuss what to do with him?'

Hera moved across and put her arm around Meredith's shoulders, 'Aunt Meredith, we don't need Inspector Campbell to help search the library. Bede is right, we're the only ones who will know if anything is out of order, and we need to start now.' She gently moved Meredith toward the shelves nearest the French doors and flung them open. She dragged one of the comfortable chairs over to the doors and pushed her aunt into it. 'I'll bring you a stack of books, and you go through them carefully. When you're finished, you can start on another. But in the meantime, sit quietly and try not to let yourself become anxious.' She smiled gently and quickly kissed Meredith on her cheek.

Moving back to the centre of the room, she and Bede exchange rueful glances. They looked around. It was a beautiful room, warm and inviting, with polished Jarrah floors and beautiful rugs from Afghanistan and Turkey. The ceiling fans at each end of the room helped keep it cool in the summer, and the bookshelves were built into the sides of the room, some reaching the ceiling. There were paintings on the walls, and a locked glass-fronted affair to house the most valuable of the antique books and first editions.

'Okay, let's get started, Hera. Maybe you could start on the desk, make sure there is nothing there out of order, and maybe I should start on the antiques. I know everything he's bought, and there should be a list as well. I'll check to make sure nothing is missing then I guess we start on the rest of the house. It's going to take days.' Bede sighed.

All was quiet for a while then Meredith looked up. 'The last time I spoke to Justin, he was looking for some old book relating to the history of the Family. See if there's anything there, Bede, he rang especially to ask.'

Bede frowned and opened the glass-fronted bookcase. Some of the books were extremely old, one illuminated manuscript from Valencia, c. 1460, *The Book of Hours*, was on vellum. It had always been one of her favourites, and even as a young girl, the beauty of the intricate miniatures had fascinated her. She carefully replaced the book in its container. There was nothing there, and she continued quietly thinking all the time.

They had been working for forty minutes when Mrs Robinson announced, 'Inspector Campbell is here. Shall I send him in?'

'Yes,' Bede answered. 'And I think we all need a cup of tea.'

# Chapter Twelve

## *Still Justin's Apartment*

Gabriel smiled gently at Kamila with a smile that sent shivers down her spine. She drew a deep breath. 'Okay, I'll tell you all I know. George betrayed Lucien in some way, and no, I don't know the details, but Lucien is furious. He wants, or maybe, needs George out of the way, possibly dead, and suspects that you, Justin, would not be averse to helping with this. George is scheming to take over some aspect of Lucien's world, I think. But that's speculation on my part. I will give you Lucien's current address and telephone number if you will please let me go now. This really is the very last job I was to do for him, and Jakub is waiting for me outside in the car. He will come looking for me soon, particularly after seeing the police arrive. I was to look for any indication of a priceless antique book you have recently bought, or documents indicating you are in the process of buying. But why Lucien thought the information would be lying around here somewhere, I have no idea. Really, that's all I know.'

Justin looked at her thoughtfully. 'Okay, the phone number and address, I will accept. The story about Lucien sending you to look for an antique book in my library is not believable, but that you know about the book, I do believe.' He regarded her thoughtfully, raised one eyebrow, and looked across at Gabriel. 'What do you think?'

'I think that we should bring Jakub in now,' Gabriel moved to the door, and called quietly to Martin.

Kamila sat frozen, not moving a muscle, her gaze on the open doorway. Jakub came through the door with Martin and two others behind him. Jakub's hands were tied behind his back, and he was scowling furiously. Justin waited while Kamila wrote something on the pad he handed her then rang the number, waited, and spoke briefly into the phone. 'Lucien, my friend, I have Kamila here and Jakub. They are a little anxious. We, my nephews and I, would like to meet tonight and discuss our mutual friend George with you. Wonderful, see you in twenty minutes.'

Looking frantically from Gabriel to the two police officers, Kamila wailed, 'The police, you bastard.'

Gabriel grinned, and said smoothly, 'Meet some of the younger members of our family.' He indicated the two men in uniform holding Jakub firmly between them.

Kamila was speechless. 'You bastard!' She turned to glare at Jakub, 'how did you come to be caught?'

He glared back at her, 'I was looking for you of course. You were taking too long. What have you got us into now?'

Gabriel smiled at his two young cousins. 'I'm amazed how frequently that works. We'll have to be careful how often we use it. It's illegal, you know, to impersonate a policeman.' He shook hands with both the newcomers, slapping them on the back in a friendly manner.

'Are you going to untie me?' Kamila snarled.

'Not yet.' Martin drawled, looking at his brother, while holding up the decanter of brandy. 'What will you all have?'

'Make them all Perrier. We need to keep a cool head here,' Gabe replied.

## Chapter Thirteen

# International Airport
# Perth Western Australia

As Gabriel came through the exit gate of Perth International Airport, he looked across at the tall, slim woman with the beautifully cut dark hair holding a placard bearing his name. It was she, the woman in his dreams over the last few months. This was obviously one of his 'cousins', or at least some relation of sorts. Bugger, he refused to become involved with anyone within the family. It was too horrendous to contemplate. But it was she without any doubt.

He and Martin moved through the crowd and greeted her. 'You must be cousin Bede, or are you Hera?' He smiled his most charming smile, the smile that never quite reached his eyes.

Holding out her hand she replied, 'Bede, and you are?'

'Gabriel at your service.'

'In that case, you must be Martin,' she said, extending her hand toward him. She looked at both of them. 'You didn't take long through customs and border control. Is that your entire luggage?'

Martin shrugged, 'Yep that's it, we left Prague yesterday. I think spent one hour in Dubai, not enough time to acclimatise to your time zone or your temperature. I think we're going to need lighter clothes.'

Gabriel cut in, 'A couple of days ago, Martin was in Istanbul and I was in London. We spent a total of two days in Prague, then flew straight here. 'After your phone call, Justin thought it would be best if we came ASAP even though', he, turning to look at his brother, 'Martin wanted to spend some R & R with friends in Prague skiing.' He paused. 'But I guess that's out of the question here.'

Bede grinned, 'Try between 37° and 40° Celsius. We can probably accommodate some lighter clothes for you both though.' She considered them carefully. 'I hope you're not too exhausted. We have the property helicopter waiting, it's easier than driving. Two days in a car is probably not what you want at the moment.'

Gabriel looked at Martin, and then turned back to her. 'Lead on, we're right behind you.'

She was magnificent, her eyes were a clear hazel with flecks of green and gold, her hair a rich mahogany with red highlights, and she moved with a dancer's fluid grace, just as in the dreams. She was dressed in shorts, a loose cotton top with long, long brown legs ending in battered leather riding boots. But he would not allow himself to become emotionally involved with anyone in the family. Both he and Martin had made that sacred vow years ago.

They walked out of Perth International Airport to a battered Jeep Wrangler in the car park. Martin strolled at her side, with Gabriel walking a few paces behind. 'So tell me about this property you own, where it is in relation to Perth, and how long will it take to get there?'

Martin, aware of Gabriel's strange reaction to this beautiful girl, was prepared to run interference, step in, and distract her. It would obviously be a while before they could speak privately, so in the meantime, he would get as much information as possible. Justin hadn't any concrete information about Australia. He had never visited 'James in his den' as he called it. He smiled down at the girl strolling beside him.

'By helicopter, it's about an hour and half northeast of here, mostly wheat country, but our property grows and exports fresh native cut flowers. We export to Europe, UK, and USA as well as the domestic market. It's a fairly large property. To be honest, I'm not exactly sure how big it is now, quite a few square kilometres. James bought it when he and Mum first came back to Australia, and he's expanded it at different times over the years. It's a bit isolated. I hope that won't worry you too much. The nearest township is about fifty kilometres south and it's tiny, but I don't imagine you will be here long enough to become stir crazy.' She looked back over her shoulder at Gabriel, and her grin encompassed them both as she led them to the waiting four-wheel drive. This was obviously a working vehicle. It was covered in red dust with two very solid looking aerials, one on the roof and another on the front bonnet of the car with 'roo bars' attached to the front of the engine.

Bede saw them looking and volunteered, 'We have a few problems with radio signals sometimes, so mostly, we rely on satellite communications on the property. Perth is fine, of course, and all the suburbs, but where we are is problematic, especially when there's a storm brewing.'

Martin drew in a deep breath. 'We both have sat phones because we travel around so much, so it shouldn't be a problem for us.' He glanced at his brother. Gabe's expression was still completely closed, although he didn't think Bede would be aware of it. Gabe was a master at controlling his emotions and was renowned for his poker face. He would continue to be charming and completely untrustworthy, while he sorted out what the problem was.

Leaning against the driver's door was a tall, rangy male. He was well over six feet with the broad shoulders and slim hips of someone who had spent a lot of time on a horse. He also was casually dressed in jeans, loose shirt, and boots. He was deeply suntanned with a hard face, probably in his early thirties.

Bede smiled at the stranger and turned to Martin. 'This is Pete, he'll drive the beast back to the farm, while we take the 'copter.'

Gabriel immediately proffered his hand, and it was grasped in a strong, almost crushing, grip. He grinned and returned the pressure. In their beautifully cut Armani suits, both he and Martin looked in this environment like a couple of pussies, so it was probably a good idea to correct the impression as soon as possible. 'I'm Gabriel, and this is my young brother, Martin. Glad to meet you.' Martin, with a grin, held out his hand. 'Don't listen to him. I'm younger by exactly ten minutes, but he's always trying to pull the big brother act.' They were both being as charming and as unthreatening as possible in this early stage.

Pete reached out to Martin and tried the same bone crusher, which Martin countered with raised eyebrows. 'You look like you spend a lot of time outdoors, and you look as if you ride a lot.' He turned to Bede, 'Do you keep many horses on the property?'

Both Bede and Pete laughed. 'Yes of course, but we also use trail bikes and have two helicopters. It's a big property,'

Bede turned to Pete. 'Martin asked me before just how big it is, but I don't know exactly. Do you?'

Pete's voice was low and gravelly with a strong Australian accent, 'No idea really, James just kept adding to it as the fancy took him, so the only one who really knows is the solicitor here in Perth. There never seemed to be any reason to check up. Maybe that's something else we need to do.' He smiled proprietorially down at Bede.

Pete looked across at the small sports bags in their hands, and with raised eyebrows, asked, 'Is that your entire luggage, or do we need to collect something else?'

'No', Gabriel answered, 'we tend to travel light, but we'll need some other clothes and probably boot.' He looked at Bede for the first time since greeting her at the departure lounge. 'I think it would make sense to go back and buy some things here, it will save time.'

She had been aware of his immediate negative reaction to her and didn't understand why. She coolly raised her eyebrows. 'Of course, sensible suggestion. You and Martin can do your shopping, and I'll ring Meredith to let her know we'll be about two hours.' She walked away taking her phone from her pocket, then paused, thought for a moment, and called after them, 'Don't forget hats, the sun can be deadly.' They slung their bags into the jeep, waved, and turned away.

As they walked back into the airport and headed for the shopping complex, Martin drew a long breath and murmured quietly, 'Well, out with it. What's happening?'

'Dreams are still my problem, Martin, and I've been dreaming about that beautiful creature for the last two months, but I refuse to have anything to do with her.'

'Bloody hell, Gabe, you really know how to complicate matters. What sort of dreams? Anything to do with this problem or purely sensual, or knowing you, they will probably be both.'

'Got it in one, and there is definitely an element of danger here in Australia, so we need to stay on our toes. What did you think of Pete?'

'Well', Martin drawled, 'he's extremely fit, not just from riding horses or trail bikes around the property. He moves like he knows how to take care of himself, and that trick with the handshake was telling. He was checking us out, and I didn't like the way he tried to manoeuvre us into driving.'

They both burst out laughing. 'We also need to know just exactly how long he's worked here, and how well he knew James. Bede seems to defer to him a little, which is also telling.'

'Well, it looks like it's going to be an interesting few days, so yes, I'll run interference if need be between you and the beautiful Bede, but I think she picked up on the chill in the air, so you will probably be fine. Mind you, you're going to owe me big time.'

Gabriel grunted, 'Jeans, T-shirts, boots, and don't forget the hat. Concentrate now, I have a feeling the very fit Pete was a little surprised with our lack of luggage. He will probably search what we did bring.'

Martin snorted, 'He has no idea of how light we can travel and still be lethal.' They both grinned.

———— •• ————

Bede turned to Martin. 'In answer to your question, both Hera and I often fly the helicopters. But mostly, it's Pete and one other employee on the property. James insisted very early in the piece that both Hera and I know every aspect of the business, so we can take over at any time. We use the 'copters for fertilising and weed control when needed. Also, we have a problem with kangaroos, so we use the 'copters to herd them away when needed. We don't cull at all. There are a few big greys that cause a lot of damage at times.'

Gabriel leaned forward suddenly. 'Can we do a sort of fly over to give Martin and myself an idea of just how large is "fairly large" and where, in relation to the house for instance, is the lake where James was sailing?'

'Of course, I'll swing by the lake, it's closer, and then we'll circle the property. We can go in low so you can get an idea of where everything is.' Bede spoke into the microphone, but the noise from the blades kept chatting to a minimum.

She was confused about Gabriel's negative reaction. Perhaps, he didn't like tall slim dark women. Martin seemed okay though. It was a pity. She liked the look of Gabriel, liked his eyes—they were a beautiful chocolate brown—almost velvety, and he was so tall. In fact, they were both really tall, well over six feet. Closer to 6'4", she thought. A relief, really, it was tedious having to wear flat shoes all the time.

She spoke into the microphone again. 'There's the lake,' she pointed through the front window and took them lower. 'That's our boathouse with the blue roof. James was apparently heading back in shore when the boat exploded. There was not much left. But there was an investigation of the remains of the boat, and a post-mortem, naturally. They didn't find anything suspicious, of course, but with everything else happening lately, we now suspect it was murder. What we don't understand is why and how.' She drew in a deep breath. 'When we get to the homestead, we'll fill you in on everything we know.'

Both Gabriel and Martin peered down through the windows at the lake below. It was much bigger than either of them had thought. Easily several square kilometres in diameter, an irregular shape—almost like a teardrop—and they could see a largish building not far from the boathouses on the shore. The countryside around looked flattish with a river meandering down from the distant hills, obviously feeding the lake. Bede continued, 'Justin said on the phone that you two are a sort of troubleshooting team. Is that true?'

Martin nodded. 'Yep, but we can leave all that until we can talk more easily.'

She angled the helicopter away from the lake and headed toward the hills in the distance. Gabriel looked back. The lake was a beautiful clear blue reflecting the amazing blue of the sky, the country around was wild with scrubby grey green trees, scattered shrubs, and red earth. There was a strange beauty about this landscape. He saw a group of kangaroos hopping through the scrub, and in the distance, there was a trail of smoke weaving toward the sky. There were no housing complex or shopping malls anywhere to be seen, just this astonishingly magnificent country. It was almost overwhelming. The beauty and majesty generated a calm and peace that sank to the depth of his soul. Even with the noise generated by the rotors of the helicopter, there was stillness around him. It couldn't be more different to the grey skies of Prague if they'd been on another planet. He felt himself relaxing. The muscles in his back and shoulders slowly unwinding, and he smiled.

He thought he could really like this place, the open spaces, plenty of room to breathe. James was probably right. This was as far away from the Machiavellian machinations of the Family that it was possible to get. Then he grimaced to himself. James was still dead, and it was more than probable it had something to do with someone from within the Family.

He had liked and respected James. He was straightforward and honest, quite like his eldest daughter, he suspected. They certainly shared the same colouring. He admonished himself. Don't get involved and don't get too comfortable, this would only be for a couple of days. He glanced across at Bede, piloting the helicopter with confidence and skill. How to keep her at a distance, but still keep her on side? They needed all the conscious and unconscious information that Bede, Hera, and Meredith had. It would be a challenge, and they would need to be careful not to give too much away. He couldn't remember if he and Martin had ever met the girls when they were young. He knew from Justin that James had brought them to Paris for one of the family Christmas celebrations, but he and Martin had always avoided them if at all possible. He had no conscious memory of meeting her before, so this impression of familiarity must be simply from the bloody dreams.

The dreams, one aspect of their gypsy heritage that could not be bred out it seemed.

Martin turned around. 'This is amazing country, Gabe, we should try to explore a bit if possible since we've missed out on our skiing R & R.' They both laughed.

Bede grinned and spoke into the headset, 'You probably had a traditional Christmas as well. I'm afraid any skiing here is done during the winter, mostly in June, July, and August, and in the Eastern states. A traditional European Christmas is a bit silly here. It's too hot for a start, and all the workers on the property with family go home for the Christmas and New Year. Mind you, the lead up to the holiday period is really busy, we close down for the full week, so we need to get the distributions out well before that.

'As I said earlier, we deliver overseas to Europe and America. They all seem to like our wild flowers, particularly the Hakeas and Proteas. We have a refrigerator truck that goes out once a week to Perth, and we have a freight contract with a Perth firm for the overseas market.'

'Was there ever any suggestion that James's death had anything to do with the business?' Gabriel gently asked.

'No, but in the initial stages, we accepted it as an accident. It was only later we, that is Hera, myself, and even Meredith, started dreaming a lot that we became anxious. When I got back here a couple of days ago, we started talking about the death properly for the first time. Then it became obvious to all of us that James had been murdered. That was when we started looking for that last contract and realised it was missing. We realised there were too many unanswered questions.' She paused. 'There's the homestead ahead.'

They peered down, and Gabriel drew in a slow breath. The sight was inspiring. They were circling, and as they drifted lower, he could see people moving around the rolling green lawn, and there were several outbuildings scattered around a large two-storey Colonial style house with veranda's shading all four sides. He could see a woman standing on the steps looking up with her arm, shading her eyes.

'Is that Meredith?' Martin asked.

Bede looked down. 'Yes, Hera is probably still at the computer. She has an assignment due in tomorrow, she's doing a masters in Biological Science.'

Martin looked intrigued. 'Obviously useful out here, where is she studying?'

'Curtin University in Perth, but since James's death she had to change to correspondence. She's needed on the property now,' Bede replied.

'Well, the sooner we try to sort out what actually happened and look at those two old books you've found, the sooner we can get at some answers,' Gabriel replied.

## Chapter Fourteen

# The Homestead

Meredith strolled across the lawn as the blades started to slow and the noise decrease. She grinned at them, while she waited quietly for them to disembark.

'You probably don't remember me,' she said, as both Gabriel and Martin came toward her. 'But I knew you when you were both quite young.'

Gabriel held out his hand. 'Very glad to renew the connection,' he said with a charming smile, still keeping a distance between himself and Bede. He would let Martin keep her entertained, while he used his charm on Meredith and Hera when they met. I'm bloody sure neither of them would throw me off balance, he mused, still very aware of Bede following behind with Martin. 'We need to get straight down to business if it's all right with you.' He smiled again at Meredith.

'Yes, of course, but won't you have something to drink and eat, it's a long flight from Dubai.' Meredith gestured toward the house.

Martin moved up beside Gabriel, and smiled. 'Maybe', he said, 'but we ate on the plane and both Gabe and I think we should move as quickly as possible with this latest development. We need to look at the books, and to hear about this missing contract. You didn't mention that when you spoke to Justin.' They both looked at her with a query on their faces.

Bede determinedly, with eyes narrowed, turned to Gabriel. 'No, at the time, we didn't really think it was relevant, but now I suspect it will fit in with whatever is going on. James was furious about something to do with it, but he didn't say what was bothering him. And the next day, he was dead, so coping with the shock and the police, it slipped our minds.' She glared at Gabriel thinking, I don't know what his problem is, but I'll be dammed if I let him try to sideline me. She fumed silently to herself.

At that moment, Hera come out onto the veranda and smiled down at them all. 'Hi, come in, we have tea waiting for you and then we can get started.' She paused and then added, 'Unless you would prefer something stronger to drink?'

Gabriel and Martin both grinned up at her. 'No, tea sounds about right then we might change our clothes!' Gabriel murmured as he moved forward to introduce himself. 'I'm Gabe, and you are Hera.' He was more relaxed now, as he took her hand and squeezed it gently.

Martin moved up behind him. 'And for my sins, Martin,' he held out his hand. They were all smiling now as they moved into the cool front hall of the house.

Martin looked around at the very high ceilings and the beautiful polished boards, the walls were painted a delicate shade of eggshell cream, and the antique furniture was lovingly polished to a high sheen. The house was open and airy with a warm welcoming feel about it. There was some astonishing artwork on the walls. He stopped in front of a huge canvas very striking, vibrant, but earthy colours reminiscent of the land they had just flown over. Bede stopped beside him. 'It's a Rover Thomas, and we're lucky to have some of his. It's beautiful, isn't it?' He continued to study the painting and was stunned by the power of the image. He moved on down the hall, seeing more by the same artist.

Hera, following being and seeing his interest said, 'They're all by Rover Thomas, a very talented indigenous West Australian painter. Dead now, I'm afraid.'

Meredith shepherded them into the living room where Mrs Robinson had laid out the tea tray with plates of scones and biscuits. Meredith indicated they should make themselves comfortable and moved to the tea tray. To Bede's annoyance, Gabriel immediately sat in the chair that had traditionally been her father's. Arrogant sot, she thought to herself. There was something about this cousin, or whatever relation he actually was, that really annoyed her. She would have to be careful not to lose her temper.

She left them drinking tea and eating scones, while she went into the library to take the two precious antiques from the locked bookcase. They may as well start now to look at the books, she thought; and then as she turned, realised Gabriel had followed her in.

He leant casually against the doorframe watching her intently, and then spoke quietly, 'I have been a little rude, I know, I owe you an apology. Can we start again?' Looking into her eyes, he continued, 'I have a problem. I am cursed with the Romany penchant for vivid and explicit dreams, and unfortunately or fortunately, I'm not sure which. Over the last two weeks, you have featured in every one. I didn't recognise the woman in the dreams, and to my knowledge, we never met as children. But when I saw you at the airport, it threw me off balance, which is not something that happens to me ever. I didn't handle it well. I turned you over to Martin and froze you out. I'm sorry.' He looked at her carefully with narrowed eyes and continued, 'I realise you are sensitive enough to have picked up on my conflict and my extremely bad behaviour, so here I am asking you to forgive my arrogance, and hope that we can work together on this? It's important.' He still held eye contact.

Bede studied him carefully. He was not strictly good looking, but with his dark well marked brows, chestnut hair, and the deep chocolate brown eyes of his gypsy heritage, there was a magnetism about him. He could obviously turn on the charm whenever it suited him.

'What sort of dreams?'

Gabriel was annoyed. 'I don't think that's important at this point,' he answered defensively.

But Bede interrupted, 'I think it is important. We all, that is Meredith, Hera, and myself have also been experiencing disturbing dreams. It's one of the reasons we started relooking at James's death.

Our dreams have all been warnings, warnings of an unspecified looming danger to one or all of us.'

Gabe raised his eyebrows, and then smiled engagingly and honestly for the first time. 'Trust me, my dreams have not been about impending danger.' He paused for a moment then continued, 'Or at least I don't think I can interpret them that way.' He looked thoughtful again. Straightening up from the doorway, he raised his eyebrows in question.

Bede looked fully into his eyes and smiled. 'Okay, apology accepted, but I have a feeling we'll have to revisit this at some time.' She picked up one of the books and handed it to him. 'Be very careful, they really are very old and quite fragile.'

He frowned down at her for a moment then turned away. He had a sinking feeling in his stomach, and muttered to himself, 'Shit, shit, shit, bugger damn, shit.'

Bede heard the muttered expletive and grinned quietly to herself. This might be quite entertaining.

They moved back into the living room carrying the books.

As they came back into the room, Martin saw that Bede was no longer scowling, so he presumed Gabe had managed to smooth over the looming problem with her. They needed her complete and willing cooperation. He glanced at the books in their arms and immediately stood up, moving eagerly toward them. The books did look old, and his spirits rose. Justin hadn't been completely convinced about the books, but had enough respect for Meredith's intelligence to send them post-haste on this amazing twenty-hours flight to the ends of the world. He hoped it would prove worth the trip.

Mrs Robinson was quietly removing the tea things and Meredith smiled at her. 'Thank you, Robby, that was delicious.' She stood up, moved across the room to spread a clean cloth on the dining table. She then produced several pairs of cotton gloves. 'They really are very fragile,' she said. 'We need to wear gloves when turning the pages. But I think, Bede, you should explain exactly what you saw, and why we were concerned.'

Bede and Gabriel put the books carefully onto the cloth, donned gloves, and they all clustered around the table. Martin picked up another pair, and leaning over, peered at the cover of the book Bede was opening.

The first book she opened, she reported was probably from the seventeenth century, but the provenance was a bit iffy according to James. He purchased it for the many references to the family name. He apparently hadn't had time to check anything, but the book was a collection of original letters, handbound by Ariane, the author of some of the letters. They were in a combination of modern and middle French with a little Latin thrown in. A beautiful collection of drawings, poems, love letters, and general correspondence between several obviously related young people. The writing was crabbed with many inkblots obscuring some of the information on several of the letters, suggesting a young person writing. The pages had obviously been folded at some point and testified to James assumption that they were genuine letters.

The young girl, whose name on the cover, Ariane Caruso-Kern, had obviously bound the book herself, and was the recipient of most of the letters and many she had written. One of the earliest letters in the book was a request for the return of letters she had written to two cousins, one Roberto and one Juliette. The book had been bound quite expertly, and had obviously not been rebound at any later date, which explained its fragility. James had made some notes in a journal he kept with the books, and some of the references he had checked did correspond to events around 1675 in France and Europe. All the letters referring to relatives were scathing of the morals and ethics practised by various named members within their family.

The three children seemed to be in their late teens, well educated, very vocal, and articulate. There were many references to the less than ethical practices of one Uncle Stefan, and how he was using his daughter, Juliette, to consolidate a business arrangement with a rival family. Not that that was an unusual practice, the problem was that in this case, the proposed husband, the Conte de Lacey, had already buried three wives and was thirty years older than Juliette. Ariane had serious misgivings about the deaths of the Conte's previous wives, but her uncle refused to reconsider the marriage.

'The letters are fascinating, almost like a novel,' Bede said. 'Hera and I became hooked, but the writing is hard to decipher in some parts and the language is difficult.'

Meredith broke in, 'I think we need Gabriel's linguistic skills to translate most of it, but it does suggest questionable morals, which given the times, isn't significant. It could be seen as an embarrassment, I think, if it's genuine.'

Bede turned to look at Gabriel. 'I thought it significant that James had actually hidden the two books in a secret section in the bookcase.'

Gabriel, with raised eyebrows and a decidedly sceptical cast to his mouth, opened the book and turned the first pages carefully. He talked or muttered to himself as he studied the writings. 'Well, the pages are all different on extremely expensive paper, which seems to bear out James's theory. The handwriting differs, but Bede is right, I need to study it all more closely for any real significance.' He looked up finally. 'It will take quite some time, and I'm not sure how significant it's likely to be. On the surface, it doesn't appear to contain anything that could be a threat to the Family. But let's have a look at the other one.'

Bede carefully put the second book onto the cloth, and carefully opened the front cover. She leaned over Gabriel's shoulder, 'The thing that I immediately saw was that there had been something inside the verso of the cover. Let me show you.' The cover of the book was bound in tooled leather with beautiful hand-coloured botanical illustrations of various flowers and much gold leaf.

Bede opened the book and showed Gabriel where the edge of the leather on the verso had been levered up. Originally, there would have been some padding within, but now, this had been filled with something from this century. She put her slim fingers carefully into the space and drew out part of a letter. The paper revealed was obviously twenty-first century, 80 grams ordinary, A4 cartridge paper. The wording looked like the end of a contract and revealed part of James's signature.

Bede looked up at Gabriel and across at Martin. 'I think someone else knew about the books, and searched the library the day of his death. Or maybe someone else was searching the library, while James was being murdered by a colleague, or there is someone else entirely that knows about the bookcase. The thing that worries me is that I wouldn't have thought that anyone knew about the secret compartment.'

Martin shook his head. 'You can't know that the books were found if they were still in the hidden compartment.'

Bede looked across at both Gabriel and Martin. 'At first, I thought this could be part of the missing contract, We use ordinary eighty-gram paper, and this piece looks the same as the rest in the office.' She continued thoughtfully, 'but this signature is on the bottom right hand side of the paper, and all our contracts are signed on the left. It's not conclusive, as none of us saw the bloody thing.' Pausing for a moment to collect her thoughts, she continued, 'This is all conjecture, as we don't have the contract. It has definitely disappeared.' She moved away from the table and paced across to the window. Turning back, she looked across at them all. 'I seem to be repeating myself, but I do know the library had been searched. I was in Sydney when I was contacted and caught a flight immediately to arrive that day. Hera and Meredith seemed too distraught to take in much, and the police were everywhere. I spoke to Inspector Campbell, and he was concerned by the state of the library. It was a mess, but sometimes Dad would get so involved in a project that he did make a mess, and Robby had orders not to touch anything. Inspector Campbell did ask me about it, but I think I was shocked as well. It wasn't until later when we were more relaxed that I realised James hadn't actually been working on anything at that time, so the chaos was really suspicious.'

Meredith got up and wandered over to join Bede at the window. She addressed Gabriel, 'I think the missing contract has something to do with the conflict that existed between George and James, but what I don't understand is why George would have anything to do with the shipping or receiving of fresh cut native Australian flowers. It would be beneath his dignity surely?'

Gabriel's lips twitched slightly and he looked across at Martin with raised eyebrows. 'It doesn't sound much like George's usual con. I'll need to look carefully at both books before I can make any sort of judgement.' He turned to face the three women and spoke sincerely, 'What you three have been through in the last few weeks is appalling and without the support you should automatically expect. That in itself is strange, and I mean to find out what's been happening. But if I'm right, there is a greater danger that someone within the committee is manipulating us all. The question I have at the moment is whether George is the culprit or whether he's the scapegoat. We all acknowledge he is a total shit, excuse my language, but he is a perfect candidate for a scapegoat.' He relaxed slightly and continued, 'We haven't been able to find him, so it seems that George is missing, or is aware of a threat and is lying low. He's being more secretive than usual, and is proving difficult to track. Justin has been looking for him as well, while ostensibly looking for what he quaintly refers to as the bloody book. An arch-rival of George's name of Lucien is also looking for him, so both Lucien and Justin are collaborating at the moment.'

Meredith laughed. 'I know Lucien very well, and yes, he and George have always been rivals of some sort, but they also collaborate on some projects as far as I remember.'

Gabriel grinned at her. 'So you know Lucien, I did wonder if perhaps you were aware of the subtlety of the relationships. You lived for quite a time in France and Paris, didn't you?'

'I only came back to Australia after Bede was born, so I lived in France and mostly Paris for over ten years.' She was thoughtful for a time then continued, 'I enjoyed my time there and the work I did, I suppose you both know about George's scheme with the stolen Turner?' Both Martin and Gabriel nodded in sympathy. Meredith continued, 'That was when James and Penny decided to get out. He was living and working in New York at the time, but he wanted Bede to grow up in Australia, so I decided to come back with them. By that time, I was missing the wide open spaces, the silence, and the colours. I don't suppose either of you can understand that.' She smiled gently at them.

Gabriel sat quietly for a few moments, then said thoughtfully, 'Do you know, Meredith, I think I have an inkling. I was stunned by the magnificence of the landscape we flew over, and there is a consciousness of freedom here that I have never experienced before, perhaps it's the incredible space, or the light you can see for miles.' He was frowning and looked pensively across at Bede. Gabriel thought again about his dreams, and wondered about this beautiful girl who had invaded them. A relative of some sort, but quite distant with a lifestyle and experience poles apart from his and Martin's.

They were self-sufficient, these three strong women. They had managed James's death, continued to run this complex business, and dealt with their grief without demanding any support from their relatives. He suspected that if not for the discovery of these two books on the table, they would have pursued their own investigation into James's death. Dangerous though he knew that route would be, he respected their right to go that way if they insisted. But he wanted to be able to direct this investigation. He and Martin were better equipped to deal with what was shaping up to be a very nasty family row. They had only suspected before an involvement from the highest echelons of the Family, but it now seemed beyond suspicion.

Gabriel put his hand gently onto the book of letters, raised his head, and frowning, looked first at Bede, then Hera, and finally Meredith. 'I think I need to study these two books carefully to see if I can make any connections to present day members of the extended family. It's not going to be easy or quick, I suspect, but I need to get started immediately.' He raised both brows and grinned. 'Can I use the study?'

'Of course.' Meredith moved forward. 'I'll show you to your rooms first. I'm sure you'd like a shower and change of clothes before you start. In the meantime, I'll get hold of Robby, and we'll set the study up so that you can use James's desk.'

# Chapter Fifteen

## *Supper*

I t was very late, Gabe had been ensconced in the study, reading and
translating for almost eight hours. He looked up as the door opened.
Bede angled through the door carrying a tray, and he smiled at her and
waited. She pursed her lips. 'I was suddenly aware that you hadn't gone
to bed yet, so thought I might see if I could help in any way.' She put
the tray on the desk and indicated with a wave, 'Coffee and sandwiches.
It's 2 a.m. and you've been at it since seven, and you probably need food
by now.'

'Couldn't get to sleep, or did something disturb you?'

She sat in the chair beside the desk and frowned at him. 'No, I
don't sleep easily at the moment, too anxious about', she waved vaguely
around the study, 'all of this, really. I just keep waking suddenly, and
worry about Hera and Meredith wondering if they're in any danger.' Her
eyes were shadowed, and she was very pale. 'I've always felt completely
safe here. We're so far from anyone. The people on the property we've
known forever, with a few exceptions of course, but a very few. If there
had been strangers around when James was killed, someone would
have noticed them.' She looked up at him suddenly. 'We're a very
small community. Even outside the property, strangers are visible, but
Inspector Campbell checked around with the locals, and the township

beside the lake, there were no strangers.' She paused. 'You do realise what that means, don't you?'

Gabriel looked across at her with sympathy on his face, and leaning back from the desk, asked, 'Do you suspect anyone? Has anyone behaved differently, seemed anxious, or worried?'

She shook her head. 'That's why I haven't been able to sleep. Obviously, this person could be anyone who knew James's habit of sailing on Mondays on his own, which means everyone on this property, in the local township, and everyone who sails on the lake, about 100 people, not including children.' Bede sighed, got up and said, 'Shall I pour you some coffee? I'm going to have one, and I've just made the sandwiches so they're fresh.'

He drew in a deep breath, flexed his shoulders, and stood up. 'Yes, a good idea, I need a break.'

He took the coffee she handed him, put some of the ham and cheese sandwiches on a plate, and moved across the room to sit more comfortably in an easy chair. He leaned back and took a bite. 'Just what I needed, a good dose of normalcy to combat the intensity of these letters, it's starting to become a bit surreal.'

'Have you been able to discover anything that could have anything to do with James's death?' Before he could reply, she burst out, 'You knew him, didn't you? You knew some of the things he was involved in when he wasn't here.' Her eyes were glistening very bright, and Gabe hoped she wasn't going to cry. He really wasn't good with weeping women. But she got to her feet and moved to the window, drawing the curtain aside. 'It's a beautiful night. I love this time of the year, the air is so clear and still, and the stars seem so low you can almost touch them.'

He stood beside her and spoke gently, 'Yes, I knew James, and liked and respected him. I also knew some of the projects he was involved in, but there was nothing that was in the least dangerous.' He paused and thought for a few moments. 'He was a very private person, almost secretive in a way, but I assume you know that better than I do.'

'Yes, sometimes I thought he missed the stimulation and intrigues of Europe. He was always a little unsettled when he got home from one of his trips. I tackled him about it after his last trip, he just laughed.

He said "Bede, I wouldn't live in Europe now for any reason." Then he hugged me and took one of the horses out for a gallop.'

She put her cup back on the tray. 'I'm for bed, goodnight.'

Gabriel watched her leave, finished his coffee, and decided he, too, needed some sleep. She really was beautiful, he thought, with that rich chestnut hair and those amazing eyes. She had obviously been asleep, and the night being warm, she wore baggy short pyjama bottoms and a skimpy T-shirt. That beautiful long expanse of leg made his mouth water, and with a deprecating grin at his thoughts, turned the lights off, and shut the door on the study.

# Chapter Sixteen

## *Travel*

'G abriel, I don't know that this was such a good idea. I'm exhausted. Maybe we should stay here in Dubai for a night just so we can sleep. I'm tired and so worried about Meredith and Hera to say nothing about Martin.'

'Take it easy, Bede, I know it was a lousy flight, but we're safe on the ground, and the flight to Paris leaves in just two hours. I promise you will sleep on this flight if I have to knock you out with my fist.' Gabriel grinned down at the beautiful, slim, and dishevelled girl in the seat beside him. He put his arm around her and gently pulled her head onto his shoulder. He was gradually becoming accustomed to the strange feeling of protectiveness toward Bede.

She looked up at him and murmured into his chest, 'I'm not usually such a wimp.' She felt herself relaxing into the warmth of his very large and powerful body.

They were sitting in the most comfortable seats they could find, waiting for their flight to be called. There was something comforting about letting him take charge for a bit, she thought to herself. I will recover my equilibrium in just a few moments and be back to my normal managing self. Bede closed her eyes and let her mind drift back.

It had been a lousy flight. There had been heavy winds and storms leaving Perth, and the turbulence had been more than she'd experienced before. The flight attendants had managed extremely well, supplying drinks and reassurance when needed. There had been constant quiet updates from the captain with details about the state of the storm and the projected abatement. It was only a ten-hour flight, but had seemed more like twenty to Bede. It was a relief when the captain finally announced they had outrun the storm and consequently were ahead of schedule. They landed in Dubai to calm pleasant hot dry weather.

It was January, and easily the most comfortable time to be in the Arab Emirates, but even so, she was thankful for the very efficient air conditioning in the departure lounge. She mused, thinking back to Gabriel's translations. He had laboured over them into the evening and early hours of the morning on that first day. Not three hours after she'd left him eating late night sandwiches. He had woken her, and Martin too, when he had literally fallen out of bed. The sound was unmistakeable, knocked over the side table with the bedside lamp, and banged into the door trying to exit the room. She had been initially stunned by the noise and the expletives, and then thinking he may have hurt himself, she raced into the hallway, switching on lights as she went. He was leaning against the doorway looking dazed and ruffled in all his naked glory. He really was beautiful.

Martin, also woken by the noise, was standing in the door of his room. He grinned at her shocked expression and turned to Gabriel. 'You really will have to start wearing something to sleep in, Gabe.' Then turned around and went back to bed.

Gabriel had been embarrassed and apologetic. He tried to explain what had caused him to wake so suddenly. The dream had been about one particular letter than was probably significant, and he needed to check it now.

Bede had suggested gently, 'Perhaps you need to put something on before starting again. Meredith will be up soon.' Gabriel grimaced and turned back into his room. It was only 5 a.m., so she, too, had gone back to bed with the after image of his magnificent body before her eyes. It wasn't a particularly restful image to take into sleep.

That had been the start of two hectic days. Gabriel headed straight to the study to recheck one of the letters he'd read. He explained the repercussions of that one letter to them all at breakfast the next morning. The name of the third letter writer, Dominic de Clario, was an ancestor of the patriarch. The particular letters he had been reading could pose questions about the current direct line of succession.

Meredith, who knew the family extremely well, explained to Hera and herself how important it was that the patriarch, in any given era, has the complete confidence of the whole of the extended family. She thought that even intimation would probably be a good reason to get rid of James! Martin was frankly sceptical, and after much discussion with Martin, Gabriel now had serious doubts. Neither Hera nor herself, even after Meredith's explanation, could conceive that as a reason for murder. To both of them, it was inexplicable.

They discussed and argued the question over breakfast, lunch, and while taking the boys to the waterhole for a swim. Again over afternoon tea, and dinner. They couldn't all agree. In the end, it was Gabriel who decided they needed to head to Paris, the patriarch, and the family archives. He explained that the patriarch, Laurent's side of the family, had always kept the records. He suggested they needed firm proof before they could proceed. He was obviously the one to go to Paris, as he had the necessary contacts. He was also the only one who could relatively easily read medieval, middle, and modern French, plus Latin and Greek.

They all objected strongly to his high-handed pronouncements. There were more arguments and discussions, but as no one could suggest an alternative, it was decided that Bede, as the eldest, would accompany him. Everything had progressed with startling speed from that point, and now, here they are. They would look into the family archives. Gabriel had access to the research facilities in Bibliothèque Nationale de France if needed.

Meanwhile, Martin and Hera would continue to look for clues or leads at the property. There was still the problem of who searched the library on the day of James's death. They needed to know exactly who had been on the property and at the house. They would start by gently questioning Mrs Robinson again, also Pete. They really needed to know more about him.

Martin thought that Gabriel was probably on a wild goose chase, and the book of letters was a red herring.

Meredith, still feeling unsettled and anxious after seeing them off, decided to take a hand. She went back into the house and picked up the phone to ring Josephine and Marina in Istanbul.

## Chapter Seventeen

France

T he flight from Dubai had been calm and peaceful. Bede slept a great deal of the time, probably more than Gabriel, really, but he didn't look rumpled or tired. He looked his elegant self, if you could call jeans and T-shirt elegant. Their winter gear was in the overhead locker, ready for when they left the plane. Apparently, it was snowing in Paris. Gabriel, in a matter of weeks, had travelled from one hemisphere to another and back again. She hoped his constitution was up to the constant changes because there would be more of it, she was certain.

As they left the customs hall, Gabriel, beside her, suddenly exclaimed, 'Good God, what now!' And quickly moved toward two elderly women waving frantically at the arrivals gate. They beamed at him as he took the shoulders of the small chubby one, and gave her the traditional three-cheek kiss.

They were chattering away in rapid French, and Bede had to take a moment before she caught up. She heard Meredith's name and realised her aunt had been doing some meddling. She felt a moment of pure rage, and then quickly suppressed it. Meredith was worried, as was she. These women were obviously relatives. Gabriel had greeted both with familiarity, and their manners, carriage, and dress were all confirmation. They were both white-haired, older than Meredith by quite a few years, she thought. They were beautifully dressed, looking smart and sophisticated as only French women can, even older women. The taller of the two, Gabriel now kissed on both cheeks and introduced as Josephine. She was slim and almost as tall as herself. The other must be Marina. She was shorter and well-nourished—was the term used these day—with sparkling blue eyes.

Bede suddenly found herself enveloped in a scented embrace with soft arms around her shoulders and soft lips on her cheeks. Marina was murmuring a welcome into her ear, and apologising for their surprise. She stepped back to make room for Josephine's embrace, and they both started talking at once. It was overwhelming.

Gabriel held his hands in the air and said firmly, 'Stop, one at a time please, we're both very tired and a little stunned by seeing you here.' He looked at Josephine. 'You explain please and make it snappy.' He put an arm around the shoulders of both of his elderly great-aunts and directed them to the entrance.

Marina chatted on, 'We have the car, and there is Phillips.'

Bede looked around and saw an elderly man, probably in his seventies, in what appeared to be a chauffeur's uniform.

Gabriel said in exasperation, 'You have the Patriarch's chauffeur? What are you both doing in Paris?' Before her eyes, Josephine turned from a dithering elderly lady into all hard edges and flashing eyes. She grabbed Gabriel's arm and turned him around, so they were all facing Bede, said quietly in accented English, 'We will talk later. Now, just behave as if you were expecting to be met by us. Phillips will report back everything we say, and it's important that we all stay with the Patriarch.'

She turned with a bright smile to Bede, and said in French, obviously for the chauffeur's benefit, 'So lovely to see you here my dear.' Then turned back to Marina, and in very loud rapid French, 'This is so exciting, Gabriel here in Paris with James's daughter. We will have to give a party tomorrow night, I think, we must start ringing around, see who's available.' She grabbed Bede's arm and almost dragged her out of the terminal, talking quietly in English, 'Phillips doesn't understand much English, but we must talk quietly and quickly. Gabriel will go along with everything I say. He's very bright and quick.

'Now, Meredith has rung, I'm sure you realise that, and told us everything that's been happening. I think she's right it all fits. The only thing Marina and I are not sure of is whether the Patriarch is involved, so we decided that it would be best if we all stayed with him while you're here in Paris. He doesn't go out much these days and does most of his business at home.' She turned back into the dithering elderly great-aunt that was obviously only one of many personas, and twinkled up at Bede, 'Isn't that a splendid plan?' in loud French.

Bede was stunned. This woman was probably in her eighties, and Marina could only be a year or two younger. They had obviously decided to become involved in something that was potentially very dangerous. She looked across at Gabriel, and he raised his eyebrows and grimaced at her. She didn't know what to think.

The two elderly ladies continued to chat in elegant French all the way back to the Patriarch's beautiful residence. Gabriel responded to their queries with calm acceptance in every nuance of his voice. He sat between them, holding the hand of each, and occasionally patting one or the other. This latest aspect of his character intrigued Bede. He turned to her and smiled. 'These outrageous women are some of my favourite people in the world, not including my parents of course. They are my mother's aunts, and in fact, they actually brought my mother up, as her parents died when she was quite young.' He was quiet for several moments, glancing at his two great-aunts and frowning slightly. 'Mind you, they are not to be trusted under any circumstances, as my mother so often reminds me.'

They both smiled affectionately at him, then Josephine turned to Bede, 'So tell me, my dear, about Meredith. How is she? And you must tell us about this property you live on. We really have no idea exactly where it is and how big it is.'

Bede was still feeling slightly stunned by these two dotty women. 'I don't know how to answer your questions,' she said. 'The property is in Western Australia and it's very big', she grinned at both of them, 'probably almost as big as Paris really, but not so densely populated. Meredith is fine. Hera is fine. Martin is staying on the property for a while. He's taking a bit of a holiday,' she improvised quickly. Phillips might not understand much English, but he would recognise names. 'It's a beautiful time of the year, quite hot, but the colours are stunning, and everyone on the property had a few days off over the Christmas and New Year. It will still be very quiet, and they can swim and explore.' She paused for breath and looked across at Gabriel.

He grimaced at her, but she saw approval in his eyes. He turned to Josephine 'You know Martin, the property is very isolated, and it's huge, completely outside his experience, he's looking forward to the challenge of exploring and some horse riding.'

At that moment, they drew up in the circular drive of a beautiful palladium house on the outskirts of Paris. Bede felt as if they had been driving for hours, but in fact, it had been only forty minutes. They were in the 16ème, but she didn't recognise anything around them.

A beautiful slim dark woman in her late fifties was descending the steps with a smile of welcome on her lips. She paused and held out her arms as Gabriel jumped from the car. 'Mother, this is a pleasant surprise. You vowed never to come to Paris in the winter again.' He swept her up and kissed her resoundingly on both cheeks. She smiled into his eyes. 'Put me down you barbarian. And where is Martin? We will talk later.' She turned to Bede, 'And you are James and Penelope's daughter, welcome, my dear. It's a pleasure to meet you at last.'

Bede felt as if she was losing the plot. These three women seemed to be shepherding both her and Gabriel. She had initially thought the two older women superficial and woolly headed as their appearance suggested, but now it was becoming obvious there was something more at work here. She looked again to Gabriel for some direction. He put his arm around her shoulders, drew her in close to his side, as they walked up the steps and murmured into her ear, 'Just play along until we can work out what's really going on here. Knowing these three, it's probably not as simple as you might think.'

He brushed his lips across the tip of her ear, sending a shiver of awareness across her shoulders. He was sending some sort of message to someone, but whom? Phillips? His two great-aunts, or his mother?

She was tired, wanted a cup of tea, and grumpily dug her elbow into his ribs. He grinned down at her, and taking her hand firmly in his, drew her up the steps into the foyer of the house. He murmured into her ear, 'All will be fine, try to relax.' Then turned with a smile to greet the housekeeper.

———————◆•◆———————

She was sitting on the edge of the bed, her place of meditation. The evening had been pleasant and totally confusing, the Patriarch had been charming. The dinner guests were relatives and friends, obviously from the 'ring around'. She had been introduced to everyone as James and Penelope's daughter visiting with Gabriel. The dinner was very formal with several servants serving the various courses, as if they were still living in the early twentieth century.

She and Gabriel had left the property with enough clothes for just the three days they expected to be in Paris, all stuffed into a carry-on bag for the plane along with necessary thermals for the winter in Europe. She had brought no formal clothes, as she had assumed they would stay in an obscure hotel while pursuing their investigations. Being met at the airport had been a surprise, and then being virtually kidnapped by the three women had really thrown her off balance, particularly Gabriel's acceptance of the event. She hadn't had an opportunity to talk to him about it. Everything had been moving so fast.

Gabriel's mother, noting the lack of formal clothing, had kindly lent her an evening dress. It was a beautiful soft black chiffon number, very flattering, and evening shoes to match. She wondered where they had appeared from; she was much taller and more slender than Gabe's mother. Seeing Gabriel in formal evening attire had also surprised her. Did he keep a full wardrobe in the patriarch's home? There was obviously a lot she didn't know or understand about him or the situation.

During dinner, the conversation had been general. They had discussed the latest films, music, and even the current exhibitions at the Louvre. The three women had made many suggestions for her entertainment all involving Gabriel taking her on a quick sightseeing tour of Paris. It was obvious she would have to disabuse them of some of their misconceptions. She was being treated as if this was a social visit to meet members of the family and various connections. She was unsure what exactly they all thought she was doing here with Gabriel, but she had an awful suspicion that they assumed some sort of romantic interest?

As the evening progressed, she became aware of the three women acting in tandem and directing the conversations, while charming Laurent, Gabriel's mother, seemed as much part of the charade as her two aunts.

She was hideously jet-lagged, her head was aching, and she desperately needed to sleep. She had just decided to drag herself off the bed when she heard a soft sound from across the room. The door handle turned slowly, and Gabriel slipped quietly into the room.

'I hoped you'd still be awake. I wasn't sure if you were aware of what those three witches were up to tonight, but they made sure the old man drank more than his usual quota of wine. He should sleep really well.' He moved over to the bed, took both of her cold hands into his warm ones, dropped a quick kiss onto her forehead, and pulled her to her feet. 'I hope you're up to a little sleuthing tonight? Apparently, the ladies want Laurent kept in the dark for the time being. We can slip down to the library. That's where most of the archives and the old books are kept these days.'

'Gabriel, I think all your family are quite mad. Those aunts of yours should be locked up and your mother seems just as bad.'

He grinned at her. 'They've been talking to Meredith, so that's where this performance originated. And yes, I agree, they are outrageous, but at least this way, we'll have most of the night to see what we can find. Now we have to be really quiet. The servants have retired, the old man is a sound sleeper, and he retired as soon as everyone left, but there are motion sensors all over the house, and we don't want to set off any alarms.'

Bede stopped. 'Motion sensors? I hope you know where they are?'

He grinned at her. 'Of course, Martin and I found most of them when we were about sixteen, I think, and nothing has changed since then. The Patriarch doesn't like change.' He tugged her again toward the door. 'I like you in that dress by the way. It suits you.'

She glanced down at the soft chiffon and snapped, 'Keep your mind on what we're doing, it would be really embarrassing to be caught.'

They didn't speak as Gabriel led her silently from the room and down the stairs to the library on the ground floor. Once inside, he spoke normally, 'There are no sensors in here, Laurent used to work at night when he was younger and his wife was still alive. He doesn't anymore. As I said, nothing has been changed for years. We can look through the relevant books easily.'

It was a beautiful room, the bookshelves built into the walls and under the long windows facing the garden. There were doors opening onto the terrace, tightly shut, and the curtains pulled across to block any light. The bookshelves were a wonderful polished wood of some sort, a lovely soft warm reddish colour with mouldings of what looked like stylised flowers and angels along the vertical struts. Bede was enchanted. Gabriel pointed to one side of the room at a shelf with large tomes in leather bindings and gold leaf writing on the spines.

He moved across the room. 'These all relate to our family history in some way. We need to go through them really carefully, but I think we start at about 1740. They're dated so it shouldn't be any problem. The writing is tedious and hard to read at times though, so it's time consuming work.' He said quietly, 'Martin and I used to pour over them when we were young, trying to find some juicy family scandal or gossip from the past. There's loads of it, by the way, but what we're looking for is confirmation of a scandal associated with a birth and any subsequent drama around 1741. So anything with details or even anything from the three cousins could be relevant. It would give us a place to start at least. There may be nothing here, but if there is any suggestion that puts the succession in question, we'll need to consider it very carefully.'

Gabriel paused for a moment, and then went on thoughtfully, 'The Patriarch is incredibly wealthy, but it's mostly inherited. He's contributed nothing personally to the Family coffers during his reign, which has always been an irritant to various factions.' He continued thoughtfully, 'I think if there was any way to shift him out of his present position, there would be several members of our loving and devoted family to jump at the chance. What I'm unsure about is whether he would care.

I don't see how he could know James had the book of letters.' There was a long silence while they both contemplated his words. Gabriel, still looking thoughtful, 'Of course, James could have informed Laurent if he thought there was a problem. It's the sort of ethical and honest behaviour I've come to associate with your father.'

Bede smiled and turned to the first bookcase. She started reading along the spines of the books. 'These are in beautiful order. The dates are very clear. Is it Laurent himself who keeps them in such order?'

Gabriel had just taken down a heavy volume. 'Mostly, but occasionally, he will bring in an expert if something needs rebinding or repaired in any way.'

'He seems more of a scholar than the head of a potentially criminal organisation. He appears gentle and slightly muddle-headed with a sly sense of humour.'

Gabe grinned. 'Bede, there is nothing potential about this family's activities. You should accept that a lot of the dealings may not now be strictly criminal, but they definitely push the boundaries of various countries' legal and financial systems.'

She raised her eyebrows at him, and grinned. 'This is all very challenging. I suppose we've always been protected by James, and we're far enough away for it not to be an issue.' She sank slowly to the floor sitting crossed-legged, while supporting the book on her legs, turning the pages of a book slowly and carefully. 'Gabriel, until recently, Hera and I were not aware of how involved we both are financially with the family. I know our name is Caruso-Kern, but your name isn't, and you're much more intrinsic to the ongoing running of the family. Or at least your mother and aunts suggested something like that at dinner tonight.'

'Yes, but my part of the family has descended by the female line, and interestingly, my mother's side of the family is patrilineal. It does get very complicated. It's astonishing that it still hangs together as well as it does. Also, the matriarchs of the family have always had a strong influence on any decisions made, or at least they did in the early days. Not so much now, but you would be advised to be aware of that small fact.' Gabriel looked across at her, sitting on the floor with the soft folds of the dress spread around her to keep it from crushing, he presumed. He held the book in his arms, and pensively continued, 'I suspect if there was less money involved, there would be more conflict. We have a strong tradition of family gatherings. I think you and Hera attended at least one in the past. These gatherings have kept all the various tendrils in close contact with each other. But I also suspect that Laurent's wife was part of the reason for the stability over the last few decades. She is a distant family connection and was a tireless correspondent, absolutely brilliant at networking. She managed to keep all the different factions in touch with each other, knew almost to the hours of any new births, made sure all birthdays were celebrated, and played the matriarch with every breath she took.' He paused thoughtfully. 'I always assumed she did this as compensation for her and Laurent's childless state. They were extremely happy in their relationship, and were obviously very much in love. Laurent misses her terribly since she died. She was a beautiful and charming woman.' He was frowning. 'This latest conflict has surfaced since she died, but I can't tie it in in any way.'

They continued in thoughtful and companionable silence for another hour.

At 2 a.m., Gabriel called a halt. 'You look exhausted, we've done enough for tonight. I'll walk you to your room. We can continue tomorrow night, or if Laurent goes out at all for any length of time, we can start again. Keep a record of where you were up to, but it's time to sleep or we'll both be knackered tomorrow.' He pulled her to her feet, and putting his arm around her shoulders, led her gently from the room. 'In case you need me at any time, my room is three doors down from yours on the other side of the hall around the corner. It's the last one on that side of the corridor if it's dark.' He was quiet for a few moments. 'I don't think there is any danger here. All this secrecy is mostly for the Patriarch's benefit. He's still recovering from his wife's death, and I don't want to worry him unnecessarily.'

They were standing outside her room, and she turned to face him. 'Gabriel, why is your mother here?'

'I'm dammed if I know. I haven't had a chance to talk to her or the aunts for that matter, and it's important to find out exactly what they're planning.' He looked down into her eyes, still talking very quietly, 'I've made arrangements for all of us to have lunch tomorrow at a friend's house. I think that's safer than going to a restaurant, and will mean being able to move around and shout if necessary.' He shrugged his shoulders. 'Shouting is often necessary with my mother. She has an autocratic streak that bugs me constantly.' Bede's lips quirked into an answering smile. Gabriel continued, 'Sarah is totally trustworthy and a fabulous cook. Mother likes her, and it would be quite normal for us to call on her. We'll leave here at about 12.30.' He kissed her gently on the forehead and opened her door. 'Goodnight.'

Bede found herself on the other side of the door before she could ask him any more questions, and she had quite a few after that statement. Who exactly was Sarah, and when had he arranged to have dinner with her? He was too inclined to go off on his own tangent following his own thought process without any reference to her. His arrogance was showing more and more and it had to stop. She could feel her anger building and drew a long calming breath. She wasn't sure what she was angry about. His arrogance, this 'friend' Sarah who was a fabulous cook, or the brotherly kiss on her forehead. She was tired, and she had no romantic interest in Gabriel, so what was her problem? She slammed the bathroom door, hoping she woke someone up, and climbed into bed.

———•—•———

Bede woke late the next morning and wandered into the breakfast room, hoping someone was still around. To her surprise, she found all three older women sitting, drinking coffee, and chatting.

'We waited for you,' Marina said. 'Come and have something to eat, the coffee is freshly brewed.'

Bede smiled at them and helped herself to scrambled eggs and toast then went to sit beside Josephine.

'Gabriel's already left, he'll be back to take us to Sarah's at about midday. We're all looking forward to seeing her again. She's a lovely girl.'

Bede smiled at Marina and asked, 'Is Sarah a relative I should know?'

Marina laughed. 'No, she's an old girlfriend of Gabe's. They're still really good friends though, and she has helped both he and Martin on some of their investigations in the past. A clever girl.'

Gabriel's mother leaned across the table and patted Bede's arm. 'Please call me Mette. I should have insisted last night. If you have nothing planned, I thought we could show you around this area before Gabe gets back, just to orientate you. I take it you haven't been to Paris before?'

Bede drew a long breath, her eyes narrowed. 'Actually, I spent a year in Europe in my gap year, travelling mostly. I was in Paris for three months over the Christmas New Year period, and I loved it. It was freezing then too, snow everywhere, a real treat for me coming from Western Australia.' She smiled around at all three women. 'No snow there ever.'

The three women stared in astonishment, and Josephine asked, 'Why didn't you contact any of the family?'

Bede shrugged, 'James wanted both Hera and me to be totally self-sufficient. Hera did the same in her gap year. We had addresses and phone numbers if we got into any real trouble, but of course, we didn't.' She stopped eating for a moment, and then continued thoughtfully, 'It was an exciting adventure, and I wanted to be completely independent. I'd just finished twelve years of schooling, and I wanted freedom. It was a great year for me. It gave me a lot of confidence, and I made a lot of real friends. I catch up with them every time I'm back here.'

The three women were staring at her in astonishment. Then Josephine gurgled, and on a hiccup, spluttered, 'Gabe doesn't know any of that, does he? He thinks you need protecting.'

Bede snorted, 'Yes, well, I've started to suspect that. He's been treating me like a slightly dopey little sister. I'm sorry I didn't mean to be rude, but he's making me very cross.'

'We'll have to see what we can do to disabuse him, and quickly. You do look very cross.' Mette smiled at Bede.

Bede, still frowning, 'I'm quite capable of looking after myself. I have a third degree black belt in tae kwon do, and I was an Olympic contestant in archery, I fly the helicopters at home, and I have been running both the East Coast and the West Coast business for three years. Why he would think I need looking after is beyond me.' She paused then grimaced. 'I've also travelled extensively for the business including China and the US. I admit I don't handle really long flights at all well. It's something to do with being locked in for almost thirty hours, I think. I tend to turn into a soggy mess, but I do recover fairly quickly.' She made a gesture indicating her alert and vibrant self. Looking around at the three women facing her, she smiled and continued, 'I'm sorry if I've been rude.'

Josephine and Marina both leaned back in their chairs, their lips pulled up into huge grins. Josephine chuckled. 'My dear, I agree with you, he needs a shake up now and then. He treats Marina and me as if we're made of spun sugar.' She continued, 'So what do you plan to do this morning, as you don't need any of us to show you around?'

'I've made a few phone calls this morning, so if you don't mind, I'll head off now to meet up with a friend. If you give me Sarah's address, I'll meet you there at one.' She pulled her phone from her pocket. 'Can you give me a contact number for one of you, and I'll give you mine.'

The three women sat in dazed silence as Bede left. This tall, straight, beautiful, and confident woman was a completely different creature from the drooping, wilting Bede at dinner the evening before.

'This puts a different complexion on this visit. I suspect she won't be deflected or sidetracked. What is Gabriel thinking? He must know what she is really, I mean, she is James and Penelope's daughter.' Mette looked across at Josephine, and they all exchanged worried looks.

'Mette, I don't think Gabe was planning on staying here. We sort of hijacked him and Bede. We may have made a mistake.'

At that moment, Laurent wandered into the room. 'Well ladies, what's going on? And what are you all up to?'

———•———

At exactly 1 p.m., outside the address Mette had given her, Bede swung off the back of the bike and handed Alain her helmet. She turned around to survey the street. They were outside a typical Parisian building in the Marais. A great many apartments, built around an inner courtyard, secure behind an imposing façade with a numeric audio pad beside the beautifully carved solid wooden entrance door. Just at that moment, a car pulled into the kerb with Gabriel at the wheel.

Mette's eyes widened in surprise and delight as she spotted Bede, and poked Gabriel on the shoulder. 'Well, he's certainly exotic, Gabe, and so beautiful.' They all turned and looked at the tall stranger lounging beside Bede. He was probably as tall as Gabriel with a wonderful head of Rastafarian braids with a few coloured beads swinging on the ends, his shoulders were broad, and his slim hips encased in tight fitting jeans. His skin the colour of milk chocolate, and the way he moved exuded sensuality and self-confidence.

Marina groaned aloud, 'If only I was fifty years younger.'

Bede waved at the occupants of the car and turned to Alain. 'Come and meet my cousin, Gabriel, and the aunts before you go, although the relationship is not as clear cut as that.'

Alain draped his arm around her shoulder and murmured into her ear, '*Votre cousin n'a pas l'air heureux et il est grand.*'

She elbowed him in the ribs. 'Behave.'

Marina was the first one to reach them. 'Oh, this is a treat, I'm a bike enthusiast,' she crooned at Alain. 'I'm too old and croppley to ride these days, but this is an Aprilla Shiver 750 GT. The Italians have made some stunning changes with this, are you pleased with it?'

Alain looked down at the elegant smiling grey-haired woman, 'Yes, Madame, I am very pleased with it.' He turned back to his bike. 'You obviously know your bikes, and dare I ask if you would like a ride, Madame.' His accented English was charming, but obviously not French, perhaps Algerian?

Gabriel moved quickly, slamming the door of the car. 'Not now, Marina.' And then turning to Bede with a lift of his supercilious eyebrows, 'We're expected, so perhaps Bede's friend could oblige some other time.' He smiled coldly, and turning, held out his hand. 'Gabriel, and you are?'

Bede was seething. He really could be an arrogant prig sometimes. 'Gabriel, meet Alain, a very old friend. He obliged me with a lift here,' she turned. 'Alain, Marina is the one drooling over your bike, and this is Josephine. And last but not least, Mette, Gabriel's mother.'

The three women exchanged smiling greetings, but Gabriel, standing with his hand lightly holding Bede's elbow, turned again to Alain. 'You've known Bede for a while, I understand. When exactly did you two meet?' He smiled the cold lipped smile Bede hated, and she turned to him angrily. But before she could speak, he continued his questions, 'You are resident in Paris?' His unspoken suggestion that perhaps Alain was an illegal immigrant?

'Oui, we met many years ago while I was studying, but now I only do research.' He held out his hand again. 'It was good to meet you.' Then with a sly grin, turned to Bede, dropped a kiss on her cheek. 'Give me a ring when you're free mon ange.' And he swung back onto the bike and roared away.

'Research where?' Gabriel frowned down at Bede. 'Perhaps you should have informed me of your proposed meeting.'

'Alain is an old friend. I explained everything to your mother and the aunts this morning.' She wrenched her arm away. 'You are so arrogant. Alain is a very well-respected genealogist. He has an impeccable reputation.'

'Bede, sometimes you are so naïve, but we need to go in.' Gabriel turned away and punched in the entry code to open the door.

Bede looked around her, as they walked through the passage and into a tiny, paved courtyard filled with potted trees and a tangle of lush green plants. Apartments rose dizzyingly all around them into the small square of blue sky above. They trooped up four flights of worn wooden stairs covered in worn red carpet, to be met at the door of a delightful apartment by Sarah. She was beautiful, slim, vibrant, and elegant, with a mass of blonde curls falling casually around her shoulders.

Bede liked her immediately. She seemed intrigued to meet Bede, and with a twinkle in her eye, took her on a tour of the apartment then left saying, 'I have to rush, but I've set the food up on the sideboard, help yourselves.' She turned to Gabe. 'Let me know if I can be of help anytime. You know how much I love being involved with your investigations.' She grabbed his shoulders in both hands, and reaching up, kissed him familiarly on the lips then rushed out the door.

Bede was stunned, and for some reason, now felt angry and off balance. 'Gabriel, what exactly is the idea of this luncheon if your friend is not even to be here?'

'I'm sorry, Bede, I felt that my relatives', he scowled at the three older women, 'need to explain themselves.' He was standing just inside the door with a scowl on his arrogant features.

Mette scowled back at him, 'Gabe, after what Meredith said on the phone to Josephine and Marina, we thought we were being very clever and helpful meeting you at the airport and arranging for you to stay with Laurent.'

Impulsively, Bede took Mette's hand. 'I feel dreadful staying in Laurent's house and searching his library.' She looked across at Gabriel. 'I think you should tell them everything that we suspect, or what we have speculated on because I'm not sure we are on the right track.'

He heaved a sigh, ran his fingers through his hair, and fell into a chair. 'Bede, I arranged for this lunch because I suspect these three will start screaming as soon as they hear what I have to say.' He scowled again at his three outrageous relative. 'In fact, I predict it, and they will want to be involved.' He turned his still scowling face on her, 'And, while we're at it, who is the creep on the bike? When did you meet him? Remember this isn't exactly a social visit.'

She felt instant anger and rage surge through her body. How dare he demand to know about Alain when obviously, Sarah was certainly not a former anything? This was turning into a nightmare. First, these three fluffy women hijacked them, and now this arrogant shit was trying to take over the whole investigation.

'Alain and I have been friends for years. I rang him this morning after you disappeared. I told you last night I don't think it's right staying in Laurent's home and searching his library, and I think Alain may be able to help. As I said, he's a professional genealogist.' She looked at Gabe directly and raised her eyebrows.

He pursed his lips thoughtfully and turned, as Josephine said soothingly, 'We may have made the wrong assumption', she looked at Mette and Marina in turn, 'and we seemed to have stepped into something that perhaps we will not like.' She turned to Gabriel. 'We may have misunderstood Meredith, as she was uncharacteristically vague. She talked about George, a couple of books, and an old scandal, and the fact that you two were on your way here.'

Mete interrupted, 'She asked us to keep an eye on you both. We jumped to the conclusion that a romance was developing.'

Gabe snorted in derision. Bede scowled at him.

Mete continued calmly, 'We assumed that George was causing trouble between you, it's what he does. We jumped to all sorts of wrong conclusions, I can see that now.'

'Yes, you've assumed too much, and all of it completely wrong.' Gabriel frowned at Bede, who scowled back at him. 'George has nothing to do with why we're here.'

The three women sat is rapt silence, while he and Bede explained why they had come. Marina finally spoke, 'Well, that's all very well, but Meredith did indicate you might be here because of James's death, and we all', she indicated the other two women sitting quietly by her side, 'feel absolutely dreadful that no one went to the funeral. We weren't even notified of the dreadful event until it was too late to do anything constructive, let alone fly out there.'

Gabriel was still frowning, but seeming a little more relaxed. 'I understand all that, but I would just ask you to trust me with this, knowing I would never do anything to hurt Laurent.'

As one, the three women stood. 'Lunch, I think, then back to the house. Marina knows where all the archives are kept. Mette and I will take Laurent out for an early dinner tonight, how does that fit?'

Gabriel crossed the room, kissed Josephine on the cheek. 'Thank you for being just as intelligent as always, let's eat.'

Later that evening in the library again, this time with Marina helping, Gabriel was translating the French aloud. He turned to Bede, 'This confirms the letters, Bede, but I still don't see it as a reason for murder. It was so long ago, and as you so rightly suspected, it would take a genealogist to work out who should be the patriarch if not Laurent. It's time we talked to him.'

Marina turned to them both. 'You found this information in an antique book in James's library, Gabriel, there has never been even a whisper in the family before today. Are you suggesting a sort of take-over bid, and how would James have been involved?' she demanded.

'That's what I don't know, or even if it has any bearing on James's murder. We're scrabbling about in the dark here.'

Bede pulled her phone out of her pocket and took photos of the relevant pages. 'I'm sending these to Alain now. I filled him in this morning, so he'll be expecting something.' She grinned at Gabriel. 'I'll remind him to be extremely discreet.'

Gabriel was now sprawled in the comfortable armchair beside the fireplace. His long legs straight out in front of him. He looked pensively up at Bede. 'We need to talk to Martin and Hera, see if they have any information about anyone acting strangely, and we are going to have to talk to Laurent about all of this. I think we need a few more facts before stirring up a hornet's nest.' He looked tired suddenly, his eyes heavy lidded with dark circles. 'Laurent is a scholar, not a murderer. He's not even particularly ambitious, and never has been.'

Marina stood suddenly. She paced across the room, then back again. 'You know, Gabe, you're right. This just doesn't make any sense.' She looked at Bede. 'Send that message and give your friend all the facts as we know them, but make sure he's discreet.' She was very pale, and her face was drawn.

Bede glanced from one to the other, 'Alain is a professional, he's always discreet. I thought we might need some professional help at some point, which is why I called him in the first place. But I'll emphasise that discretion is needed.'

Marina suddenly rose from her chair. 'I heard the car. They're back, I think we should finish in here and wait for your friend's report, Bede.' She hurried from the room.

Gabriel, still sprawled in the chair, looked up across and Bede. 'Why didn't you tell me you had spent a year in Europe and months in Paris?'

He thought for a few moments then continued slowly, 'To say nothing of a triple black belt in tae kwon do.'

Bede grinned at him. 'It never occurred to me to be honest. It wasn't until you started treating me like a halfwit that I got angry, and blurted out all that stuff to your mother and the aunts. I suppose you now expect me to apologise or something?'

Gabriel grinned. 'No, I was thinking you might appreciate a training session with me downstairs. There's a fully-equipped gym set up in the basement. This racing between hemispheres has played havoc with me. I need an hour of decent exercise.'

Bede grinned back. 'Love to. Shall we go? It's not even midnight.' She surged to her feet.

# Chapter Eighteen

## Back at the Homestead

Hera was sitting at the breakfast table, looking pensively out of the window. In the last three days, she and Martin, with Meredith's help, had entertained most of their nearest neighbours. They had decided that was the easiest way to start asking questions.

Martin has been presented as a long lost 'cousin', to be introduced to everyone in the area. Meredith had carefully selected the individuals to be invited to lunch at the sailing club, dinner at home, and finally a huge BBQ for the staff, and a general invitation to anyone who would like to attend. Of course, everyone who could, did any excuse for a booze-up on the weekend.

The weather was perfect, not too excruciatingly hot with a cool breeze. Martin had performed brilliantly. He had asked leading questions with a subtlety she admired, but there had been no surprises. He had introduced James's death in a way to inspire sympathy. He had looked forward to meeting him, but had left it too late, etcetera. It had been a perfect ploy, everyone had been sympathetic, and willing to talk about James and that 'dreadful day', but there were no surprises. Nothing to add to what they already knew, there had been no stranger anywhere in the district, no strange cars seen at the sailing club or in the area at all.

Hera felt heaviness in the pit of her stomach. It confirmed what they all suspected. Someone he knew well, or at least someone who was no stranger to the district, had killed James. At that moment, Martin wandered into the room and helped himself to scrambled eggs, sausages, toast, and coffee before he sat down opposite her.

'Well', he said softly, 'I think we can assume that unbeknown to either Gabriel or myself, someone from the Family has been keeping an eye on James for a very long time. There have been no new comers to the area for the last two years, is that right?'

'Yes', Hera frowned, 'what do you mean unbeknown to you and Gabriel?'

'Well, I think, in the interests of future relationships, you should know a few facts. Gabriel and I are, for want of a better word, fixers. I'm sure Meredith has told you about the structure of the Family. Justin has been a fixer for years since before my parents were married. It's how he knew how my mother and father were feeling about each other, and seriously talking marriage. Part of our job description, if you like, is to know what all the disparate members of the family are doing. We have a fairly comprehensive network of informers set up all over the world, and they report to either Gabe or me every day by e-mail, SMS, or if it needs to be dealt with immediately, by phone.' He paused, then continued, 'Hence, the sat phones.' He held up his hand to stop Hera's interruption. 'Now, the most salient facts are, given what we've learned or rather not learned, your family has obviously been under observation for at least two years, and not officially.'

'But you just said Justin is a fixer.'

'I said he was. He hasn't been for about five years now, certainly not officially.' Martin put down his knife and fork, and looked across the table at Hera. 'Justin was relieved of his position when he turned sixty as a sort of retirement, but unofficially mostly because he had been making deals with some questionable people. No one wanted to make too much of a fuss if you like.'

'Well, you've certainly been discreet. What you're saying is that Justin is not to be trusted. If that's the case, what was the thing about you and Gabriel chasing around Prague after him and some bloody book?' She looked closely at him. 'And if you have been keeping track of everyone in the family, surely you've been keeping track of us as well.' She was furious and felt as if she wanted to push his face into the scrambled eggs on his plate.

'Hera, I can see you're upset. In fact, your cheeks are very red and your eyes are spitting sparks, I think I need to take the knives away from the table.' He grinned at her then continued, 'I'm sorry, but you do look very cross. I'll explain, no, we didn't keep tabs on your family because James kept us up to date. He made sure we knew mostly everything relevant here. Although we didn't know Bede had spent a year in Europe in her gap year.' He was very thoughtful. 'James was obviously circumspect with some of his information.'

'How did you know about that?'

'I talked to Gabe, and I didn't know about the triple black belt either. She must be pretty good.'

Hera settled back in her chair and grinned at him. 'Well, should I tell you about my gap year as well, and my single black belt?' Hera was now feeling more relaxed. She raised her eyebrows at him questioningly.

'Shit, I asked for that, I suppose. You obviously spent it in Europe getting into trouble and having a wonderful time?'

'Yes, of course, Bede came over for some of it. And yes, we did have a great time. James wanted us to learn how to be completely independent. I suspect that's why he never did tell us much about the family. I don't think he trusted everyone or maybe anyone.' She looked thoughtful now.

'No, he liked and trusted Gabe. I didn't see as much of him as Gabe, but they always caught up when he was in Europe or the UK. In fact, he and Gabriel spent a lot of time together and have a couple of business arrangements together.'

Hera was silently fuming. She would have to speak to Bede. Had Gabriel told her any of this? She smiled sweetly across at Martin. 'He didn't mention any of that. He certainly didn't say anything to Meredith. I know he was secretive, and he probably thought that keeping us in the dark was keeping us safe. But there is a part of me that would like to strangle him.'

Martin looked at her and wondered about the girl. She was young, early twenties, but obviously James's daughter. She was as stubborn and determined as Bede.

He had spoken to Gabriel earlier, learned what they had found, and probably confirmed by now what they suspected. But did any of that have anything to do with James's death? He suspected, as did Gabe, that it didn't.

They would have to wait for Bede's friend's official report. But in the meantime, they really needed to find the mole here at the property. He turned back to Hera. 'I suspect the spy has been in residence here at the farm, or very near for several years. How well do you know your employees? We need information on everyone employed here. We need to look at when each and every one of them started and to check their references. Can we do that now?'

Hera sighed. She suddenly felt ill, her stomach was churning, and she pushed her plate away. 'Yes, of course, we keep the records in the office. We can go there now. Most of our employees have been with us for at least two years and some of them much longer. The aboriginal workers are all part of the same community and have lived on the property for generations. In fact, they were here first. I don't think they would be a party to anything to hurt James. They're friends more than employees, and totally loyal.' She felt like snarling. 'For a start, when would they have been approached and to do what? They would have told James immediately if anyone started asking questions, or suggesting anything for that matter.'

'I tend to agree with you. Having observed them at the BBQ. But it might be a good idea to talk to them quietly, see if they've observed anything that has puzzled them in the past. In fact, anything that has puzzled them over the last few years.' He paused, looking out the window as if thinking, then turned back. 'Particularly over the past six months, can we do that discretely?'

Hera looked thoughtful for a few minutes. 'Of course, that's not a problem we can go tomorrow, to look at some of the artwork and the craft stuff they produce. While you look around and buy something,

I'll go talk to one of the elders. We'll need to take the truck, I think, to make it look as if I'm doing the tourist thing for my distant cousin.'

'Tell me about the art centre we're going to. Where is it in relation to this property, and why do I have to buy some artwork?' He continued to eat slowly.

'It's about thirty kilometres north of here, and you'll love the artwork. Some of the young people work with us at different times. They stay here when we need extra hands. The centre is 100 per cent indigenous owned and run by the community. It's an incorporated, not for profit organisation, managed by an executive committee, mostly the senior people. It's a fairly small group, but they're totally dedicated to their art. There is some support from the local council of course, and a small amount from the state government, but they're working hard toward being totally self-sustaining. We try to help in any way we can. For instance, if someone from overseas buys a really large canvas or two or three, we package them up safely and include them with one of our shipments, either down to Perth, and even overseas if it's called for. There are quite a few overseas visitors from time to time around here, staying at the sailing club mostly. Just wait till you see the paintings, you'll just love them.' Hera, smiling at remembered delights, reached across and patted his hand.

Martin looked at her thoughtfully for a full minute, and then spoke carefully, 'Hera, you've never mentioned overseas visitors before. When was the last lot, and how close to James's death was it?'

Hera surged from the table, cursing, 'I never thought of that.'

Martin got up, and gently placing his hands on her shoulder, turned her to face him. 'Take it easy, Hera, it may not be important, but we do need to explore everything. Did your inspector check that out? Do you know?'

'It never occurred to me to ask, Martin, there's too many things none of us thought to check out. It was the shock I think.' She turned and headed to the office. 'We can look at the employee records now, I think, if you've finished eating. They're all on computer, so it shouldn't take long.'

Martin looked up from the computer printout. 'You have employed more staff than I realised from the socialising we've done over the last week.' He looked at the list thoughtfully. 'There are three males and one female who have left in the last year, and the excuses listed all seem to be a little spurious.' He glanced up at Hera. 'Do you know anything about them, and what they've done since leaving here?'

Hera glanced down at the list: Damian Black, Gerald Watson, Peter Watson, and Sienna Watson. 'Well, the three Watsons' behaviour was always a little strange. Bede and I suspected that Peter Watson and Sienna Watson were not brother and sister for a start. We thought perhaps Gerald was actually Sienna's father, and that she was running away from something, probably an abusive husband. Although Peter was nothing to write home about, and he wouldn't have been my idea of a protector, but he did seem to care very deeply for Sienna.

Of course, we could be wrong about all of them. Neither Bede nor I were sorry to see them leave. They didn't actually do anything suspicious. It was their manner. They were arrogant and stand-offish, probably kept to themselves for a good reason. They were all good workers though. And, no, I have no idea where they went after they left here. Damian Black', she paused to consider her answer, 'he was a bit of a mystery as well. He was an extremely good worker and very knowledgeable about Australian natives, especially Grevilleas, but his leaving wasn't a mystery.' There was something about the way she didn't quite look at him while talking about Damian that Martin found disturbing.

'Tell me more about him. I can arrange to have the Watsons checked out, but Damian interests me.' Martin looked hard at her, and Hera was looking uncomfortable now. Her colour was high, and her eyes very bright.

'Well', she said almost defiantly, 'he was young and good looking, and we had a connection of sorts.' She cleared her throat, and drew a long breath. 'James seemed to take exception to him suddenly, if you must know, and asked him to leave.'

Martin frowned thoughtfully at her for a moment then asked her to explain. 'When was this exactly, and forgive me, but how did you feel about him?'

Hera's colour was very high now, and she shrugged. 'I met him at Curtin. He's in the middle of a PhD and we became friendly. He was always very quiet and reserved, almost shy. He didn't seem to know many people and obviously hadn't been in Australia very long, although his English is very good. He is also really dishy looking, so I invited him to a few parties. He never seemed to have much money either, and I felt sorry for him. So I suggested that he look at applying for a casual job here in the summer break. He really is brilliant at what he does. His thesis is on the medicinal uses of various native plants. We were never intimate if that's what you're implying.'

Martin had tensed slightly, and she looked at him defiantly. 'But James didn't completely trust him, and offered no explanation for dismissing him. He never said, just insisted that Damian leave. So he left here almost a year ago, but he was only ever here for a few months over that summer.'

'You speak about him in the present tense. Do you know where he is now? And when was the last time you actually saw him?'

'I saw him in the city a few months ago. I attended a symposium, which he also attended. His research is in some ways parallel to mine.' She thoughtfully moved to the window and continued quietly, 'Sometimes, I wondered if that had something to do with why James threw him out.' She rubbed her eyebrow worriedly then continued, 'But I'm sure he is totally ethical. The symposium was before James's death. We talked a little, but I don't know where he's living now. It wouldn't be hard to track him down. He's certainly well known at the university. I can't believe he had anything to do with killing James. He was always completely immersed in his research, to the exclusion of everything and everyone around him.'

Martin was frowning now. He wandered over to the window and stood leaning on the windowsill, gazing thoughtfully into the distance. Then he straightened up and turned back to her. 'Do you know why James didn't like him? Was it simply that he didn't approve of any intimate involvement that might develop between you, or was it something more subtle? Did he give any indication that he thought it was anything more?'

'No, at the time I thought he was being overprotective. We argued about it. I was really angry, if you must know, it didn't make any sense. I liked Damian, we spent a lot of time together, but I wasn't interested in him in that way.' She sat quietly thinking back. 'At the time, I couldn't understand why Dad was misreading the situation so badly. He was usually very perceptive. So perhaps there was something else behind his actions.' She suddenly looked tired and defeated. 'Honestly, Martin, I have no idea. James never gave us any indication that he thought he, or any of us, was in any danger.' Her eyes were very bright. 'We always felt completely safe and secure here. We know everyone and any stranger in the area is instantly a source of endless speculation and gossip by everyone. I might add including the police, we're almost a closed community.' She got up from the desk and wandered across to the window.

Martin put his arm around her and gave her shoulders a gentle hug. 'Take it easy. I'll set one of my people to make enquiries. We will keep a watch on Damian for a while, the Watsons might take a little more time to track down.'

Hera scowled up at him, 'Do you have people here to do that sort of thing?'

He grinned. 'Of course, that's what Gabe and I do. We have a network that functions anywhere and everywhere we need it to.' Sitting back down at the computer, he frowned across at her. 'I need you to tell me everything you know about Pete. There's no real background information here. His references, where he worked before he started here, or when he started.'

'Why? I know you and Gabriel both had a sort of macho clash with him when you both arrived, but he's been one of the mainstays on the property well before James was killed. He's also become very protective of Bede and me since Dad's death, so I can't think why you would suspect him of any involvement.' Hera scowled at him.

'Hera, at this point, I suspect everyone and no one. It's nothing personal, really.' He continued after a moment, 'Despite that incident when he tried to mount me on a half broken horse.'

Hera laughed outright. 'It's a sort of favourite joke out here when someone with your accent says they can ride. The fact that you can actually ride and managed beautifully made the joke backfire. It can be dangerous actually, and has proved a bit of a problem in the past. I was with Meredith at the time. We were watching from an upstairs window, and she was amused more than anything. She would have put a stop to it if she thought even for a moment that it could be dangerous.' She chuckled. 'I was about to shout down to Pete, but Meredith's reaction convinced me that there wouldn't be a problem. She actually laughed outright and told me to watch Pete's face.'

'Yes, well, she knew we spent quite a lot of time on a property in the UK when we were teenagers, training and exercising Arabians.'

'Wow! Tell me about it.'

'Nothing to tell, really, it was just another of the more bizarre aspects of our education. Sheik Ali Pasha Sherif, a good friend of our father, has an interest in an Arabian breeding stud in Sussex in England. Gabe and I spent some of our favourite summer holidays working on the stud.'

'Well, getting back to Pete, there should be copies of his references in his employment file.' She moved across to the filing cabinet. With uneasiness in her voice and a puzzled frown, 'Martin, the file is empty, there is nothing here.' She looked up worriedly. 'James employed him as he did everyone on the property. None of us would dream of questioning him. Pete just arrived one day, but James was expecting him, and said he was the new manager and would be managing most aspects of the business when he, James, was away. That was about five years ago.' She continued to frown. 'He's certainly competent, flies the helicopter for spraying, and seems to be protective of both Bede and me. I don't know how Meredith sees him. I've never discussed him with her. He is obviously another one that needs investigating. But I can't believe he had anything to do with murdering James.

'Where is this all going to end? I'm starting to suspect everyone I see of not being who they say they are. There is a tendency not to ask too many questions about people's background out here. It's the perfect place to disappear for a while if you need to, but he's always seemed to be very loyal, and he's been invaluable since James's death.'

'Hera, you're exhausted. This is enough for me to go on with for the time being. Why don't you go for a ride? Try to relax a little. I'll make some phone calls and contact my people to see where we go from here. We'll have to put off going to the camp for a couple of days. Tracking down the Watsons, making enquires about Pete and Damian Black is more urgent.' He put a hand gently on her shoulder. 'I'll need to go to Perth to arrange some of this, so I'll get Pete to fly me there. It will probably take a few days to set some investigations going. In the meantime, you need to act as normal as possible. Try not to worry, and try not to let Meredith see how disturbed you are, she seems to be badly affected by all this tension.' He smiled at her. 'Don't let it get you down. I'll send Pete back immediately with the helicopter. He won't suspect I'm investigating him.' He walked out of the room without a backward glance, leaving her exhausted and worried.

## Chapter Nineteen

# Bede and Gabe in Paris . . . Still

After the vigorous training session, they both collapsed onto one of the thick training mats used for more contact exercise. Gabriel handed Bede a small bottle of spring water and opened another for himself.

'I think we need to consider another aspect of this, Bede, Laurent would not ever countenance any violence against James even if his position was threatened.' He paused, and took another swig of water. 'It's just not that important to him. Admittedly, he was raised from childhood to fulfil the role.' He continued thoughtfully, 'Besides, Laurent, as everyone in the family knows, would step away with alacrity if the opportunity arose. He's really a scholar at heart and would welcome the chance to retreat into his books.' He rolled over onto his elbow and looked down at her sprawled beside him. 'I'm thinking about George, Justin, and Lucian. The terrible trio as my father often called them. They've been friends since Eton really, although rivals might be a better word.'

He turned to Bede and pulled absently at one of the wisp of hair springing up around her face from the heat and perspiration of their vigorous workout. He twirled it around one of his fingers, and then lightly caressed her cheek. He continued thoughtfully, 'Lucien is Czech, or rather, he was born in England. His mother is English and a very distant connection to the family, but his family are all Czech. They did have a difficult time during the Second World War, but I think they've managed to reclaim most of their ancestral land. He's definitely not the most trustworthy of persons, I probably should tell you about the last time I saw him and Justin in Prague.' He looked across the room deep in thought, then turned around bent down and kissed her softly on the lips. He drew back slightly, raised his eyebrows in question, smiled into her eyes, and bent toward her again, slowly. This time, the kiss was a more definite statement, and Bede responding, wondered why it had taken him so long.

Much later, she murmured, 'You were going to tell me about Lucien, George, and Justin in Prague.'

Gabriel pulled himself up and away from Bede. He relaxed back against the wall, reluctantly releasing Bede, and pulling her up beside him. Prague seemed like a lifetime ago, but was in fact only a matter of days. He recounted the bizarre evening at Justin's flat, and then thoughtfully went on to recount his previous association with Kamila. He slowly slid sideways down the wall until he was lying flat on his back and gazing up at the ceiling. 'I think I will sleep here. I'm too buggered to move.'

Bede laughed, jumped to her feet, and grabbing his hand, dragged him to his feet. 'Come on, you need a shower and a proper sleep in a soft warm and comfortable bed. You've been galloping around the world with very little relaxation between flights.' She gurgled deep in her throat. 'You saw what I'm like on one twenty-four hour flight. I would be a physical and mental wreck if I had tried to do what you've just done. In how many days?'

He draped his arm around her shoulder and pulled her close. 'Do you know', he murmured, 'I have no idea, I've lost track. I've changed time zones so often my body is having trouble keeping up, let alone my brain.' He grinned down at her. 'You could come to bed with me and help me work it all out.'

She laughed. 'Not going to happen, you would get no sleep at all.'

He snorted, and kissed her soundly.

She reached up and cupped his cheek. 'You are a constant surprise to me. Is now a good time to ask you about those dreams you spoke of?'

'No, not yet, and you're right, we both need some sleep, my pet.'

# Chapter Twenty

## Introduce Damian

Damian Black slipped quietly through the dark streets. It was 2 a.m., and he was reasonably certain it was safe now for him to venture into the streets. He had been moving to a different hotel every night for the last week paying with cash, but was now seriously short. He couldn't continue for much longer without another infusion of cash, and he needed to get back to his laboratory. He had plenty of cash stashed there, but was anxious they would have someone still patrolling the area waiting for him to re-emerge from hiding.

He headed to the deli on the corner. It had been days since he had eaten a hot meal. Staying in crappy, cheap hotels meant no room service. The constant moving around from suburb to suburb was finally taking its toll. He was almost ready to let fate, or whatever went for fate these days, take control. He wasn't fearful for his life, or not so much, he was fearful for his research. He needed to get back to the laboratory. His notes were all there, and of course, all his available cash.

He cursed fluently in several languages, and thought passingly of ringing Hera or Bede. He felt sure if he told them the whole story, they would help him, at least with enough cash to disappear properly for a couple of months. He felt certain that although 'they' whoever 'they' were, knew the general area of his laboratory, the specific location was safe. He just had to keep away long enough for them to give up looking.

He was still racking his brain for some way to get more cash when a hand landed heavily on his shoulder. His head dropped to his chest in defeat.

'Damian, my friend, I've been looking for you.'

He drew a long shaky breath, cursed softly under his breath, and turned slowly around. A grin spread slowly over his face, and he launched himself at the person standing in front of him. 'By all that's holy, Martin, you're a sight for sore eyes. What the hell are you doing here? I didn't expect to see you in this hemisphere.' He grabbed Martin again in another bear hug.

Martin extricated himself. 'Why are you here? But we will discuss all that later. We need to leave quietly I'm afraid. Your friends are not that far behind me. You haven't covered your tracks as well as I would have expected of you.'

They were grinning at each other, and Damian punched him hard but playfully in the shoulder. 'Where's Gabe?'

'Talk later, let's go.'

They turned and walked quickly out of the store, both hyper alert to any disturbance or unexpected movement in the street. Martin hurried Damian around the corner to a sleek black sports car parked discreetly at the curb.

'Get in quickly. I don't think anyone has spotted me at all yet, but one can't ever be certain. We need to talk about what the hell you think you're doing.'

'Martin, someone tried to grab me a couple of days ago, and I've been running ever since. I've run out of cash, so I hope you're loaded.'

'This whole thing is a shambles, Damian. Gabe and I have been trying to find out what happened to James. Did you have anything to do with that?'

Damian looked at him in astonishment. 'Christ, no, James was always helpful', he was silent for a moment and went on, 'until he got this thing into his head that I was interested in Hera. Then he went ballistic. He wanted everything to do with the Family kept well away from the two girls. He'd be furious if he knew you were here.' He went on after a moment, 'They probably told you about me working on the property for a few months. James helped me collect specimens without it being obvious, that's all. I though his death was an accident until I realised I was being stalked. Then I shut down the lab and went into hiding. The lab is safe, but I don't think I am, and I'm bloody hungry. Do you have anything to eat in this beautiful car, which I assume is stolen.'

'Of course, back seat for food, and yes, it's stolen. Do you have any idea who's stalking you?'

As he reached into the back seat, Damian replied, 'No bloody idea, I haven't actually managed to see them clearly. It's more that awful sixth sense that is so well developed in me. I do research that's all I know, and yes, I probably should have been more careful. I hope the rest of James's family are all right. Meredith was always really nice to me. I was just considering asking the two girls for some cash, but was unsure how much they know.'

'Believe me, they know nothing at all about James's activities. That's how he wanted it. But Gabe and I thought it was a mistake from the start. I'm staying there at the moment, and Gabe's in France with Bede. There is a major conspiracy of some sort happening, but I can't seem to work out what at the moment. Hera thinks I'm in the city to try to track you down, and a couple of suspicious character employed on the property over the last few years.' Martin paused for a moment, and then went on thoughtfully, 'Do you know anything about the Watsons?'

Damian opened a packet of crisps and paused. 'Say all that again . . . no, don't bother. No, I don't know anything about the Watsons. They were always more than a little reticent about where they were from, and I don't believe for one minute that they're father, son, and daughter. For a start, they practice incest if they are, although that could always be the case. No, the so-called son and daughter are no relation to the father, and I suspect he was using them as camouflage, but I could never get a handle on what he was up to. How did you find me?'

'You used your real name at the property, and why does Hera think you may be interested in her personally? Also, I know your habits quite well, and managed to pick up your trail three hotels ago. You need to be more resourceful. I thought we had taught you better.'

Damian scowled, 'Potato crisps? Couldn't you have found something more substantial? I might add I had to run with very little money in my pocket. I know I should have been more prepared. Bloody hell, Martin, I didn't expect any problems here. As for Hera, well, I think she's great, she's almost as smart as I am with her research, and she good to look at.'

Martin turned and scowled at him, 'Just don't go there. At the moment, she's still suffering from the realisation that James was murdered. Gabe and Bede are in France checking out another aspect. It could be related, but we think it's a separate issue. Not completely unrelated, but separate. In the meantime, we have to get you to a safe place. And I assume we need to get your research notes from your lab.'

Damian, opening another packet of crisps, mumbled under his breath, 'Yeah, that's about it, any ideas?'

'Several in fact, but the first question, can you fly a helicopter?'

## Chapter Twenty-One

# *Paris Again*

B ede woke to the phone ringing beside her bed, and she groggily picked it up. It was early for Alain to ring! She sat up, pushed the hair out of her eyes, and croaked into the phone. 'This had better be important. It's not yet 7 a.m., and you know how I hate to wake early.'

'We need to meet, and this morning if possible, I need to be at work by twelve.' He paused for a moment, then continued, 'How do you feel about that rather large cousin, or whatever he is, of yours?'

'Why?'

'Because I've found some interesting information, and if you trust him, I think he should be there as well.'

Bede could hear a microwave pinging in the background and the news blaring—from the television probably. She thought for a moment. 'Yes, I do trust him.' She was a little surprised to acknowledge that. It had been creeping over her slowly for a number of days. It had started on the flight from Perth when he had been so sympathetic and helpful, caring really, when she had been such a wimp. She smiled to herself. 'Yes', she said again, 'I do trust him, so where and when do you want to meet?'

She was smiling to herself, as she climbed out of bed and headed for the bathroom. She wondered what Alain had found and hoped it would prove to be significant enough to give them some direction, but not turn out to be too dramatic. She'd come to appreciate Laurent's quiet, subtle, slightly sarcastic sense of humour. She felt instinctively that he was honourable, and didn't really want to discover otherwise. Sighing, she stepped into the shower and let the hot water wake her completely.

Dressed in jeans and a light woollen pullover, she wandered into Gabriel's room and plumped down onto the end of his bed. 'Gabe, wake up.' She reached across to shake him, and suddenly found herself being pulled across the bed and tucked under Gabriel's chest. 'So you are awake, then I have news.' She tried to pull away from him, but he kept her anchored to his side.

'It's dangerous to come into my room when I'm sleeping,' he said into her ear. 'You might find yourself looking at a knife, or even a gun.' He grinned down at her. 'Be warned.' Without any seeming physical effort, he swung her out of the bed and put her onto her feet. 'What's this news?'

Bede raised her eyebrows at him. 'That was an impressive move. Alain wants to meet this morning. He seems to think he's found something significant, but will not talk over the phone. He's always a little paranoid, so I wouldn't take too much notice of that, but I do think we should go. He's suggested we meet at my favourite park at ten. The park is close to where he works.'

Gabe frowned. He was lying back against the pillows with his hands behind his head. 'I wonder what he's found. I have to make a few phone calls this morning, and we need to ring Martin and Hera to see if they've found anything significant. What time is it there at the moment?'

'It's about 3 p.m., so a good time to call, but maybe we should ring the mobile just in case they're not at the property.' She pulled her phone out of her pocket and sat back down on the end of the bed.

Gabriel looked at her. 'If you turn your back, I can get out of bed and have a quick shower, while you catch up on the gossip from Hera.'

Bede grinned at him. 'You should wear PJ's to bed like everyone else.'

'Piss off, I get too hot, now either turn your head or close your eyes.'

She turned away. 'Hera', she yelled, 'this is not a good connection, where are you? Can you ring back on Skype?' She listened for a few moments. 'Okay, fifteen minutes, talk to you then.' She turned back and yelled into the bathroom. 'Did you hear that?'

'*Yes*, I think the whole house heard you. I'll see you in the office in fifteen.'

Bede strolled to the bathroom, leaned on the doorframe, and gazed at Gabriel with pure lust in her eyes. She took in his beautiful back and shoulders, tapering to a small firm, and very hard backside. She willed him to turn around, so she could see him from the front. Her breathing was affected, her mouth was dry, she glanced into the mirror opposite the shower, and her eyes met Gabriel's in the reflection,

'I think you should join me', he said, 'so that I can perve on you. It's about time, don't you think?' He turned fully toward her, and she saw his broad chest and his fully aroused cock. Bede took two steps into the bathroom, pulling her jumper over her head as she moved. Gabe was smiling that wonderful seductive smile she had come to love. The one she had seen only a few times in the last few days. 'I've been waiting for you to finally acknowledge how you felt,' he said in a gravelly voice. 'But I didn't want to frighten you. Come here.' He caught her hand in his and pulled her into the warmth of the cascading water.

It was much later, lying in the warmth and comfort of his arms, with the doona pulled over their cooling bodies, that Bede remembered the call she was supposed to make to Hera. She sat up suddenly in bed, turned to Gabe, and saw him grinning at her. He was now lying back with both arms behind his head, looking more relaxed than she had seen him ever.

'Hera', Bede gasped, 'she will be wondering what happened.'

Gabe pulled her back down. 'Forget Hera for a moment, now, I can tell you about those bloody dreams of mine. They were vivid, but nowhere as spectacular as the reality. When I first saw you at the airport, I had an instant hard on. I could scarcely move. You looked so beautiful. Then when the reality of who you were hit me, I wanted to smash something. I think I fell in love with you in that moment.'

Bede scowled, 'You were such an arsehole. I was so angry with you, you were ignoring me, and you were the stranger in my dream, the one who rescued Hera and me. I recognised you immediately, and wanted to throw myself into your arms, but you were such a shit. I hadn't been able to tell Meredith or Hera, but the kiss in my dream was sweet, so sensual, and when you left, I was bereft and lonely.' Her arms were crossed on his chest, and her fingers were sifting through the hair there. She nuzzled his throat and nipped at his chin.

He pulled her closer and nibbled at her lips, ran his tongue over her mouth, and deepened the kiss. 'Bede, you know this is not really the smartest thing either of us has ever done. Martin and my position in the Family make any association with your family a little difficult to say the least. It's why James kept our dealings a secret. I'm not sure he would approve, but I'm not letting you go now, I hope you realise that.'

'Well, the feeling is mutual you know, and I might add I have a very jealous streak, so you had better subscribe to the theory of monogamy.'

Gabriel threw back his head and shouted with laughter, he wrapped his arms tightly around her. 'God, you're beautiful, I can't seem to get enough of you. And Hera and Martin can wait. Now just stop talking.'

Later, still wrapped securely in his arms, Bede murmured, 'What time is it? We haven't rung Bede and Martin, and we're to meet Alain at ten, but I'm loath to move at the moment.'

Gabriel smiled gently down at her, tucked securely into his side with her head resting on his chest. He sighed, 'Come on, we need to move, we can continue this later. And believe me, we will.' He leapt out of the bed, pulling Bede after him. He slapped her smartly on the backside and turned to pull on his jeans.

Bede, already dressing, turned. 'Do we have time to ring Hera before we leave? She is going to notice because she notices everything!'

'Perhaps it would be best to send her a text, tell her we're about to meet with Alain, and we'll ring when we find out what he has to say. It makes sense at this point, and I do need to know what Martin has been up to. He's following a strange trail at the moment, I haven't had time to tell you about it.'

Bede sat down on the end of the bed, and then raised her eyebrows. 'You can tell me on the way, we need to get going. Alain hates to be kept waiting.'

———————•———————

Martin watched as Hera walked down the steps of the homestead. She had waited until the blades stopped rotating before walking toward them. He took a few moments to consider how to explain Damian, and then decided to play it by ear. He greeted both Hera and Meredith with a cheery smile. 'We had to hire someone to bring us back, as we needed to get here quickly. There have been some surprising developments.' He indicated Damian, now climbing slowly down, and at her startled expression, continued, 'I'll explain inside, I'm glad you're both here. We really need to talk.'

———————•———————

They caught the metro to St Paul, and Bede dragged Gabriel in her wake, along the Rue de Rivoli toward one of the most strange and beautiful parks in Paris. On Rue Payenne, bordered by Rue de Sévigné and Rue du Parc-Royal.

Bede said, 'You're about to see my favourite park. I found it the first time I came to Paris. I was eighteen, and it was the middle of winter then too. It was all so beautiful and romantic, everything covered in inches of deep snow, and I was on my own, free at last.' She grabbed his hand and pulled his along. 'After finding this place, I went looking for as many other quirky parks as I could find. There are lots of them just tucked away in out of the way places. I'm sure they all have some significance, but mostly to their local community, I would think. Anyway, on that day, Alain was taking photos and we just started talking. That's basically how we met. The park was like a fairyland for me. Pristine white covering everything, even the cars parked on the side of the road had a foot of snow on the bonnets. There were children throwing snow balls, making snow men, and generally having a great time leading up to the Christmas season.'

You'll see the ancient roman ruins scattered around the periphery, and in one corner, the remains of a temple complete with ionic columns and a frieze incorporating a roman warrior and an angel, perhaps Gabriel? There was a free-standing semi-naked Diana, the huntress, sculptured in marble, standing in the centre of the garden surrounded by dormant rose bushes. The most startling aspect of the park was the trees planted around the perimeter, beautiful and straight, looking silver in the winter light. The trunk of each tree had a wooden kitchen chair attached about three metres from the ground, looking as if the trees had grown straight up through the seat of each chair. Some of the chairs were painted bright colours and others varnished, but all the chairs depicted a previous era and use. There was no indication of the intent behind the statement made by this amazing exhibition. A very post-modern experience!

Gabriel and Bede looked around in delight. This challenging and exciting park was the perfect place to meet, particularly at this time of the year. It was too cold for most to be outside for any length of time, and so the park was empty, but there was no snow.

Gabriel looked around in astonishment. 'This is really something. A pity there are no chairs in the trees now, it must have been an astonishing sight. I had no idea this park existed, and I've lived in Paris.' He turned to her and smiled. 'You continue to astonish me, Bede.' He pulled her gently into his arms, and kissed her softly on the lips. 'Thank you.'

Bede draped her arms around his neck and lifted onto her toes ready to explore that kiss, but was interrupted by a greeting from behind them.

'I see you two are on time, merci.' Alain smirked, and clapped Gabriel hard on the shoulder as they pulled apart. 'I asked you here because I knew we would not be disturbed, and it is very close for me, I can walk from here.' He looked around himself and smiled nostalgically. 'Just as beautiful as always.' He was looking at Bede.

Gabriel scowled, 'Stop playing games, Alain, you are being paid very well for this information. What do you have to report, and why not just send it by e-mail?'

'Ahhh, I just love this place. It's been a while since I was here, and I thought it would be Bede, not Bede and her large cousin as well.'

Bede raised her eyebrows, but her lips were curved. 'Come on, Alain, what do you have?'

'Yes, I have news, although I'm not sure it's what you expected. My research has been very extensive on your family tree, and although, Bede, you're were right, there was some reason to suspect that Laurent may not be the legitimate heir.' He paused dramatically, then spread his arms wide in an expansive gesture; and with a grin, continued, 'But it seems that he actually is.' He turned to Gabriel. 'Your family is indeed complicated. It's like an exercise in Algebra, but in reality, Laurent is the legitimate heir.' He looked so pleased with himself. 'I'll explain even if as you suspect, the child intimated in your strange journal is illegitimate by a series of bizarre pairings over the years. Laurent is still the legitimate patriarch to the Family.' He continued, 'I might add that you have some very famous or infamous figures in your family tree including several suspected criminals from not so long ago. Some that I personally would not boast about.' He smirked at them both then continued thoughtfully, 'Although now it appears most of the business enterprises are indeed legitimate.' He went on. 'I have spent a week on this, and it's been one of my most intriguing and rewarding challenges. I've had to go screaming off all over Europe to get a look at some documents and have enjoyed every moment.'

Gabriel was looking more relaxed now, lounging against the remains of the Roman Temple. He held out his hand. 'Thanks for that. I don't think we could have achieved as much in as little time even with the records in Laurent's library. Send your bill in, and I'll see it's paid quickly.'

Alain gazed at him for a moment. 'Dare I ask where you hoped this would lead?'

'It's not really appropriate to say at this point, but be reassured you've helped Bede and Hera enormously.'

Alain still looked thoughtful. 'I hope so.' He pulled a rolled-up scroll of papers enclosed in a transparent plastic cylinder from his backpack, and held it out to Gabriel. 'This is the family tree from before the dates you requested, so you can study it at your leisure. Even if the child in question was not the legitimate child of that marriage at the time, by now, it's all come full circle. The only family tree I've ever found more complicated than this one is the legitimate succession of any royal family.'

Gabriel took the scroll and unrolled it carefully. It was quite substantial, not something easily read, and certainly not standing in the middle of a park covered in snow. 'I was starting to suspect what you would find.' He turned to Bede. 'I'm convinced that the reason behind James's death is indeed in Australia, but probably originating from within the Family. We're looking in the wrong direction.' He paused thoughtfully then turned back at Alain. 'As I suspect, we were meant to.' He turned fully to Bede. 'We need to return to Australia, and I think very soon.' He held out his hand to Alain. 'Thanks again for your help in this, don't forget to send in your account. I don't want you to be out of pocket in any way. You must have worked like a Trojan to come up with this so quickly.'

Alain drew a long breath. 'Yes, but I knew how important it was to Bede, and for her, I would do anything. I am happy to have been of service.' He turned to Bede. 'Cherie, I think perhaps you will go home now. Be safe.' He suddenly caught her shoulders, pulled her close, and kissed her sweetly on the lips.

Gabriel stiffened. Bede put her arms around Alain and hugged him close. 'I will call you next time I'm in Paris. Thank you so much for all you've done.'

Gabriel watched him walk away with a frown on his face, and then turned back to Bede. 'Well, I can see you two have a history?'

She smiled sweetly at him, and took his arm. 'You're not jealous, are you?'

'Don't be ridiculous,' he snapped. 'We need to go.'

Bede smiled to herself.

They were all gathered in the library that evening, sitting quietly around the fire. Laurent looked up from the glass of brandy he had been studying and across at Gabriel. 'Are you going to tell me what's been going on over the last weeks?' He slid his eyes across to the three women, then lastly at Bede.

Bede cleared her throat. 'I feel it should be for me to explain everything,' she said.

Gabriel climbed easily to his feet, put his glass on the table by his chair, and took a few restless steps toward the fireplace, then turned back to Bede. 'No, I think it should be me that explains to Laurent what we have been doing, and what we hoped to achieve with the investigation.' He turned fully to look at Laurent. 'We have been investigating James's death, which we strongly suspect of being murder. More than that, I personally suspect that it was a planned assassination controlled from within the Family, and for a while, we suspected you were implicated in the cover up. We never suspected you of being part of the original plot.' He held up his hand as Laurent started to speak. 'Wait, there is more. There is a book, an antique book that James has in his library. The book is a book of letters written in the seventeenth century, which cast suspicion on your legitimate claim to the position of patriarch of the Family.' He held up his hand again as his mother tried to speak. 'Wait', he turned back to Laurent, 'we have now confirmed, with the help of one of Bede's friends, that this is a false premise. I am slightly embarrassed now by that suspicion and for staying here in your home, while we investigated.' He paused for a moment. 'But in my defence', he looked across at Bede again and continued, 'in our defence, I felt it important enough to investigate fully. I might add that I have always thought it highly unlikely that you would have been the instigator of such an underhand assassination of one of our own.'

Laurent sat unmoving in his chair, gazing thoughtfully, but not speaking to Gabe as he continued. 'Although to be fair, we had initially no intention of staying here.' He looked across at his two great-aunts. 'We were in fact, effectively kidnapped,' and he smiled ruefully.

Laurent held up his hand. 'I thought it was something like that. I could have saved you the trouble, you know, that rumour has been around for several generations now. My father looked into the matter very quietly not long after he assumed the mantle. He was determined to put the rumour to rest for all time, but in the end decided to let it stand. You may not know it, but he had a decidedly peculiar sense of humour.' He looked at Josephine, Marina, and finally across at Mette. 'You ladies do tend to interfere at times, but in this case, I forgive you.' He turned to Bede. 'It's given me the pleasure of meeting you, my dear, and if I'm not mistaken, to welcome you solidly into the family.' With a completely expressionless face, he turned to Gabriel. 'Am I mistaken?'

Gabriel's face, also expressionless, lifted one shoulder, but remained completely impassive.

'What are you two talking about?' Josephine demanded.

'Jose, sometimes you're not as astute and clever as you think you are.' Laurent climbed to his feet. 'I'm for bed, goodnight all.'

Gabriel, startled, said, 'Wait, don't you want to know all the details?'

'No', with a lift of his hand, 'I know most of it, but I expect you to keep me fully informed. James's death is inexcusable.' And he left the library.

They all sat quietly for a few moments. Mette was the first to speak. 'We should have known that he would have worked out what we were after. He was always the analytical one, never did let emotion cloud his judgement, and his father was even more astute.'

'Yes,' Josephine sighed. 'Laurent's father would never leave anything to chance, and although he was a ruthless bastard, he was always scrupulously honest when it came to the succession. He always insisted that it had to be kept pure because so much else in the family wasn't.'

'So, where do we go from here?'

He was pacing now and he turned back. 'There has to be some connection with the book. Otherwise, James's death doesn't make sense. Someone planted the idea that there was a potential problem. Where did James get the book? Did he buy it? And from whom?' He looked at Bede. 'We need to ring Martin and Hera, see if they can dig up information. A bill of sale perhaps, there has to be some sort of document stating the provenance of the book. It's obviously a valuable antique.'

Bede looked down at the drink in her hand, still untouched. 'Well, I do know he often attended the auctions at Christie's in South Kensington when he was in the UK,' she said thoughtfully. She was sitting cross-legged on the floor with a snifter of brandy dangling dangerously from her right hand. She looked up and her lips twisted into a half smile. 'Gabriel, the easiest thing is to ring Hera, but by my calculations', she looked at her watch, 'it's 5 a.m. tomorrow morning. It's too early even for you to ring. They won't appreciate it, especially if you're going to ask then to scrabble through old files.'

He grinned. 'Okay, so we all go to bed and sleep on it.'

He held out his hand to pull Bede to her feet. 'Come on, it's been a long day. You need your beauty sleep, as do I.'

Bede allowed him to pull her to her feet, putting the untouched glass of brandy on the table.

He turned to his three female relatives still sitting quietly and scowled, 'And you three need to stop plotting.' He followed Bede from the room.

The three women sat in silence for a moment, and then all three simultaneously burst into laughter.

# Chapter Twenty-Two

## Surprise at the Homestead

Martin's cheery greeting reached Hera and Meredith as they were slowly descending the steps.

'Damian?' Meredith's startled exclamation rang across the clearing. She scowled, and with narrowed eyes, watched Damian climb carefully down from the helicopter. 'Martin, what is going on? And why is Damian here?' She turned angrily to Hera and demanded, 'Do you know what this is all about?'

Hera, looking anxious, stopped abruptly and turned back to Meredith. 'No, I have no idea why Damian is here. Don't shout at me.'

'Calm down everyone.' Martin hurried across the lawn. 'I need you all to come inside, and I'll explain everything, but perhaps you could relax a little and smile at Damian. I assure you he hasn't done anything to warrant this aggression from both of you.'

Hera scowled, drew a deep breath, and massaging the back of her neck with one hand, made a huge effort to relax. She swung around to Damian, and with a frigid smile on her face, 'Shall we start again? Damian, so good to see you, do come inside and tell us what you have been doing lately.' She turned back to Martin, and with raised eyebrows, 'Was that better? Now, perhaps you will come into the house as well and explain.'

Martin strolled up and draped one arm across her shoulders. 'Much better, and yes, you have every right to be anxious and worried. I will explain everything, but perhaps inside would be wise.' He turned her casually to look across the lawn to see Pete and another of their workforce leaning against the fence outside their sleeping quarters, quietly smoking, but watching the proceedings with obvious interest.

The helicopter took off just then with a deafening roar, making any more speech impossible.

Meredith was the first to speak. They were all more relaxed now with she and Hera drinking tea, and Martin and Damian holding ice-cold glasses of beer in their hands. 'Well, Martin, perhaps you would like to explain exactly what's going on.' She speared him with her gaze. 'James asked him to leave, and I'm sure he had a very good reason.' She turned her cold gaze onto Damian. 'Why is he back here?'

Damian started to speak, but Martin waved him to silence. 'Meredith, James asked Damian to leave because he thought Damian has designs on Hera. I don't think that's true, but what is true is that James was funding Damian's research into the medicinal properties of various native Australian plants.' He held up his hand at Hera's gasp. 'Wait, Hera, James continued to fund his research after he dismissed him from here.' He paused. 'And he continued up until his death.'

Meredith looked thoughtfully at Martin.

Hera looked across at Damian, and with her mouth compressed into a thin line, 'Perhaps you, Damian, should tell us why James threw you out.' She put her cup carefully down into the saucer and looked fixedly at him.

He responded slowly, 'Hera, what Martin said is true. He was determined to stop any romantic interest that might develop between us. He knew my background, and I think was a little wary of me.' He looked suddenly uncomfortable. 'He knew my research was running parallel to you, and I thought maybe he thought I was trying to poach. But nothing could be further from the truth. James was actually helping me by funding some of my research. He knew I was really very short of funds.' He slumped into the chair.

'Is that what he found out was that what you were really doing here, poaching, I was trying to help you, you bastard.' Hera bounded out of her chair and lurched across the room. 'Did you have something to do with his death? What do you mean he knew your background, are you a murderer?' Gesticulating wildly, she continued, 'Get out of this house, now!' She rounded on Martin.

Martin sprang quickly to intercept her and pulled her into his arms. She was sobbing now and snarled at Damian. She was screaming and struggling in Martin's arms, and then turned on him. 'Why did you bring him here? You're involved in this somehow, aren't you? You didn't take long to find him, you knew where he was all the time.'

Martin was trying to hold Hera without hurting her. 'Hera, calm down, you've got it all wrong. Please have some faith in me, and listen to what Damian has to say. Give him a chance, and for Christ's sake, stop shouting.'

Meredith was on her feet now as well. She, too, was trying to calm Hera down. She took her gently by the shoulders and pulled her into her arms. 'Quiet,' she whispered.

Hera continued to struggle and pulled away from Meredith. Then picking up the empty plate previously holding biscuits and started threateningly toward Damian again, shouting. 'You bastard!' She was trying to hit him over the head with the plate, screaming at him, while Damian, with his arms up protecting his head, was slowly backing across the room.

Martin was shouting for everyone to calm down. He grabbed Hera and thrust her into a chair, while taking the plate away. 'Sit down everyone, and I will explain.' He turned to Hera. 'For God's sake, what do you think you're doing? Damian hasn't done anything. He didn't kill James! Think, woman, you're being hysterical!' He now turned to Damian. 'Sit in that chair, and don't say anything.' Then turned back to Hera, sobbing quietly. 'Hera, I don't know what James was thinking, I don't know why he was funding Damian, but I'm sure Damian has nothing to do with James's death. He had nothing to gain and everything to lose.' He was exasperated by all this emotional turmoil. 'Now listen to me, all of you. Damian has had someone stalking him

for over a week now, and he has no real idea who it is, or why he's
suddenly become a target for these thugs. He has been attacked twice
and managed to escape, but is covered in bruises and needs help, and
somewhere to stay for a while. That's why I brought him here.'

Hera snarled, 'Tell him to go to the police then, or the hospital.
Why bring him here? He's betrayed us, me, and now it's obvious Dad
has been less than honest with all of us.' She turned back to Martin
and snarled, 'And who exactly are you? You prick. And why are you
defending this thief?' She next snarled at Damian, sitting quietly in the
chair with his head in his hands. 'You've stolen my research, haven't you,
you, you . . .' she spluttered into silence.

He surged to his feet. 'No, I did no such thing!' He swung around
to Martin. 'I think this was one major mistake. I'm grateful for your
help, but I think I'll leave now.' He headed for the door.

Martin, in exasperation, held up his hands. 'Will you all just shut
up and let me explain!' He pointed his finger at Damian. 'And you,
stay where you are. You're not going anywhere, or you're likely to end up
dead.' Martin felt he had presented the arguments calmly and coherently,
and was stunned by the reaction. He cursed under his breath. He should
have been more conscious of the anxiety and stress they had been under
over the last weeks and handled the situation better.

Meredith was sitting very quietly and looked thoughtfully and
intensely at Damian.

Hera, although very red in the face and shooting angry glances at
both Damian and Martin, was no longer threatening Damian with
bodily harm.

'Now, can we be calm everyone, please,' Martin spoke firmly, but
quietly, and indicated the couch and armchair. 'I'm going to tell you
a story, some of which you all know, but it's relevant and I think
important. I'm not sure it has anything to do with James's death though.'
He paused, looking thoughtfully at the three people facing him then
paced slowly to stand in front of the unlit fire.

The two women sat quietly with Meredith holding Hera's hands in
hers, and gently stroking, while Damian looking dejected, sat slumped
in the armchair facing them. Martin looked at Meredith first and then

turned toward Hera. 'I'll start at almost the end of the story. I can't prove any of this at this point, so it's all surmise, but I think I'm right. Firstly, I suspect James's dismissal of Damian wasn't for the reason you think Hera. I think he had learned somehow that Damian's past had caught up with him, and he wanted him off the property quickly. I don't know how he would have known about Damian's past, but I suspect Gabe. He allowed you to think it was because he didn't approve of any relationship developing between the two of you, although that could have been part of it.'

'What truth?' Meredith asked. 'I'm starting to think James was much more involved with that side of the Family than he ever allowed any of us to know. But I would have thought he would take some precautions if there was any danger threatening.'

Hera now surged to her feet and started to pace. She could never sit still if agitated, then swung around to glare at Martin. 'Are you saying now that James's murder was because of Damian?' She swung back and glared first at Damian then at Martin. 'Have you suspected all along what this is about, and the books have nothing to do with it?'

Martin, still exasperated, walked toward Hera. He put his arm around her shoulder and briefly hugged her. 'No, I'm not saying either of those things. Come on relax a little, will you? This story is about Damian, and in my opinion, has nothing to do with James's murder.' He gently led her back to the couch, and she allowed herself to be seated. Martin continued, 'As you informed me before, Hera, Damian is a brilliant biologist. He has always had an almost uncanny ability to identify the medicinal properties of various plants. You said he was doing research toward his PhD?' Straightening his shoulders, he looked at Damian and drew a deep breath. 'Damian, I'm sorry everything has to come out now. It's too dangerous not to.' He paused for a moment. 'I feel sure once they hear the full story, they will keep your secrets. I don't think they really want you dead.'

Damian, still slumped dejectedly in the chair with his head in his hands, looked up; and with a small gesture of his hand, urges Martin to continue.

'In fact, Damian already has a PhD from Charles University in Prague under his real name.' Hera gasped, sat up, and looked across at Damian in astonishment. Martin continued, 'A PhD he finished when he just turned twenty, but because of a rather silly, immature, and dangerous prank he and some of his friends pulled immediately after graduation, he had to disappear totally.' He looked across at Damian, sitting quietly now with a resigned expression on his face. 'It was really stupid because it involved the Czech Mafia, and a great deal of money.' Martin paused again, frowned as if in thought, then continued, 'Fortunately for Damian, Gabe and I were in Prague at that time, and we heard about the scam. To be honest, we were impressed, but knew there would be some substantial fall out.' He looked at Meredith. 'Lucien was also involved, but not directly,' he shrugged. 'You know Lucien, involved to some degree, but not technically Mafia.' He turned back to Damian and smiled. 'Neither Gabe nor I had met Damian at that point, but as I said, we had heard some of the details. That night, we had been out to dinner with Justin, and were walking back to our hotel when we heard screams and a loud splash. Gabe and I between us managed to pull him out of the Vltava. He had been thrown from Charles Bridge by some very irate Czech thugs. He had been badly beaten, was almost unconscious, and bleeding from a nasty head wound. We took him to a discrete doctor we knew, and later helped him disappear. Both Gabe and I kept in touch, mostly, but over the last couple of years, we lost touch. Neither of us knew he was in Australia, let alone here on the West Coast.'

Meredith was looking at Damian thoughtfully now, and Hera was visibly startled. 'So you're some kind of genius.'

Damian just curled his lips and didn't answer immediately. He stood up. 'I think I should tell you the rest of the story. We, my friends and I, were really stupid. We pissed off a rather nasty gangster, and he is a ruthless bastard. He had one of my friends killed the same night they beat me up. They hadn't expected me to survive, so although I thought I had just set myself up for a life of ease working for one of the drug companies, doing the research I loved, I was now about to be killed by one of the most devious criminals in Europe.' He drew a long breath and continued, 'Being pulled out of the river by Gabe and Martin was the luckiest thing to happen to me. They had the contacts and the resources to help me disappear. They set me up with a new identity.' He made a sweeping wave of one hand down his body and continued, 'But I couldn't use my academic credentials. They did manage an undergraduate degree from Charles for me in my assumed name, but even that was dodgy. In a word, I had to start again, I had to get out of the Czech Republic, and be very careful to not shine above the radar. I eventually enrolled at Comenius University in Bratislava for a master's then used that to come to Australia to do another PhD at Curtin. I just wanted the facilities really, and to be able to finally settled down. I thought Australia was far enough away from the past to be safe.' He looked across at Martin. 'I had no idea really how hard it is to really disappear. The past is always there like a bad smell.' He looked tired.

Martin now took up the tale. 'That's the bones of it. James knew the story because he and Gabe have', he paused and looked with compassion at Hera for a moment, then continued, 'have a really good relationship, and in the last few years, he stayed with Gabe whenever he was in London.'

Hera was sitting upright and quivering. 'Just how well did you and Gabriel know my father?' she demanded. She looked across at Meredith. 'And did you know any of this?'

Meredith was slumped slight in her chair. She drew a long and painful breath before she answered. 'No, Hera, I knew nothing of any of this. I suspected James kept in touch with some of the family, but I had no idea with whom exactly. He made it clear particularly in the last few years that it was best if I didn't enquire too closely. He wanted to make sure you and Bede were protected from any of the family machinations as much as possible.'

Martin cleared his throat. 'We both knew your father really well, and as I said, especially Gabe, but he never mentioned anything about either you or Bede. He made it clear that you both were to be kept far away from the family. But because of that connection, we were stunned by Laurent's apparent lack of interest in James's death.'

They all sat quietly for several moments, each sunk in their own thoughts. Finally, Hera lifted her head and looked across at Damian. 'So you're being chased by these Czechoslovakian gangsters, is that it?'

Damian shrugged and glanced across at Martin. 'I don't know who they are, but I don't think they're Czech. I'd guess Russian, if anything.' And with a curl of his lips, 'And one of them is definitely a cowardly Pom.' He touched the bruise on his left cheekbone.

Hera suddenly grinned. 'You have absorbed enough of the Oze's distaste for our English cousins, I see.'

Damian grinned sickly and shrugged. 'So, what do we do now?'

Meredith stood up. 'I think we need some time out. This has all been a bit too emotional for me. I'll go and see Mrs Robertson. We should have something to eat, an early dinner is in order I think, then afterward, we can sit down calmly and try to make some sense out of this chaos.'

Hera sank more deeply into the chair, Martin wandered across the room to the window, and stood with his hands clasped behind his back, while Damian's head fell tiredly against the back of the chair.

'Meredith's right,' Martin said from the window. 'We have been reacting instead of being proactive. Finding you, possibly involved with this, has thrown me a little, and I've allowed myself to be sidetracked.' He turned back to Hera. 'We need to be calm and think this through. We'll leave it until after dinner.' He turned to Damian. 'You probably haven't eaten properly for a while now.'

'Four days, in fact,' Damian lifted his head. 'I've been eating crap food.'

Hera grinned at him. 'Poor baby, you haven't had anyone to look after you.'

Damian picked up a cushion from the chair and threw it across the room at her, but he was smiling quietly now. 'It's nice to be back here anyway for whatever reason.'

Meredith and Hera chatted throughout the meal, keeping the conversation flowing with anecdotes about the local community, bringing Damian up to date on all the latest romances, births, and one marriage since he was last there.

Martin was sunk deeply into his own thoughts, not taking any part in their conversation. As the meal finished, he finally lifted his head. 'We need to ring Gabe and Bede, but first, we'll all sit down and sort out exactly what you each know about the time James asked Damian to leave. We'll go through into the living room, and then one at a time. I want you to recount everything you can think of, and I mean everything regardless if you think it has any bearing on what happened.'

Damian was the first to speak, 'I don't know how they found me if it really is the same crowd. I've changed so much since that skinny, arrogant kid I was back then. I wouldn't recognise me, so I don't know how anyone else could. I've grown four inches, put on several stone, and most of it muscle, thanks to you and Gabe. I've learned how to defend myself, and how to keep a low profile.' He looked at Martin. 'Again, thanks to you and Gabe. I have the feeling my problem has nothing to do with James. My credentials are as legitimate as is possible under the circumstances, and they've never been questioned, not even by immigration.' He shrugged his shoulders and slumped back into his chair.

Hera looked at him. 'What about your parents, or any other relatives, could they have slipped up?'

Martin shook his head and answered for him. 'Damian's an orphan with no close relatives at all. His parents were killed when he was about six, I think. His education was paid by the state, particularly after they realised his potential. Gabe and I made sure his death was reported with graphic details, and although his body was never found, we made a good story of what we had seen.' He continued, 'I'm inclined to agree with Damian, I think this is a separate issue, but maybe not unrelated.'

Hera scowled, 'What do you mean?'

'Well', Martin continued, 'I suspect, as I said before, that someone has been watching James for a long time. Damian spent a few months here last summer, and then was publicly thrown off the property. It would have been relatively easy to find out what Damian was doing, what his research involved, and how Curtin felt about it.'

They were all silent, thinking through what he had said. And then Damian stirred. 'Martin, that makes more sense than the Czech mob catching up with me. It would also explain why they were so stunned when I made it clear I didn't want to talk to any of them. They seemed a little surprised initially, then they just got nasty.' He touched his cheek again. 'They're just another bunch of crooks wanting me to work for them somehow. I seem to attract them like flies.' He groaned. 'They're probably just thugs trying to set up a lab to make ice or something equally lethal, and thought I would jump at the chance because I had just lost James's backing.'

Meredith smiled. 'Damian, you poor thing, you really do need someone to look after you.'

He scowled at her, 'You think me completely inadequate.' Then sighed. 'Well, you're probably right.'

'Don't be an idiot Damian, Meredith was joking, but it wasn't meant nastily.' Hera slowly stood. 'Remember Meredith's weird sense of humour from before and ignore her. It's her age, I think.' She turned to Martin standing idly looking out of the window. 'Well, Sherlock, what do you think?'

'Damned if I know. I think Damian's right, but it doesn't get us any nearer to solving James's death. I really need to talk to Gabe. I'm going to ring now and wake him if necessary, then we're going to have a long session of recollections regarding James, what James said, what James did, and when.' Just then, his phone rang. 'Hopefully this is Gabe,' he said, taking the phone out of his pocket. He looked at the number and frowned, looked across at Hera sitting quietly now, and spoke into the mobile, 'Do you have any news?' He looked surprised. 'Really. Keep me informed.' Turning back to the three eager faces looking at him, he shrugged, 'Sorry, that was from the guy I have looking for the Watsons. They seem to have disappeared.' Meredith gave a startled gasp and turned to Hera who shrugged her shoulders wordlessly.

Martin left the room heading for the library, and a quiet place to think and make the call to Gabe.

Martin returned to find Hera and Meredith deep in conversation. Meredith looked up, 'Martin, we seem to have gotten away from our original thoughts about the missing contract and James's rage against George.' Hera cut in at that point. 'We've been grasping at straws, I think, that book of letters wasn't the clue we thought it was, but perhaps the other book with the scrap of paper with James's signature was more important than we thought.'

Damian looked up. 'What books are you talking about?'

Martin sprawled in the armchair deep in thought, while Hera talked. He cleared his throat then sat up. They all turned to look at him. 'I had already thought that we could be on the wrong track, so I asked Gabe to check the auction houses in London for information about both books. He and Bede flew out of Paris this morning. Apparently, James favoured Christies in London, but let's not discriminate. So yes, bring out the books Hera, and we'll look at them now then I'll recount what Gabe said on the phone. We'll go back to the beginning, as I suggested before, and perhaps each of us should write down our impressions of James, George, and Lucien over the last few months. There has to be a connection somewhere.'

Hera carefully put the book of botanical illustrations onto a clean cloth on the desk. She thought Damian would appreciate the beauty and skill involved in producing this exquisite tome. She was right. He slowly lost the colour in his face, as he bent over to examine the book. His hands were trembling slightly, as he inspected first the cover, and then carefully opened it to the illustrations within. They were beautifully executed in watercolour, ink, and pencil, not the etchings that he had expected. These were original paintings with handwritten notes in explanation. The writing itself was a work of art, and Damian was stunned. He looked up and said in an awed voice, 'This is priceless. These are originals and it's been handbound. Where on earth did it come from?'

'That, Damian, my friend, is the question of the moment,' Martin said quietly. 'The book is beautiful and valuable, but I can't see it as a reason to kill anyone. The potential in the book of letters has more gravitas, but Gabe has now put that one to rest.'

Hera interrupted. 'You mean Gabe and Bede, don't you?' she said challengingly.

Martin grinned. 'Sorry, point taken.' He turned back to Damian. 'Gabe and Bede, between them, have confirmed that there is no conflict at all with Laurent as patriarch of the Family.' He grinned across at Hera, 'Better.'

She huffed and sank back quietly into the chair.

'I suggest we all find somewhere quiet and start thinking. Write down all your thoughts and memories about the last time you saw or spoke to James, then we compare notes.' Martin moved quietly toward the door and continued, 'Damian, you use the desk in the office.' And turning, added firmly, 'It's important to be completely honest, no keeping anything back because it's embarrassing or think it's not important. Hera, you should put the books away safely.'

She snorted at him, 'Martin, I'm quite capable of working that out for myself.' And left the room holding the books carefully in her arms.

# Chapter Twenty-Three

## Justin Arrives

**M**eredith was looking a little stunned after picking up and answering the telephone. She turned to Hera. 'That was Justin. He's on his way here. In fact, he's already landed and has hired a helicopter. He should be here by lunchtime.'

'Did he say why he's here?' Martin asked mildly.

'No,' Meredith answered. 'He just said he had arrived and was on his way.'

Martin quietly left the room, pulling his mobile from his pocket as he went. Hera heard him talking to Gabriel. She couldn't hear what he said, but he sounded serious.

Coming back into the room, he looked at the three. 'I've suggested to Gabe that he and Bede had better head back as soon as they can get a flight.' He paused, and then continued thoughtfully, 'I don't like the idea of Justin suddenly packing up and flying here. It smacks of knowledge we don't have.' He turned to Damian. 'Have you met Justin?'

Damian got up from the couch where he had been sitting and moved restlessly about the room. 'No, I've heard a lot about him from Gabe, of course, and also strangely, James. He spoke about him a couple of times just before he chucked me out.' He shrugged. 'Not that it means anything. Why the anxiety?'

Martin smiled. 'It's just strange, really.' He turned to Meredith. 'When was the last time he was here?'

Meredith pursed her lips and looked across at Hera. 'I can't remember, can you?'

Hera was looking worried now. 'No, it was years ago, I was at boarding school. What can he want?' And turning to Martin, 'Do you think he had some news, something we haven't heard about?' She jumped to her feet and started pacing around the room then turning back to Martin, 'I'm frightened for some reason.'

Meredith put her arm around her shoulders, and drew her to the door. 'Hera, it's okay, it's just a strange thing for him to do. And there has been a lot happening lately, and you haven't had a chance to process it all. Justin is a friend as well as a relative. If he's come he's here to help, it's simple. Let's make sure Mrs Robinson prepares a bedroom for him, he'll be jet-lagged. He's not a good traveller, and over twenty-four hours on a plane really knocks him around.'

Damian looked across at Martin. 'You're not sure about that, are you?'

Martin still looked thoughtful. 'No, I'm not sure at all, but he's on his way. What exactly did James say about him?' And the two of them left the room together.

⎯⎯⎯•⎯⎯⎯

Gabriel put his phone back into his pocket and turned to Bede taking her hand, and turned her away from the painting she was studying. 'We have to leave now. We need to get a flight immediately and take you home.'

She smiled into his eyes. 'What's happened now? Or is this just an excuse for you to get some quality sunshine?'

He put his arms around her. 'That sounds great actually, but Martin just called. Things have been happening back on the farm, as they say, and Justin has just arrived in good ole Oz.' He paused. 'And that's surprising really, so Martin wants us back. We don't actually need to be here anymore. We can still follow up the investigation on the two books by phone and e-mail.'

Bede sighed. 'Well, it's been nice having you to myself for a while.'

He grinned down at her. 'The feeling's mutual. Come on, we'll collect our things from the hotel and head for Heathrow now. I'll see what's available leaving immediately, and hopefully with just one stop.'

———•◦•———

Meredith was waiting on the veranda when the helicopter landed, and Hera wandered out to stand beside her as Justin climbed down. He waved to them, as the rotors finally stopped spinning.

'Hi, you two, good to see you,' he called, as they came down to steps toward him. 'I hope I haven't caused you any trouble just arriving like this. I wanted to surprise you.'

At that moment, Martin wandered out and stood on the top step. Justin faltered briefly walking across from the stationary helicopter. 'Martin', he smiled his old smile, 'I didn't realise you were still here. I thought you'd gone to Paris with Gabe.' He continued across the grass more slowly now.

'Good to see you, Justin, what brings you this far south?'

Justin came up the steps, holding out his hand first to Meredith then Hera then taking Hera by the shoulders, looked into her eyes. 'My dear, you have grown to be a beautiful young lady.' He bussed her briefly on both cheeks. Turning again to Meredith, he smiled down at her and kissed her on both cheeks in his usual smooth manner.

Meredith took his hand, drew him up the last steps, and into the house. As she looked back toward the helicopter, she saw Pete talking to the pilot. They were deep in conversation. They obviously knew each other really well—not surprising—it was a relatively small community, but Pete seemed to be disturbed about something, almost angry.

Later that night, Meredith, Hera, Martin, and Damian were all gathered around the living room. Justin, as Meredith had predicted, had retired early to bed. He really wasn't a good traveller, and had looked exhausted during dinner that night.

Martin was the first to break the silence. He looked across at Meredith. 'Did Justin give you any indication why he was really here?'

'No, in fact, he very cleverly avoided any mention of his motives except to say that he felt it was time.'

Hera, sitting quietly on the sofa, spoke for the first time since dinner, 'I don't have a good feeling about this. Something is going on that I don't understand. How did he arrange for the helicopter so quietly without someone from Perth notifying us that we were to expect a visitor? There are only so many options, and mostly they should have let us know. Justin must have insisted we not be notified. We could have been away from the property for all he knew unless he did know, and that's a worry as well.' She looked at Martin leaning quietly on the arm of the sofa.

Martin shrugged, 'I suggest we all get an early night. I've heard from Gabe. He and Bede managed to get a flight from Heathrow immediately, so they'll be here within the next two days. I suggest we not mention to Justin that Bede and Gabe are heading back.' He raised his eyebrows in enquiry at Meredith. She moved her head slightly in acknowledgement and smiled.

Martin left the room quietly saying he though a walk in the cool of the evening would help him think. He moved quietly and casually out of the room and to the front door. Once outside, ever indication of relaxation left him, and he moved silently across to the outbuilding where Pete and the rest of the workers slept. He silently moved across the veranda to Pete's door, and knocking quietly, waited for an acknowledgement. He slipped into the room looking around. He hadn't actually been here before and was interested. It was a large room, comfortably furnished with a combined bedroom and sitting area, air conditioning, and through an open door, he glimpsed a modern pristine bathroom. Pete had all the comforts of home. The paintings on the walls looked like originals, and he moved over to one depicting the waterhole they usually swam in. Looking across at Pete still sitting in front of his computer, and indicated the painting. 'One of yours?'

Pete shrugged, 'One of many. That one actually worked. You're curious about how our visitor got here?'

'Very, I thought you had an arrangement that no one from any of the firms out of Perth would fly anyone here without notifying you first?'

'It's true, but Les, our friendly pilot, thought he looked innocent enough and he'd spun a romantic story about wanting to surprise Meredith after many years. He also paid triple the going rate. Les took a chance, one he will never do again if he wants to keep our business.'

'So do we actually know when he arrived?'

'No, he could have been in Perth for days. It didn't, of course, occur to Les to ask, but he'll do some checking for me. I thought he would have rung by now. Sit down and I'll ring him. We need to know, don't we?'

'Yes, it's out of character for him. He's devious, and although I've known him all my life and he's my uncle, I don't actually trust him and never have. Neither does Gabe. He's too slippery to ever take at face value.'

Pete had picked up the phone, dialled, spoke briefly, looked surprised, then hung up. 'Well, your devious uncle has been in Perth for a week staying at the Rydges. He's kept his room and reception think he'll be away for a couple of days.' Pete continued to look thoughtful. 'I think we need more information. I'll get someone on it, try to find out what he's been doing for a week.'

Martin, leaning against the door frame, nodded. 'Thanks, let me know if you come up with anything, I'll also get my guys to check a few of our contacts. I don't want them tripping over your lot.' He moved to the door quietly.

Pete cleared his throat. 'Does Damian know your uncle?'

'No, he knows of him, but to my knowledge, they've never met. Justin has no idea of the connection to myself and Gabe. He thinks he's just a friend of Hera's. Why?'

'Don't know, just a feeling I have. I think it's important somehow that he doesn't know. Goodnight.'

Martin left just as silently as he'd come. He drifted across the clearing then turned and wandered back to the front of house. It was quiet. Everyone in bed, he thought, but he was still restless. Taking out his phone, he sent a long text to Gabe. There was something not quite right about Justin's sudden visit.

# Chapter Twenty-Four

# Gabriel and Bede Return

Two days later, Justin was sitting quietly on the veranda, reading, when he heard the telltale sound of a helicopter. He put his book down and called into the house. 'Incoming visitor, are you expecting someone?' He was relaxed, and looked slightly better than he had the day before. He still felt lethargic and tired, but he'd been in Western Australia for over a week, he should be feeling better by now, but his mind was still not as sharp as usual. He really hoped the visitor, whoever it was, wouldn't stay too long. He had been sitting there thinking about what he needed to say to Meredith, and wandering how to get her alone for a couple of hours. He was pissed that Martin was still here, and he couldn't quite decide what he thought about the young lad, Damian. There was something about him that raised the hackles on his neck. Getting up slowly, he put his book down on the table beside his chair and moved to the front steps.

Hera came bounding out the front door. Really, he thought to himself, her energy level was very trying. Meredith was following her with a huge smile on her face. Maybe he was missing something here. He really hated the fog that jet lag left him in.

Martin was ambling in that loose-limbed way of his from around the back of the house, and Damian was following him like a little puppy, he thought irritably. He looked across at the outbuildings and saw Pete, that long-limbed foreman, or whatever he was, lounging against the door of his home. Really, did he do nothing around the property?

The helicopter had landed, the blades had stopped spinning, and to his rage and consternation, he saw first Gabriel and then Bede step out. Hera was running toward them, and threw herself into Bede's arms. She was jumping and almost shouting in her excitement. He looked at the tableau with exasperation. This was an unexpected hitch in his plans for Meredith. Hera, he could have managed, but Bede was a stubborn miss and always had been. He needed to be very careful about how he was going to manage these young people. He plastered a welcoming smile on his face and moved down the steps.

Later around the table, after dinner, the energy was still high. Bede was still giving Hera and Meredith an account of everyone they had seen in Paris and London. Gabriel was quiet, which was unusual for him, sitting back and smiling whenever his eyes rested on Bede. He seemed indulgent at all the excitement around him. He and Martin had disappeared earlier, which still worried him. Neither of them had volunteered anything about what they had discovered. Bede seemed to be concentrating on the family. What had made them stay with Laurent for God's sake, and why had Mette been there as well as those two old biddies?

Gabriel suddenly turned to Justin. 'Do you know, Justin, I think I caught a glimpse of George in Perth. Do you know what he's doing in Australia? I thought he and Lucien had something happening in Prague. You've just left there, haven't you? Do you know what they are up to?'

Justin could feel his face blanking. 'No, that's impossible, you're mistaken. George wouldn't be here. Lucien had spoken of him just before I left Prague. He had plans that included George's full cooperation, a project that Lucien thought George would jump at. Mind, I'm not sure exactly what Lucien's motives were, and I didn't actually see George. I don't trust either of them, but I'm sure it couldn't have been George you saw.' Justin was quite pale, and ran his hands through his hair. A telling gesture, Gabriel thought.

Bede looked up at that. 'Justin, I saw him too, it was across the concourse, but it certainly looked like him. He saw me looking and quickly turned away and disappeared into the crowd. Both Gabe and I tried to find him later, but he'd disappeared completely.'

Meredith, startled, turned to Gabriel. 'Surely not, what would he want here? I don't think he's been here for nearly twenty years.'

'I'll make some enquiries, Meredith, but he could have business interests here.' Gabriel grinned. 'Because we don't trust him, and assume that he wouldn't venture into this hemisphere doesn't mean he hasn't.'

Justin suddenly felt faint, almost panicky. What the hell was going on?

Later that night, in Gabriel's bedroom, Bede was sitting on the side of the bed, and Hera was lounging in a chair by the window when Martin slipped quietly into the room. Gabriel moved across and stood behind Bede with his hand resting possessively on the back of her neck.

'Okay, spill all Gabe. What have you really discovered, if anything?' He looked across at Bede, frowned, and then turned back to Gabriel. 'What's Justin up to, and did you really see George at the airport? Coming or going?'

'Coming. And it was definitely George. I saw his face when he realised Bede had spotted him. He did a double take and lost that high colour of his. It was while we were going through customs control, and I was distracted for a moment by the customs officer. I couldn't very well tell him to wait, and go tearing off. By the time I looked around again, he'd disappeared. We both looked for him later, but couldn't see him. But if he didn't have to collect any luggage, he could easily have grabbed a taxi. He was ahead of us by about five minutes.'

Martin pursed his lips. 'This is becoming interesting. We now have Justin and George here, and all we need now is for Lucien to turn up.'

Two days later, all sitting around the breakfast table, Meredith turned to Justin and spoke quietly with a smile in her voice. 'Justin, you seem to have finally recovered. I suggest an excursion for today. Lunch at the club is called for. You didn't manage to get there the last time you were here, and it's become very civilised over the last few years. The food is delicious.' She looked across at Bede. 'Gabriel and Martin would enjoy the day as well. We can arrange for you all to go sailing with the Wellards. They seem to be there every day now they're retired, and Justin might enjoy a trip on the lake. It's a very peaceful way to spend a few hours.'

Hera and Bede grinned, then Bede spoke, 'We can drive. It's only a couple of hours, and that way, you'll get some idea of the country around here at ground level.' She looked across at Gabe and then Martin.

They exchanged glances, and Martin slowly got to his feet. 'Sounds an excellent idea, this is west we're talking about, toward the coast?'

Hera grinned. 'Yes, very different country to that around the waterhole.' She turned to Meredith. 'I'll let Robbie know we won't be here for lunch, and maybe dinner either. We can drive back in the cool of the evening. It's quite beautiful at that time, and the stars are absolutely stunning, I love it.' She looked across at Damian. 'Do you feel confident showing your face at the club?'

'Well, I can't hide forever, so yes, a day swimming, sailing, and eating good food sounds great.' He drew a deep breath, but was frowning slightly as he stood up.

Gabe gazed across the table at him, them murmured, 'Take heart, Damian, it's unlikely any of your crims will be members of the club, so you'll be fine.' He continued thoughtfully. 'We will need to draw them out at some time in the future though.' He paused, and looked at everyone sitting around the table. 'And while we're all here, might be a good idea.'

Bede turned quickly toward him, frowning now as well, but didn't speak.

Justin looked around at the breakfast remains littered across the table. He wasn't sure he wanted to drive for a couple of hours through what was virtually desert for a swim in a lake and a questionable lunch. He preferred the cool of the house and the chance of a quiet word to Meredith. He was feeling increasingly frustrated, and needed to get her somewhere on her own, so they could talk. There would probably be no chance at the bloody club. He turned, smiling brightly. 'That sounds wonderful. I just need to make one phone call, and then I'm ready.' Getting up, he moved around the table and left the room.

'He's not all that pleased,' Martin turned to Meredith. 'I know that overly bright smile of old. What's going on, do you know?'

'No, I'm puzzled. He's not easy to read. I thought the trip might push him in some direction.' She was thoughtful. It was obvious to her that Justin wanted something. There had to be a reason for him to make this trip, and this particular time seemed suspicious. She was starting to feel almost anxious. There was a feeling of tension in the air, almost like the build-up to the wet season farther north. This day, away from the property in a pleasant non-threatening environment, would be perfect. Getting up from the table, she turned to Bede. 'Will you let Pete know we'll need the Land Rover for the day, and make sure he monitors the phones.' And left the room.

They were gathered in the living room, ready to leave, when there was the sound of a vehicle drawing to a halt at the front steps. By the sound of the engine, Gabriel thought a large 4W drive. He listened to doors slamming and footsteps mounting the front steps. Then as one, they turned and looked in expectation toward the front door.

## Chapter Twenty-Five

# Inspector Campbell

M eredith wandered out to greet their unexpected visitors. Bede looked across at Hera. 'We're not expecting anyone, are we?'

Hera shrugged. 'Not to my knowledge, and that sounded like the police Land Rover.'

At that moment, Meredith came back into the room, followed by Inspector Campbell and Sergeant Morris. She was very pale and tense; Bede and Hera, looking puzzled, stood up. Meredith spoke quickly, as if to interrupt anything they had been about to say. 'There's been an accident out on the Wills Track early this morning, and the driver and passenger were both killed.' She looked across at Justin, then stated baldly, 'The passenger was George!'

She was very pale. 'I've told the inspector that George is a relative, and he thinks we might know the driver as well. His name was Edmondo De Amis.' She automatically gave the name an Italian pronunciation.

The assembled company turned and looked at the inspector with varying expressions of shock and confusion. He quietly surveyed them all, and there was no doubt from the shocked expressions on all their faces that they were stunned.

Meredith now slipped quietly into a chair, while Gabriel shot to his feet. 'Good gods, are you sure?'

Inspector Campbell looked at the young man facing him. He saw a tall, dark, obviously very fit man in his late twenties or early thirties. There was an aura of command about him that he noted as he spoke, 'And you would be, sir?'

Bede spoke quietly from where she was sitting. 'I'm so sorry, Inspector, this is Gabriel, a distant family connection.' She indicated Martin, 'His brother, Martin', and turning to Justin, 'and this is another family connection, Justin. You know Damian of course.' She indicated the policeman standing just inside the door. 'Inspector Campbell, everyone, and Sergeant Morris from the local police.' She drew a deep breath and turned back to Gabriel. 'Inspector Campbell is the detective who investigated Dad's death.'

'To answer your question, yes, we're sure. We've checked both passports and various documents they had on them.'

Gabriel, still on his feet, moved around to stand behind Bede's chair. 'Inspector, Bede and I have just returned from Europe. We thought we saw George at the airport in Perth, but he disappeared before we could speak to him, so we thought we must have been mistaken. He lives mostly in Paris.' After a short pause, continued, 'Or Prague?' He turned to look with enquiry at Justin.

Justin looked up. He was pale with a faint sheen of perspiration on his forehead and cleared his throat. He looked uncharacteristically confused for a moment. 'Yes, George was in Prague recently, and of course, I knew Edmondo. He's a long-time associate of George.' He looked for a moment, as if he would say more, then cleared his throat and looked away.

The large policeman frowned around at them all. 'Perhaps you can all tell me the last time you saw and or spoke to either of the two victims.'

Gabriel, still standing behind Bede with his hands resting gently on her shoulders, spoke again, 'Can we assume there is something suspicious about the deaths, Inspector, and that's why you're here?'

'The grapevine will spread the news fairly quickly, so yes, they were both shot with a pistol, point-blank range between the eyes. If this was Sydney, I'd say a gangland killing without a doubt, it was very professional, but this is Western Australia.' He looked around at them all and continued, 'Old Jerry Harding, taking his camel train across country, found them very early this morning. He saw the car as he crossed the track. It was parked at an odd angle, so thought he should have a look. He sent his young son overland to the Drummonds place to make the call to me. This is definitely not the usual scenario we're used to out here.' He spoke coldly and succinctly and waited for a reaction. There was a stunned silence, and when no one spoke, he turned to Justin. 'You said you knew both of these gentlemen. When was the last time you saw them, and where would that have been?'

Justin was not his usual calm, controlled self. His hands were shaking slightly, and despite the early hour, he moved across to the drinks table and poured himself a hefty glass of brandy. Then turning around, spoke quietly and sincerely, 'As Meredith said, George is a family connection, probably closer to me than anyone else here. But I haven't seen either George or Ed for quite some time, probably months. I can't remember exactly. They live in Paris for most of the year, but have been in Prague quite recently.' He paused briefly at that point, then continued, 'Prague being my home city. Ed is Italian from Genoa, I think. I've always thought of him as being slightly shady, but he was a long-time friend of George's. Was there any indication of what they were doing there?'

'No, nothing, they hired the car at Perth airport, but it had been booked from Paris, France. They apparently arrived on an Emirates flight three days ago, and picked up the 4WD immediately. We don't know where they've been, or what they've been doing since.' The inspector turned now to Bede and Gabriel. 'You said you thought you saw him at Perth Airport. Tell me exactly what you think you saw and where?'

Bede spoke slowly, 'Inspector, as Gabriel said, he and I arrived three days ago from London. We thought we saw George at the airport, but later couldn't find him and assumed wrongly, it seems, that we had been mistaken. At the time, we couldn't understand why he would be here. He hasn't been to Australia for years, and he certainly didn't contact any of us.'

The inspector glanced around at the assembled company then turning to his sergeant, 'We'll need to get statements from everyone here.' He turned back to Meredith. 'Can we use the library? We'll need to interview each of you separately. It's routine really, nothing to worry about.'

Meredith, still pale, but recovering quickly, 'Of course, I'll ask Robby to set up the desk for you. And would you like anything? Tea, coffee?' She now grinned at him. 'Water, whisky?'

'Tea would be great, thanks.'

The inspector and his sergeant followed Meredith from the room, leaving silence behind.

Justin, very pale, but with his face set, turned to Gabriel. 'Do you know anything about this at all?'

Gabriel, now sitting quietly beside Bede, drew in a deep breath and climbed slowly to his feet. 'No, as far as I know, George had no financial dealings with anyone in Australia.' He continued thoughtfully, 'But knowing George, he could be involved with someone as a silent partner. He's done that sort of thing in the past, and last time, it took some fairly deep digging for me to uncover what he was up to. Since then, he's made it a point to avoid me completely.' He raised his eyebrows and smiled slightly. 'I suspect you've probably seen him more recently than either Martin or I.'

Justin leaned forward with his arms on his knees. 'We all assume that his reasons for being here were financial, and the fact that he's been shot seems to confirm that. Before I left Prague, Lucien was talking about some financial deal he had going with George, or a potential of a financial deal with George. He was gloating, really, that he had something that would really tempt George to commit himself for a change. But as usual, he gave no real information.' He looked up and across at Martin first and then Gabriel. 'I didn't take much notice, as you are all well aware. Lucien and George have been rivals for years. It was obvious from that stupid abortive break-in at my place by Kamila that Lucien was up to something, but I didn't get to the bottom of it. Lucien just apologised, said it was information gathering because both you and Martin were in Prague. I didn't pursue it, as I thought his explanation was feasible.'

'Whatever, it's obvious Martin and I will have to investigate this. George might have been a devious shit, but he's our own personal shit.' He was thoughtful for a moment, glanced across at Martin. 'Any thoughts?'

'Yes, but in fact, it will be a little complicated. We have no authority here, so we'll have to cooperate with the police. In the meantime, I think we should give Lucien a ring.' He continued thoughtfully, 'Perhaps we shouldn't mention Lucien yet to the inspector, or the fact that we're here to investigate James's death on behalf of the family. Locals don't like private investigators at the best of times. They definitely won't like our particular brand.' He quietly left the room.

Bede, looking worried, glanced searchingly at Gabriel. 'This is starting to be worrying. I don't remember much about George, but I don't like the sound of this at all.'

Gabriel drew Bede into his arms briefly then turned around to Hera pacing again. 'Don't get too agitated, Hera, until we have more information. We just need to take it easy. I'm going to talk to Meredith and see where we are with the inspector.' He left the room, thinking, thinking, this was starting to have a very definite Family feeling about it. He and Martin had worked with Justin for years, and in fact, Justin had trained them both to some degree, so he knew how he worked. He had been genuinely shocked by George's death, but there had been that calculating gleam in his eyes. He was up to something, and it had something to do with either Meredith or the two girls or both, was something he would not countenance. It was something personal he had no doubt. But knowing the subtlety of Justin's mind, made him very uneasy. The way he felt about Bede, the protective feelings he had for her meant he would put her well-being before anything the Family dreamt up, and the realisation shocked him more than a little.

He was still struggling to come to terms with this shift in loyalty, but it was solidly there, and he acknowledged this with a grimace. It encompassed both Hera and Meredith, but mostly because anything affecting them would impact on Bede's well-being. He probably needed to discuss this with Martin, but from the looks he'd intercepted, Martin already suspected. He hoped this wouldn't cause any problems with his twin; they'd been inseparable since conception.

Gabriel quietly walked down the hall and out of the house. He took his phone from his pocket. There was information he needed now, and he really didn't want anyone in the house to hear this conversation.

## Chapter Twenty-Six

# Lucien is Stunned

Lucien was stunned, George dead, it didn't seem possible. George had been one of his sparing partners for years. He hadn't envisaged a violent end for George, not yet at least; in fact, it didn't fit. There was more to this than appeared, so forcing himself to relax, he sat back and allowed his mind to drift.

With a glass of 20-year-old brandy in his hand, sitting in his favourite chair in his beautiful and comfortable living room, he closed his eyes; and using his surroundings to anchor himself, sank into a meditation. It was pure indulgence to have an open fire these days, but he found the heat soothing. Smiling gently to himself, he thought of his daughter constantly trying to bring him into the twenty-first century, trying to instil an awareness of the planet's vulnerability. He was so proud of her, so beautiful, intelligent, and principled.

Staring into the fire, he listened to the crackle of the flames devouring the wood. He felt the warmth seeping gradually through his limbs, starting at his feet. He absently examined his feet, still allowing his mind to drift. His shoes were off, and he contemplated his socks, not matching, an affectation that had started years ago at university. That was where they'd all met; he, Justin, and George—the 'terrible trio'. They had been known by that appellation since. There had been several others in their little group, hangers on, really, but the three of them had remained friendly competitors.

Those heady days of insanity at Charles University were still clear in his mind. The scams the three of them had pulled, the constant juggling for supremacy between them. They were all competitive, all highly intelligent, and all with the morals of an alley cat. Their constant competition around women in particular had been intense. As soon as one of them had found a new woman, the other two would move in, trying to seduce and undermine. Consequently over the years, he had learned to be very circumspect. Neither of the other two had any knowledge of his wife and daughter. He chuckled to himself briefly. He had learned very early in his career to keep his private life very private indeed. He made certain that neither Justin nor George had ever suspected how domestic his life now actually was, and neither of them had ever discovered where he really lived. They had tried over the years, but never succeeded.

He had accepted that he couldn't trust either after the disaster with Justin's fiancée. He had never known the full story. No one would ever discuss it, certainly not Justin, or his brother who was somehow involved. Justin had never really recovered. He denied this, of course, and always intimated it was something to do with his brother. But the facts were he had never married, and although over the years there had been many beautiful women hanging off him, he couldn't or wouldn't make a commitment to any of them. That family was riddled with jealousies and power struggles and had been for generations. Because of the Second World War, and the demise of most of his own family, he had a degree of autonomy that they had no concept of.

He thoughtfully took another sip of brandy. He remembered Justin's fiancée. She had been a beauty, all long legs, startling blue eyes, and those cheekbones; she was the epitome of feminine beauty even within the Caruso-Kern family, and they were a startlingly good-looking lot.

George had fallen for her first, but in his arrogance, had frightened her. She had just arrived in Paris, a beautiful teenager, her parents were dead, and she and her brother were staying with relatives. But George, the alley cat, had tried something with her, and that brother of hers had beaten him almost senseless. George had never forgiven that one, but he'd backed off; then Justin, a few years later, predictably had moved in. What was her name? Meredith.

He never did learn the details of why that engagement had been broken. It was all so long ago, but George had been talking about it before he left, reminiscing like a lovesick schoolboy. Now George was dead, Justin was in Australia, and staying with the former fiancée and James's daughters. One had to wonder about the timing of all this. George was devious and dangerous, as was Justin.

Over the years, Justin had managed to obscure most of his illegal activities from his family. But he managed to implicate George in some of those activities. The most significant was the Turner affair. Justin had been the original instigator of that one, but had arranged for George to run with it—of course expecting to receive a percentage of the profit. Justin must have known that it would fall apart. It had been an insane undertaking from the start. George had panicked when it started to unravel and had managed to implicate James. Stupid really, even he realised all those years ago that one didn't mess with James. He was young, but there had never been anything weak or indecisive about him. All those qualities when young had coalesced into the James of today. He was a canny investor, quick, and determined with an almost supernatural ability to make money. He had no need to be involved in any underhand swindle even all those years ago.

George was clever and devious with a mind convoluted and mischievous. His schemes were always inventive and imaginative, but quite often badly executed. Justin was always there to rescue him and to subtly skim the top. But George had trusted Justin completely in their financial schemes, and George had been the perfect scapegoat for Justin. Lucien had often thought that Justin had secretly hated George. On the surface, Justin was the more successful, but George had the more creative mind. He was almost a genius in his analysis of people, and his ability to manipulate people and situations to his advantage.

So the question was why had George really gone to Australia? He had to have some scheme in hand. He hadn't mentioned Edmondo when chatting about his latest schemes. In fact, he had been unusually circumspect, not even mentioning where he was heading. Lucien suspected Justin had no idea George had even left Europe. Why was he dead, Edmondo as well? For Christ's sake what was it all about? It didn't make much sense at this particular time. He could almost suspect Justin of finally disposing of him, but that didn't fit either. If anything, Justin needed to keep George alive. For all his brilliance, George had never suspected Justin's machinations.

He continued to gaze into the fire, speculating and thinking. It must have something to do with the past. Justin, George, and those twin nephews of Justin's all in the one place, this definitely smacked of Family business.

Closing his eyes briefly, he couldn't shake the conviction that he was missing something. There was a memory just out of reach. Finally drinking the last of his brandy, he got to his feet and moved to the stairs. Tomorrow, he would put some feelers out. He knew he was missing something vital, but in the meantime, his beautiful and gentle wife was waiting for him, warm and snug in bed.

# Chapter Twenty-Seven

## The Club

Justin was still sitting quietly, frowning at his own thoughts. Bloody hell, this development put his plans for George into total disarray. How dare the little shit get himself killed, and at this particular time too?

Martin, standing quietly, watched first Gabriel leave, and then Justin. Gabriel came back into the room and paused in the doorway. Martin raised his eyebrows in query and Gabriel nodded, they were in accord as usual. Justin was up to something.

The inspector and his sergeant had just left.

Bede suddenly stood up. 'This is hopeless. I suggest we continue with our plans for lunch. We've all made our statements. We can't do anything here.'

Meredith, sitting quietly in an armchair, agreed. 'Yes, we should all go. Damian go, and tell Pete we're leaving in half an hour. There'll be time for a swim and a late lunch. We'll keep in touch with the inspector by phone.' She got to her feet and moved to the door.

Bede was driving the big 4WD with Gabriel beside her and the other five comfortably in the back. Hera was holding forth on what she was planning for lunch. It would be an hour's drive, but the three women didn't think twice about it, treated it like a trip to the supermarket.

Justin was uncharacteristically quiet, and Damian seemed to have fallen asleep.

Gabe, watching the landscape through the open window, was again mesmerised by the stark beauty, the space, and the rugged low-lying mountains on the horizon. The colours were not the colours of Europe. He catalogued them as they raced past grey, green, red, black, silver grey, ochre, deep purple, blue, deep green, but again, not the deep green of Europe, but a blue green very rich. He had an overwhelming desire to ask Bede to stop the car and walk toward those distant mountains. Across the flat plain, they were now transecting. The soil looked more like sand than soil, again a deep red, coarse, and gritty. A lot of iron ore in that soil, he thought to himself.

Leaning across to Bede, he murmured his desire to walk toward the mountains. She laughed gently. 'Be very careful, Gabe, it's the magic of the desert calling. Once you succumb, you'll never be free. It's calling to you.' Just at that moment, a mob of red kangaroos streaked past, hopping in their strangely graceful, rhythmic movement that ate the distance, and a herd of feral camels fifty metres back from the road. He was enchanted.

'What do you mean once you succumb?'

Bede glanced across at him. 'Well', she said with a decided twinkle, 'it has been known for travellers to get out of their cars, leave them on the side of the road, and walk toward the mountains and just keep on walking.' He snorted in disbelief. She turned to him. 'Seriously, trackers have had to be called in to find them, it's happened more than once. The trackers call it magic. I call it people being unhappy with their lives, and needing an excuse to opt out of life for a while. It's very effective, but you had better not try it, or I'll personally track you down and beat you.'

He looked across at her grinning, and to his astonishment, saw not a hint of humour in her face. She was deadly serious. He sat back in the seat, and gazed at her for several moments before speaking again. 'You really are serious?'

'It's partly something to do with the isolation, I think, but there's something else, another element, something almost mystical. Not to be ignored.' She looked thoughtfully out of the widow. 'The last guy, and it always seems to be guys, was an engineer stationed in Kalgoorlie. His wife had just left him, and he was driving back to Adelaide when he suddenly stopped the car and just walked into the desert. He was found after two days, and recovered nicely apparently, but it happens.'

Hera spoke up suddenly from the back seat, 'Hey, you two, you're being morbid. This is an excursion geared toward relaxation. Gabe, put some music on.'

Justin spoke, 'Not some loud raucous modern stuff please, Gabriel, something classical. Beethoven would be nice.'

Martin snorted, Meredith sighed, and Hera giggled.

Gabriel, ruffling through the CD's, said, 'What about some of his piano concertos? There's a disc here, you would probably approve of Jean-Bernard Pommier playing.'

'Perfect,' Justin relaxed.

Bede said quietly, 'I don't know where that came from, but it will keep Justin and Meredith happy.' She called into the back seat, 'Sorry Hera, Martin, and Damian, I think you'll just have to put up with it.' She chuckled, and Gabriel reached across and cupped his hand around the back of her neck, gently massaging. Bede sat back and concentrated on driving.

The rest of the trip passed in companionable silence.

The lunch was delicious, and the swim before, refreshing and relaxing. Hera had arranged for them all to go out on a friend's sloop after lunch, but Justin declined, and then Meredith became involved in a game of bridge with several friends, so it was just the five of them joining the merry crew—all school friends of Bede and Hera on the halcyon for the afternoon. They enjoyed themselves enormously with Damian becoming the butt of much gentle ribbing, as he had never sailed before. Bede wondered in passing if there was anything Gabriel and Martin didn't excel at. But there wasn't the slightest arrogance in either of them, at least not that she'd seen yet.

It was a perfect day, the sky was clear, and the wind gentle, just enough to ensure a very pleasant afternoon. By the time they docked and wandered up to the clubhouse, they were all feeling mellow despite the dreadful shock earlier in the day. Justin signalled to them imperiously, as they entered the bar. He had obviously been waiting for them, and by the scowl on his face, he was irritated and waiting to take that irritation out on someone.

Gabriel turned back to Martin and murmured, 'He's not pleased about something, and we really need to find out what he's actually doing here. Stay alert.'

Martin slapped him on the back and laughed aloud, as if they were still joking about something on the boat, then turning, waved to Justin and called, 'We'll just order some drinks for our hosts and then join you.'

Gabriel herded them all to the bar where Bede introduced him to the barman, David, another old school friend. Orders were called with gay abandon, and then they turned on mass to join Justin. He'd managed to smooth the scowl from his face as he stood to greet them all. Without any preamble, he stated, 'Meredith is still playing bridge if you can believe it. She's been at it for hours, and doesn't seem inclined to finish in the near future. I thought we might make arrangements to have dinner here before we drive back.'

'That's fine with us.' Gabriel turned and then caught sight of Damian's face. He had lost colour and was rigid in his seat. Gabriel and Martin both turned to see what he was looking at when to their astonishment, Damian surged to his feet, charged across the room, and threw himself at the waiter who had just entered. He hit the man under the nose with the heel of his hand, and followed it up with a knee to the groin. The waiter went down without a sound, simply collapsed, and lay writhing on the floor, groaning, surrounded by broken glasses from the tray he dropped.

There was stunned surprise on the faces of all who had witnessed the incident. Damian was almost dancing in his excitement and rage. He yelled, 'You fucking bastard, what are you doing here? Did you follow me?'

Drawing back, his foot was about to kick the writhing man when Gabriel strolled up and caught his arm, and drawing him away, spoke calmly. 'Ah, Damian, he isn't going anywhere, I assume this is one the crooks chasing you in Perth?'

Bede looked on in astonishment. Damian's face was almost purple with rage, and he was shaking. She looked toward Gabe and realised he was completely relaxed, not shocked in any way; in fact, he looked almost amused by the incident. Glancing at Martin, she saw the same expression on his face. There were times she realised when she really didn't know either of them. Hera, obviously stunned, had bounded to her feet and was now holding Damian's arm trying to drag him away, while he was still snarling and muttering.

Damian turned back to Gabe. 'Yes, this is the prick who broke my arm, beat me up, and drove me crazy. He's the one that drove me into hiding. I think he's got something to do with drugs.' He got in another swift kick before Hera finally dragged him away.

Justin, looking around the room, spoke, 'Well, Gabriel, I suggest you remove him somewhere more private before someone else comes in.' He looked across at their friends, and David, the barman, all calmly watching the proceedings.

David murmured, 'He's an arrogant sod.' And turning to Gabriel, 'He has a friend who usually comes in around now for a drink. Tall, thin English chap, you might want to take him out of here fairly quickly.'

Gabriel now grinned. 'Thanks, friend, appreciate your help.' He hauled the waiter to his feet, and he and Martin hustled him out of the lounge.

Hera was still trying to calm Damian down when their friend behind the bar slid a glass of brandy down the counter. 'Damian, calm down and drink this, your friends seem to have him in control. Is the Pom involved with this as well? Because he'll be here soon, you might want to make some plans.'

They were now all sitting around the table, and David brought the drinks over. Bede asked, 'How long has he been working here, David? You obviously don't like him much. What do you know about him?'

'He's just started working here in the last week or so, but he's been around before. No, I don't like him, he tried to chat up one of the girls, and turned nasty when she turned him down.'

'You've been working here for months now. Were these two here when James died?'

'No, I don't think so, but I can't really remember. They've both been asking questions about you lot, and particularly Damian. I don't think anyone has said anything to them, but the Pom has been throwing money around, trying to find out what's happening at your place.' He paused for a moment then continued, 'It's not as if they could just turn up out there.' He grinned, and turning to Damian, 'That was great, you know, I've wanted to sock him for days now.'

Just then, Martin came back into the lounge and signalled Damian to join him and Gabe.

Justin turned to Bede and murmured, 'Perhaps you should round Meredith up. I suspect we will be heading home instead of staying for dinner. Just give her a gentle hint perhaps. It's been an interesting day.'

Bede left the lounge, and instead of trying to find Meredith and her friends, went looking for Gabriel instead. She found him in the billiard room talking on his phone to the police, by the sound of it. She waited calmly, leaning against the side of the billiard table until he'd finished.

'Well, what's happening now? Who is he, and what have you done with him?'

Gabriel smiled, and sliding his arm around her waist, drew her slowly to him. 'Damian and Martin have him and his friend trussed in the back of the car. I've just informed Inspector Campbell about what's happened, and he's asked us to bring them into the police station now. It seems they have been causing a bit of trouble with the locals, and they've had a few complaints about them. Damian isn't sure who they are, just that they've been hassling him in Perth. The inspector can sort it out.' He kissed her softly on the lips. 'But I need to talk to them for a bit before we drive them to the station, so do you think you can keep everyone happy here for half an hour?' He raised his left eyebrow in query.

She frowned at him. 'I think you've practised that in front of the mirror for years.' She smiled into his eyes, and then continued thoughtfully, 'Justin wants to go home now, but we can stall him for a bit. I know Meredith wanted to stay for dinner.'

He waggled both eyebrows at her. 'I can do one at a time.' He kissed her swiftly. 'Are you all right with all this?'

'Yes, just go, I'll find Meredith.'

Driving back later, Bede thought back over the evening. Gabriel, Martin, and Damian had taken the two troublemakers to the local police station, and Damian had laid charges of harassment and assault against them both. Gabe had warned it probably wouldn't stick since Damian had attacked one of them unprovoked, but then, Damian could prove the assault in Perth as he's landed in Charles Gardiner Hospital with his broken arm and cuts and bruises. He had reported the attack to the police at the time.

It was an uneventful drive back, and they weren't prepared for the uproar that greeted them as they pulled up. It took the combined voices of both Gabriel and Martin to achieve quiet from everyone milling around, all talking at once. Gabe pointed a finger at Jonathan, one of the young workers on the estate, to tell them what had happened. He also demanded to know where Pete was.

# Chapter Twenty-Eight

## Thieves Again

Meredith came quickly down the steps. At that moment, calling out, 'Pete is on the floor of the library, unconscious. Come quickly.'

The library had been ransacked, books scattered all over the floor, with Pete lying on his back. Meredith was crouched down beside him, gently helping him to his feet. Most of the staff had followed them into the house; and Jonathon, a pleasant youth, reported, 'There were two of them. They came in a black Toyota 4WD with Perth number plates.' He stopped for a moment, and then continued sadly, 'Unfortunately, I didn't get the number plate. It was covered in dirt.'

Pete, climbing slowly to his feet, revealed, 'Christ, sorry about this, but I was too slow. There were two of them, and they knew what they were after. They took the two antique books. They've only been gone a few minutes, so if you take the copter, you should be able to track them. They're driving a big, black 4WD with Perth number plates.' He paused, grimaced, then continued, 'But I didn't get the number.'

There was still blood trickling down his forehead, and Gabriel thought he seemed to be trying to convey something else, but at that point, he collapsed back onto the floor, his legs simply crumbling under him. They were all furious, Bede and Hera were confused and concerned about Pete, and Justin was simply stunned as he gazed around at the shambles.

Hera immediately went across to Pete's side. She helped him to his feet again, and asked Jonathon to help her assist him onto the sofa. Meredith came in at that moment with a bowl of warm water and some soft clean cloth to bath his head. 'We need to look at this without the blood,' she said. 'You may need stitches.'

Pete cursed softly under his breath and watches as Gabe, Martin, and Bede raced from the room. Still cursing softly, he suddenly yelled, 'Be careful, you three.'

Gabe waved to acknowledge the warning, as they pelted across to the hanger with Bede in front. 'It's all fuelled up,' she shouted. 'Pete was going to spray early tomorrow morning.' The three of them wheeled the machine onto the pad and quickly climbed aboard.

It took only a few moments for Bede to have the engine revving and then they were airborne. They started circling. It was coming on dark, but would be a good hour before they lost all the light. There was still the spotlight they used for shooting brumbies when and if they needed it, Bede thought. It didn't take long to spot the vehicle. It was racing down the Wills Track at about 100 kilometres an hour. The road was a secondary road, but in good repair.

Bede spoke into the intercom, 'They're heading west. The track meets up with the Great Northern Highway just north of Newman, but it's about 250 kilometres, and there's nothing between here and there, so I don't know how they think they're going to get away.' Just at that moment, there was the sound of a shot pinging off the fuselage. Bede pushed the control forward, and they immediately started to climb out of range of what had obviously been a handgun.

Gabe swore in a language Bede didn't understand, and Martin put his hand gently onto her shoulder. 'Stay out of range, and we'll just follow for the moment.'

In the meantime, Gabriel reached across and picked up the radio controls, noting with approval the latest in French communication technology. 'We need to speak to Inspector Campbell, and get him to set something up.' He looked at Bede with raised eyebrows. 'Road blocks?'

She grinned at him. 'It's easier out here. There is nothing and almost no one for miles. We can notify the couple of homesteads between here and Newman, and notify Newman itself.' She shrugged, 'They won't get far, they're idiots if they think they can.'

Gabe continued to talk over the radio, while Bede and Martin watched the speeding car. 'Who do you think they are, Martin?'

'Well, I'd say someone from Europe not used to the distances out here, and I think opportunists. They couldn't have known we'd be at the club until late.' He paused thoughtfully. 'Unless they have some connection with those two idiots at the club.' He paused again and exchanged a glance with Gabe, still speaking to Inspector Campbell.

Gabe nodded, then with a wicked grin, 'The inspector asked if you're carrying a rifle. He seems to think you probably do for culling brumbies, and suggested we try for the tyres. What do you think?'

'Well, I have to fly this thing, and I'm not a good enough shot. We don't want to kill them.'

Gabe grinned again. 'But I am. If you can keep it steady, I'm sure I'll manage.'

Bede indicated a compartment at the back of the passenger seats. 'It's in there, not loaded, but you'll find the ammunition in a separate locked compartment behind the seat.' She handed a key back to him.

Gabe set about loading the rifle. It was a L1A1 SLF. 'Nice rifle', he said with a grin, 'and in good condition.' Bede snorted in derision, but took the helicopter lower and parallel to the speeding car. Martin moved out of the way, sliding the cabin door open; and Gabriel positioned himself in the opening, wedging his left shoulder securely, and with one foot, keeping him balanced on the landing skids. He raised the rifle to his right shoulder. 'Okay, Bede, keep her steady.' He took careful aim.

His first shot hit the road just in front of the car, and they skidded to the left. He aimed quickly again, this time hitting the front tyre, causing the vehicle to swing crazily across the road. The driver was fighting the skid, trying desperately to keep the car from rolling over. Bede brought the copter lower and prepared to land in front of, and as close to the damaged car as possible. She held her breath, hoping that the driver and the passenger they could see were not hurt. They needed information, and potentially, this pair knew quite a lot.

'Keep back, Bede, they're likely to start shooting. We've got the greater range, but they might be a bit impulsive.' He prepared to leap down as soon they touched, and had the rifle to his shoulder. He fired one more round into the back tyre this time, as the Toyota finally swung to a stop.

The passenger and driver both erupted from the car, swearing and cursing in Czech. Martin, grinning, climbed down to join Gabe. 'Well, well, well, I recognise these two. Things might finally start to make some sense.'

Gabriel was scowling, but keeping a tight control on his rage; and with the rifle held loosely beside his leg, crossed to confront Kamila and Jakub, both still cursing. Bede switched the engine off, and as the rotor of the Robinson slowed, she too climbed down, watching the drama unfolding.

Kamila stormed toward Gabriel, while Jakub tried to calm her down. 'You pig, Gabriel, you could have killed us. Are you still jealous of Jakub?' She rushed at him with arms flailing. Jakub finally caught her, as Martin stepped between her and Gabriel.

'You bitch', he snarled, 'why do you think Gabriel would be jealous, and where exactly do you think you were going? You stupid cow, do you really think you could get away with such a stupid robbery here? In the middle of the Australian bush?' He drew a deep calming breath.

'Calm down everyone,' Gabriel sauntered up, still casually holding the rifle at his side. 'Now perhaps Jakub', he looked toward the tall, dark man still holding the still struggling Kamila, 'would like to explain what's going on? Which of you two fired on us, and I agree with Martin's question, where did you think you were going?'

They were all caught in the spotlight from the helicopter, as Bede switched it on.

She thought they were speaking Czech. She didn't understand anything said, but obviously, they all knew each other well. The beautiful, slim woman trying to attack Gabe confused her, and her tall companion trying to restrain her, was not having a great deal of luck. Martin seemed furious, but Gabe, as usual, was his cool unruffled self. But he was pale, and he still had his finger on the trigger of the rifle. 'Could you *please* all speak English?' she said mildly, as she strolled to Gabriel's side.

Gabriel turned to her, and transferring the rifle to his left hand, put his arm around her shoulders and drew her into his side. 'Bede, meet Kamila and Jakub, I told you about them. They're dubious associates of Justin and Lucien, which raises interested question. Did you notify the inspector that we'd caught them?'

'Yes, and Pete is fine by the way.' She glanced at the two irate seething Czechs. 'Which one of you smashed him over the head?'

'My guess is Kamila,' Martin hissed.

'Right', she snarled, 'he deserved it. He knocked me out the last time I saw him, the bastard.' Kamila was sulking now.

Bede was startled and had to close her mouth quickly. What the hell was going on? She moved away from Gabe, turned frowning to look first at him, then Martin, and lastly, the two book thieves. She was suddenly very cold and frightened. 'I don't know what the hell is going on here, but it's obviously not what I thought,' she said as she grabbed the rifle from Gabriel's loose grasp before he had time to react; and moving several steps back from him, brought the rifle up quickly to cover all four. 'Don't move, any of you, and don't think I won't use this.'

Gabriel, frowning but still relaxed, took one step toward her. 'Bede, take it easy, don't overreact. I, we, can explain.'

'Stop, don't move. What exactly do you plan to explain?' She was furious and shaking with rage. 'This has all been some sort of swindle, hasn't it? And you're all involved.' She moved another step carefully back toward the helicopter. 'Which one of you actually killed my father, or was it Pete, the ever loyal employee, that Kamila knows very well of old. You all obviously know each other well.'

There was an awful stillness now. All four were facing her quiet and watchful even the sulky Kamila had straightened.

'Keep your hands where I can see them, all of you.' The light from the spotlight keeping them all in sharp relief. 'I may not be the sharpshooter as you are, Gabriel, but I'm quite capable of firing off two or three shots before any of you can grab me. And believe me, from this distance, I can't miss, and I'm not sure which of you four I'll shoot first.'

She continued to move backwards, slowly and carefully, sliding her feet across the loose stones on the road. It wouldn't be a good move to stumble at this point. She moved the barrel of the rifle carefully from one to the other. She couldn't believe she had been such a fool, but couldn't allow herself to think about any of this yet. She had to get to the helicopter, take off, and call Inspector Robinson. She also needed to disable the Toyota more completely. It was a hire car, so probably had more than one spare tyre in the back. Without the car, they wouldn't be able to escape. She could fly on to Newman, and get the police from there to come out and pick them up.

'Bede, this is not what you think.' Gabriel held out his hand. 'Please, Bede, let me explain.' He took a step toward her.

'Stand still, I said don't move.' She was moving more quickly now, only a couple of steps and she'd be able to get the cabin door open, then she needed to somehow take off before they reached her.

'Bede, listen to me, please. This really is not what you think.'

'Yeah sure, your former girlfriend is in Australia and steals the two extremely valuable books, while we're away from the homestead. How did she know we would be away? And Pete, loyal Pete, she knows Pete from before, before when and where? Before Pete killed James, or was it one of you two? Or perhaps it was the very versatile Kamila or her husband.' She was sobbing now, raised the rifle quickly, and blew out the other back tyre of the hire car, then swung it back to still keep them covered. All four were still, Martin quietly watching Gabriel. 'I suggest you stay put. There are no waterholes around here. The police will pick you up.'

'Bede', Gabriel was seething he'd lost all the colour in his face, and his hands were clenched so hard the knuckles gleaned white in the light from the helicopter, 'for Christ's sake, stop this now. Martin and I had nothing to do with James's death or the stupid theft of those bloody books.' He swung around to Kamila and Jakub. 'Tell her, or we'll be stuck here all night.'

Kamila shrugged her shoulders, and her face took on a mulish and sulky look, but she did speak, 'It's true, Gabe and Martin had nothing to do with this. They had no idea we were here.'

Bede was at the cabin door now. 'You'd say whatever he told you to. I don't believe you.'

Martin, quiet until now, finally spoke, 'Bede, Gabe is telling you the truth. We, neither of us, knew these two were in the country. We suspected Justin was up to something, but had no idea these two were here.' He swung back to Gabriel. 'I told you before, you should have levelled with her from the start.' Turning around to Bede, 'Just take a moment to think, Bede, you know Gabe is besotted with you. He wouldn't have allowed these two anywhere near you if he'd known what they were up to.'

'How can I believe you? You've been lying to me from the start.' She was looking at Gabe now, but still keeping the rifle levelled at them all.

'No, Bede, I haven't lied to you at any point. I admit I haven't been completely honest with you, but I've never lied to you.' He was quiet for a few moments then continued gently, 'It's finding out about Pete that's rattled you, Bede, but think. He's been on the property all this time on James's invitation. He's been protecting you all. James tended to be a little paranoid, and as it turns out, he was right to be worried, but Pete is completely loyal to all of you.' He moved one step toward her. 'Bede, I would never let anyone or anything hurt you, deep down you know that. When we arrived, Martin and I were suspicious of Pete's role here, so we did some checking. He was just as suspicious of us initially. Yes, Pete has a connection to the family as you've guessed, but you've jumped to the wrong conclusions. James obviously had been concerned about something for a long time, but he didn't let on to anyone what it was. He just went ahead and arranged for Pete to be here, and keep an eye on you all particularly when he was away. The reason there are no details in his file is because Pete has in the past had a similar role in the family as Martin and me.'

Bede was at the helicopter now, and paused.

Gabriel held his hand out toward her palm up. 'It's Pete's story, Bede, but I can tell you a little. He had a difficult and messy relationship break up and left Europe. That was a long time ago, and he'd been wandering around the Middle East when James bumped into him. He asked him to come here and live on the property, keep an eye out for any potential problems, but he didn't tell him exactly what he was concerned about. James was always paranoid and far too secretive.

'Bede, you're the only one who can fly this thing, so you're completely safe. We need to go back to the homestead and try to work this out. You can't really mean to leave us stuck out here all night. Please?' He seemed more relaxed, his colour had returned, and the corners of his lips twitching slightly. 'Please? The whole day has been one shock after another, starting with George's death, and then the nonsense at the club. You do know me, Bede.'

Kamila yelped, 'George is dead?' She swung around and punched Jakub in the shoulder. 'I knew we shouldn't get involved in any of this. Now, we won't get the rest of our money.'

Jakub spoke for the first time in heavily accented English. 'Shut up,' he said and turned to Bede. 'We had nothing to do with any killing.' And more gently continued, 'You don't know either Kamila or me, but believe me, we have killed no one. It's not my scene.' He was thoughtful for a moment. 'I'll admit to stealing the odd item or two, and spying, maybe some rough stuff, but definitely no killing.' Taking a deep breath, he continued thoughtfully. 'Well, not unless Kamila's life was in danger.' He paused again. 'Or mine, of course.'

Both Gabriel and Martin looked amused by this speech, and Gabriel said, 'Jakub, I suggest you just stop talking. It's not your thing.' He turned back to Bede. 'What he means is that he's a thug, Bede, but not a killer. Kamila is tricky, unscrupulous, and with very few morals, but she's not a killer either.' He met her eyes, and there was a depth of pain there she hadn't seen before. He leaned toward her, but other than that, didn't move. 'Bede, I'm sure you've worked out over the last few weeks what we do within the Family. Martin and I are both capable of killing without remorse if the situation requires it.' He kept eye contact with her. 'But neither of us had anything to do with James's death. We really are here to sort it out.' He gestured to Jakub and Kamila. 'These two idiots have just muddied the waters a little.'

Suddenly, into the silence, Gabriel's phone rang. He cocked an eyebrow, 'Can I answer that?'

Bede felt exhaustion pulling at her shoulders, and felt the nausea in her stomach rise. She wanted to believe him, she knew she had been falling in love with him over the last few weeks, but there really had been too many questions and no answers. They needed answers to the questions. Pete had seemed completely loyal and supportive, particularly over the last few weeks. Yes, James had always been secretive, even Penelope right up to her death had complained about James's paranoia. The phone was still ringing. 'Okay, answer it, but put it on speaker.'

Gabe let out the breath he hadn't realised he was holding. He pulled the phone from his pocket and switched to speaker. Pete's voice came out loud and clear. 'Gabe, where are you? Have you caught those two idiots yet, is Bede all right? Meredith and Hera are just about beside themselves. They're so anxious about all this.'

Gabe spoke clearly, 'Yes, we've caught them, but there's been a development. Pete, I need you to come totally clean about your role on the property since you've been here. Bede is freaked as Kamila confessed to knowing you.'

'I knew this would happen. Bloody James and his need for secrecy, put Bede on.'

'We're on speaker, Pete, just talk.'

As Pete talked, Bede relaxed slightly. The tension in her shoulders slowly releasing, and the tight band around her forehead unwinding slightly, so that she felt she could think properly. His gravelly voice rolled on, and many of the unexplained and puzzling incidents over the last few years became clear. Pete had arrived on the property just twelve months before her mother's death. It had been a shock, an aneurism, not something any of them could have foreseen. Pete had supported James through his grief over Penny's death and kept Meredith, Hera, and her stable in the months following. He had taken over the running of the farm, and even travelled overseas on one occasion when James had been unable to complete the contract. He had always been more than an employee. James had trusted him completely, but not enough to tell him what it was that he feared. Today really had been a day of startling developments. Drawing a deep breath, and trying relaxing her shoulders, she spoke to Gabe. 'I want to talk to Hera. Ask Pete to put her on.'

'Did you hear that, Pete?'

'Yep, we're all here including Justin. Damian is with Inspector Campbell and his young constable in the library. They arrived soon after you lot.'

Bede felt the tension drain out of her body, and she signalled for the phone.

Gabriel took the five steps across to her and handed her the phone. His eyes held such sadness and compassion. She could feel the sting of unshed tears, but simply shook her head and took the phone. Her finger still on the trigger of the rifle now held more loosely in her right hand.

The phone, still on speaker, Hera's voice came strong and steady. 'Bede, everything here is fine. Inspector Campbell arrived about half an hour ago, he'd been on his way here anyway. Pete has a lump on his head, but he's okay now. It's all been a bit of a shock.' There was a pause, then her voice continued, 'I can imagine what you're thinking, Bede, honey, but you need to get back here so we can start to sort it all out.'

Bede switched the phone off and handed it to Gabriel. 'Okay, everyone into the copter.'

Hera had used their childhood signal for 'it's okay to come home, Dad has calmed down'. Bede had a sudden memory of the time Hera had stayed hidden in the bush for two days when she'd really strained his patience. She had taken the short wave radio apart, convinced she could fix the crackle that annoyed her so much, only to discover she'd damaged one of the valves, and they had no replacement. She never had managed to fix the crackling.

'I take it "honey" is a code word between you two,' Gabe spoke softly into her ear, making sure no one else heard him as he climbed in.

'You really don't miss much, do you?' she said frowning slightly.

He didn't answer, but gazed deeply into her eyes, then nodded slowly, his expression sombre.

Before getting into the helicopter, Bede removed the remaining clip from the rifle and put it into her pocket. She was the only one of this lot able to pilot this thing. She felt quite certain no one wanted to cause an accident here in the middle of nowhere, but was taking no chances.

---

They were gathered in the living room. Bede sitting quietly in her favourite chair, watching and listening, she could almost see the emotions roiling through the ethers. Would they ever get to the bottom of James's death? It seemed to be submerged beneath a miasma of peripheral events. But someone had ordered his assassination, she was as sure of that, as she was of sitting in this chair. Did it have something to do with Damian's research? Was he trying to produce a new designer drug, and had James been somehow involved? She really didn't believe that for a moment, but at this point, she was prepared to look at any and all options.

She looked across the room and frowned. What exactly was Justin doing here? He had still not said. She was suspicious about his motives and didn't trust him, but so far, she hadn't shared that with anyone, not even Hera. She looked thoughtfully across at Meredith and wondered. And then these other two inept thieves; it seemed obvious they were connected to George, who was now dead, murdered too. This seemed to suggest another player or players somewhere. She was so confused. The events over the last few weeks had shaken her. She had always felt herself to be a good judge of character, but in the last twenty-four hours, things had been moving so fast, she felt she couldn't quite trust her reactions to either the events or the people involved. She felt there was some undelaying affair, some sinister motive, or events that would explain everything!

Looking around the room again, she managed to catch Gabriel's eye. Did she really trust him and Martin? Hera certainly had reservations about Martin. And added to that, Gabe's confession that both he and Martin were capable of cold-blooded murder had shaken her. But being honest with herself, she had known deep down that he was dangerous, but not to her or Meredith or Hera, she was quite sure about that.

At that moment, Gabriel caught her eye. He smiled slightly, not that she would call it a smile exactly, that slight curve of one side of his mouth and the lift of one eyebrow, but it was so familiar now that she felt the warmth of the familiar expression wash over and around her. She felt herself relaxing, and with a slight tilt of his head, he indicated the door. She nodded and climbed slowly to her feet.

## Chapter Twenty-Nine

# Inspector Campbell Is Concerned

Inspector Campbell looked around the room. He took note of Bede and Gabriel moving out of the room, but ignored them at this time. He had done some very intense checking through official channels including Interpol on that young man and his brother. And although the small amount of detail he'd managed to uncover had startled him, he was confident they both had the three ladies interests at heart.

He cleared his throat loudly and looked around, as all eyes focused on him. 'Well, I think it's time that a few facts were made clear to all of you present.' He paused. 'Firstly, these two thieves.' Kamila bristled and opened her mouth to say something, but Jakub elbowed her in the ribs; and with a sulky scowl and a shrug, remained silent. Inspector Campbell continued mildly, 'These two thieves are well known to several of you.' He turned first to Justin who nodded his head in agreement, then Martin, and finally Gabriel, just leaving the room. They all acknowledged the statement, and he continued, 'We know they arrived in Perth in company with Mr George Caruso-Kern and his friend about three days ago, and have been staying in the same hotel in Perth.'

He turned to the two Czechs and raised his eyebrows.

Kamila almost squirmed in her seat, but lifting her chin, looked directly at him. 'Yes, you're right of course. We arrived with George and Edmondo on the same flight. George wanted those two books.' She indicated them, now lying on a small round antique piecrust table across the room. 'I have no idea what or how he knew about them.' She continued thoughtfully after turning to Jakub, 'He knew where they were kept and the spring to release the secret compartment. He warned us they were fragile, and to be very careful with them, which is why he gave us that special backpack.' She indicated the leather satchel/backpack on the floor. It was open, and they could all see the padded interior divided into two sections.

Jakub now took up the tale in his strangely accented English. 'I didn't realise they would be as large as they are until George arrived with the satchel. He explained exactly what they were, but couldn't tell us much more.' He drew a long breath. 'I searched online to find more information, but didn't get much except an estimate of their value, which is quite substantial.' He looked around the room, particularly at Justin. 'But in my opinion, there has to be more to it than the money. It's quite a bit, but not enough. I wouldn't have thought to justify bringing us all this way, let alone a murder or two. George paid us really well, but not enough to go to jail for him.' He slumped back onto the couch beside his wife, and picking up her hand, kissed it absently.

Kamila patted his hand in a familiar and somehow touching gesture. She spoke now, 'I think somehow Lucien is involved with those books. He laughed when he talked about Lucien, and we both got the impression that George was up to something devious again. You could never trust him, that's why we insisted on half our money before we left Prague.' She gestured at Justin and almost snarled. 'He probably knows more than either of us. Lucien told us before we left that he had something planned with Justin.' She looked defiantly across at him.

Justin, now looking startled, spoke, 'Well, not planned exactly, at least nothing concrete. Lucien did intimate that he had a plan involving George and suggested that it would finally compensate him for the many times George had lied to him, and tried to double-cross him. He also said I would be delighted when I heard about it, and he would call on me at some point. He didn't give me any details, so to say that his plan involved me is technically incorrect.' He was looking a little hunted now, but continued, 'He laughed when he talked about it, and said he didn't want to disclose any details just yet. I thought from the little he did say that it would be embarrassing more than dangerous, something George wouldn't be able to talk his way out of, and would finally expose him as the scheming bastard he really is. I didn't get the impression that Lucien was planning anything violent. It's not the way he works. He's devious, but tries to stay inside the radar of the law. Killing someone even in Prague is problematic.' He looked across at Martin who was standing quietly, leaning against the wall.

Martin studied him thoughtfully. 'Lucien may have thought no one would ever suspect he was working with George.' He turned to Inspector Campbell and continued quietly, 'You may have realised by now that George has pissed off so many people over the years. It's not surprising he's finally been killed, and to be honest, I don't think too many people will miss him. It's possible one of his old adversaries may have spotted him and Edmondo in Perth and decided to get even.' He shrugged. 'Edmondo was as bad as George at pissing people off. It's even possible he was the initial target.'

There was silence in the room as the inspector surveyed them all. Christ, what a family, he thought; and he probably wouldn't get much more out of this lot tonight, he may as well deal with the Czechs.

Straightening his back and rising from the chair, he turned to his young constable. 'Let's get these two back to the station and question them more fully there.' He could have sworn there was a combined sigh of relief at this announcement, but he felt sure that those two young fellows would start to put the screws on their uncle now.

Gabriel and Bede wandered back into the living room. No one had moved since the police had left with their two grumpy prisoners in tow. Bede moved across to sit beside Meredith, and took her hand gently. 'Meredith, this has been very trying for us all and particularly for you. I know you didn't care for George, but he was a relation, and you had known him for a long time. Do you want to talk about it now?'

'Not particularly,' she said with asperity. 'There was a time when both James and I considered ways of disposing of George. I told you about that, but over the years, we, or at least I, put him consciously out of my thoughts. I forgot about him. It now seems that perhaps James had something to do with him, but I find that very hard to believe.' She looked down contemplating the glass in her hand, almost as if she didn't really see it. 'How did he know about the books, and who told him how to open the secret compartment? I didn't even know about it until you girls told me, and that was only recently.'

Bede worriedly took the glass from her and placed it on the coffee table. Meredith was suddenly looking pale and fragile, something she had never been.

Hera crossed the room and sat down on the other side of Meredith, putting her arm around her shoulders. 'Come on, I think this night has gone on long enough. It's time for bed, we can continue this discussion tomorrow after a really good breakfast.' She looked hard at Justin for a moment. Both Bede and Hera drew Meredith to her feet, and quietly left the room.

# Chapter Thirty

## Justin Confesses

It was very late now, the sound of the police Land Rover pulling away from the house created a disturbance for a moment, and then all was silent again. The room was lit softly. They hadn't turned on all the lights. After the noise of the helicopter, the arrival of the police, and the anger and rage of everyone concerned in the attempted theft, keeping the lights low had seemed a way to reduce the furious outbursts and accusations flying around.

Justin suddenly lurched to his feet. He hadn't liked that look from Hera. 'What exactly is going on here Gabe? Have you any idea?'

'Not so much', he quietly replied, 'but I think it's time you come clean, Justin. Just why are you really here, what do you want, and what do you know about James's death?'

'The reason I'm here is none of your business, and I know nothing about James's death, or George's either.'

Martin, slowly straightened away from the wall, and moved casually to stand beside Gabe. 'Justin, neither Gabe nor I believe you for one moment, and we need to know what you're doing here. We suspect it's something to do with Meredith. Do you have some plans of resurrecting your earlier relationship with her, moving in on her now that James is dead?'

Justin spun around snarling, 'Don't you dare try to pressure me. I knew more about extracting information from people before you were born, so don't think you can manage me. This whole situation has got completely out of hand.'

Martin, still relaxed, regarded him thoughtfully. 'I've never seen you lose your cool before, Justin, and believe me, we', he nodded towards Gabe, 'are very aware of what you're capable of.'

Gabe slowly straightened beside Martin. There was something cold and unyielding in his eyes, and finally, Justin realised these boys he had known since their birth had moved well beyond his influence. He wondered when he had stopped seeing them as they were, instead, seeing only what he wanted to see. He reminded himself he was twice their age. He would be able to manage this, he wasn't ready yet to give up. He'd been planning this for too long, had invested too much, and he'd be dammed if he'd let these two sidetrack him. He would tell them as much as he thought they would accept.

He sat back down, steadying his breathing, and pulling his control around him like a blanket, raised his eyes and looked at Gabriel. He would have to tread very carefully here. Keeping his expression bland, he gestured for Gabriel to continue. At all costs, he needed to keep these two relaxed and directed away from his ultimate goal.

'Start talking, Justin, you told us in Prague that you knew more about James's death than you've let on to Meredith. We suspect you also know something about George and Edmondo, and why they were in Western Australia? And even perhaps what's been going on here on the property for the last few years.'

Gabriel watched Justin's eyes very carefully. They had always been his most vulnerable point. Even when lowered as they were now, they told him a lot. For a moment, he thought Justin was going to continue with his protestations of innocence, but then, he lifted his eyes and slowly relaxed. His shoulders lost their rigidity, and he slumped against the back of the sofa.

'You're right of course, about most of that. I shouldn't have come here when I knew the two of you were involved with the investigation, but I've been planning this for a number of years. And in the end, I decided I would continue with my plans.' Pausing for a moment, 'I've kept an eye on Meredith for a long time now. I've paid for information for the last few years from various sources, but the most recent was someone that worked here for a while.'

Martin, moving slightly away from the wall he had been lounging against, interrupted at that point, 'Gerald Watson and company?'

'Yes, you seem to have deduced most of it. They were a particularly inept lot, not very bright posing as a family, especially as bloody Peter was screwing Sienna. When I realised what was really going on, I told them to leave immediately. I knew James would have twigged and would be watching them very closely. I thought that with the three of them, they could divide their time between various members of the family. I even suggested that Peter try to chat up Hera.' Lifting one shoulder in a familiar gesture, he raised his eyes. 'Ahh, it was a stupid idea, and not very ethical. And of course, Hera couldn't abide him. She is an excellent judge of character. Very intuitive as they all are.'

'What about Damian?' Gabriel seemed calm, but his eyes were narrowed to glittering slits.

Justin knew this deceptive calm, and sat up straighter, put his shoulders back, and started talking quickly. 'No, I had nothing to do with Damian. I knew his history of course. Your father told me the story a few years ago, but I never actually met him, and I had no idea he was in Australia, let alone here.' He drew a deep calming breath. 'Okay, I'll tell you everything I know and everything I suspect. But I know nothing about George and Edmondo. But yes, you're right about Meredith. When I heard about James's death, I thought I would finally have a chance to make amends for my stupidity all those years ago. I've never been able to completely forget her. I tried to talk to her at the club, but she just kept avoiding me. While James was alive, he would never let me near her or his girls either. He simply didn't trust me. Once you stuffed up with James, there was never a second chance. He didn't ever forgive. He didn't allow for mistakes, and he's brought the girls up the same way, so take care, Gabriel.'

'Still trying to influence and manipulate, Justin. It won't work, continue with your story.'

Justin raised his eyebrows, shrugged his shoulders, and sank into his thoughts. He finally looked up. 'When I heard about James's death, I did think initially that it was an accident.' He paused thoughtfully. 'It was only later I considered the circumstances, and realised it couldn't have been. James would never make a mistake with the maintenance on his boat. I contacted the Patriarch and discussed it with him. I said I would arrange for someone from the family to go to the funeral and make sure everything was all right. I actually intimated that I would go.' He had the grace to look embarrassed at that point.

'But you didn't, did you? You made sure no one from the family even heard about it until it was too late for anyone to attend, then you muddied the waters again making it seem that Meredith had refused to allow anyone on the property. If it hadn't been for me and Martin asking questions about why we hadn't been instructed to look into his death, the Patriarch wouldn't have any idea of what you were up to.'

Justin was very pale now. Damn, he thought, they knew much more than he suspected, and they had been talking to the Patriarch about it. He was furious, but he had to stay calm.

Gabriel continued, 'You had no idea how close Martin and I had become to James. You had no idea that I had business interests with James, and had for a number of years. You didn't know that James stayed with me in London whenever he was there. You're definitely slipping, Justin.' Gabriel paused for a moment then continued quietly, 'Now tell us about George.'

Justin was definitely rattled now. He couldn't seem to think straight. Gabriel and Martin had been suspicious of him from the first, and the Patriarch? What did he know, and why had Gabriel taken Bede to Paris? What had that really been about? He suddenly felt much too warm. He could feel perspiration starting to form on his upper lip. He had to get out of here and think. Maybe Gabe was right. He was definitely losing the thread. What could he tell them about George that they'd believe? He had to tread very carefully here. How much did they know about Lucien? Christ, he needed time to think.

He cleared his throat. 'I told you I don't know anything about George, or why he was in Australia. I know even less about why he would have been murdered. You know George as well as me. He had more than his share of people who hated him.'

Martin had taken the phone from his pocket; and Justin could feel panic rising in his throat, but asked quietly, still in control, still staying calm, 'Whom are you calling at his hour?'

'Lucien, of course, remember the time difference, it's early evening there, he'll be delighted to hear from us. Particularly if the police haven't managed to speak to him yet.'

Justin spluttered, 'What do you think he can tell you that I can't?' He thought quickly he could still handle this. 'All right, I'll tell you what you want to know.'

Martin glanced across at Gabriel with a question in his eyes and acknowledged the quick nod. He carefully returned the phone to his pocket, and turning back to Justin, waited quietly.

Justin was unsure where to start. He needed to keep as close to the truth as possible; but looking across at his nephews, he felt a fission of fear. They knew some of the 'games' he had been playing over the years that was patently obvious now, so he would have to be very careful. He had taught them long ago to look beneath the surface. He had instructed them in the technique of watching for the tiny telltale signs of lies. The slight twitch of the eyebrows, the tightening of lips, and the tremor of the hands. Drawing a steadying and calming breath, he turned to Gabriel, rose from the chair, and paced across the room. He could let them know he was agitated, and then perhaps they wouldn't look too closely, wouldn't suspect his real motives.

'I assume you've guessed that I'm here to try to convince Meredith to take another chance with me. I was a fool all those years ago, and although I did try at the time to repair matters, Meredith would never speak to me. And over the years, James made sure we didn't meet.' He continued to pace. 'Neither of us is young anymore, she has never married, and of course neither have I.' He was quiet for several moments, looking deep into the past. 'I made a mistake all those years ago. I behaved badly to everyone, I have no excuse to offer for what I did, and to be honest, have never been able to look too closely at it. I didn't even have the excuse of being particularly young. I was certainly much older than Meredith and James. But I was immature and arrogant.'

Gabriel was still lounging quietly against the wall, while Martin sat in the chair with an expression of calm boredom on his face. Neither of them spoke. A very effective technique he knew, and he felt their combined compulsion to continue with his recital. There were a few beads of perspiration blossoming on his forehead, and he resisted the urge to wipe them away.

'I haven't been completely honest with Meredith or the girls, and I certainly haven't spoken to her about my wishes for the future.' This was proving even more difficult than he had imagined. Looking around him at the beautiful room, warm and inviting, he suddenly knew there was no other option now. He felt the tension leave his shoulders, and drawing a very deep breath then letting it out slowly, he moved to sit down again. 'I really had nothing to do with James's death, but I suspect George of having some involvement. But it's only a suspicion and I have no proof. George never did forgive James for the beating he received, and he's always made a point of gloating over the fact that I didn't manage to make off with Meredith either. He's carried a grudge for years and has consistently made threats against James to both Lucien and myself, but usually when he'd had too much to drink. I never took it seriously.' He looked across at Martin. 'Lucien will confirm everything I've said.'

Gabriel pushed casually away from the wall. 'Justin, you haven't said anything that Martin and I didn't already know. What we would like you to tell us is what you know about why George was in Australia, how he knew about the two books, and why you set him up to steal them?'

Martin leaned forward in his chair. 'And we would like you to explain what you know about why George and Edmondo were shot. It has all the earmarks of one of your operations', he paused briefly, 'an operation that went wrong.'

Justin was stunned, and now felt perspiration trickling down the back of his neck and beading over his eyebrows. He shot to his feet in rage and panic. 'What are you talking about? And what are you accusing me of?'

Gabriel moved across the room now, and putting his hands quietly but firmly onto Justin's shoulders, pushed him gently, but inexorably, back into his chair. 'Justin, we've been tracking your movements since before you left Prague. We've already spoken to Lucien, and although he tried valiantly to keep your confidences, he realised it has become critical. There are now three deaths to account for to say nothing of the attempted theft of two valuable antique books. You're up to your neck in the conspiracy against James and his family and have been for years.'

Martin interrupted at this point, 'It was you who employed the very ineffectual Watson family, and although they're no longer technically on the property, they have been keeping a watch on everything that's happening. They're camped just a couple of miles from here, and are taking turns with the binoculars. They really are an incompetent lot.'

They were playing him, and he was exhausted. It had been a very long day. Maybe he really was getting old, he had no idea these two were so on top of all his machinations. He tried desperately to think. He really had no idea who had killed George and Edmondo. It didn't make any sense, but it did point to him. He knew he hadn't had them killed, and he hadn't had James killed, but if he didn't sort this out, these two would tie him up. Admittedly, he hadn't been honest with anyone for a very long time. He had allowed his penchant for deception and intrigue to finally undermine his natural caution. It was impossible, if George hadn't had James killed, there was no one else, and there had been no whispers of anyone targeting George or Edmondo for that matter, except him.

His mind was reeling. He had, in the past, used George as a scapegoat. George, although brilliant in many ways, was surprisingly naïve in others. George had trusted him and Lucien completely. They had all been rivals when younger, but over the last few years, they'd often worked together to a common goal. Always financial, of course, they were now all incredibly wealthy in their own right, completely separate to their respective families. He was missing something, but his gut kept insisting this was Family business. Taking a long and calming breath, he turned to Gabriel. 'I know you think I had something to do with James's and George's deaths, but in fact, I didn't. I don't say that I haven't, over the years, speculated about both, but ultimately, they were both more valuable alive.' He paused, shrugged, 'Actually, that's not strictly true. I would love to have done away with James. He caused me problems quite a few times, and he kept me solidly away from Meredith all these years, but I did not order his death.' Glancing up, he saw Gabriel briefly nod at Martin.

'Actually, Justin, Martin and I didn't think you had anything to do with James's death, but George and Edmondo's are connected in some way, and as you and I know, you are untrustworthy and devious. You have some reason for being here, and although I can almost believe you about Meredith, I don't think that's all.' He now strolled across the room, and parting the curtain, signalled to someone outside.

Justin was aware of the cold brittle blackness of the desert streaming through the window. The radiance of the stars was almost terrifying. They were glittering diamonds scattered across the heavens so close one could almost touch them. There was no ambient light to cloud the intensity, and suddenly, he felt the hairs on the back of his neck rise. This alien country was unforgiving in its primitive grandeur. He really didn't belong here.

Pete appeared at the open window. 'The Watsons have left, packed all their gear, and driven off. We'll still keep an eye on them. They can't disappear out here, but they were definitely freaked when Bede took off in the copter and the police arrival.' He grinned, and poking his head through the window, said, 'Justin, I think you've lost your little spies,' Chuckling quietly to himself, he turned away.

Gabriel turned to Martin, 'I need to talk to Bede, I think.' And with that, left the room abruptly.

Justin sighed, 'Oh, to be young again.' He scowled after Gabriel's retreating back, 'I'm going to bed.'

'Before you sleep tonight, or what's left of the night', Martin quietly spoke, 'I suggest you do some solid thinking, Justin. There's something you're not telling us, and I suspect it would be in your interest to reconsider. Gabe might be besotted, but he's not stupid, and all those women are incredibly intelligent and resourceful. Keep that in mind.'

## Chapter Thirty-One

# Gabriel Grovels

G abriel knocked, gently and quietly opened the door. Bede was just a lump in the bed covered by a light sheet, but he knew she wasn't sleeping. It was a very hot night, and he could just see her through the mosquito netting hanging over the huge bed. The ceiling fan was whirling softly, and the window was wide open with the light from the moon shining straight onto the bed. He felt his groin tighten.

'Well, my love, what exactly have you been up to? What was your paranoia with those two idiots Kamila and Jakub? You've been listening to my aunts, my mother, and perhaps Meredith.' He raised his eyebrows in question.

Bede surged up in the bed, threw the mosquito netting back, and glared at him. 'Yes, I bloody have. What exactly do you do for the family, Gabriel? Are you one of the so celebrated assassins?'

He laughed gently. 'No, my sweet, but if you want to have any sort of rational discussion, you need to put some clothes on. I can't concentrate with all that smooth golden skin glowing at me.' His voice had deepened as he moved silently across the room.

'As for those two idiots, you were desperately in love with Kamila at one time. You asked her to marry you?'

'Bede, I was nineteen, a hopeless romantic, hardly to be credited given my family. I was more than a little naïve, certainly about love.'

He moved suddenly, caught her shoulders gently, and pulled her against him. 'Now back to my earlier question, what have my aunts and my mother been up to? I can find out, you know, but it would just make it a little easier if I didn't have to spend time digging around within the family. Laurent is not pleased with all this drama. He doesn't like the family name appearing in any newspapers, and this has the potential to make the media worldwide. I may not have liked George or Edmondo for that matter, but both of them were very well known in international finance.' He smoothed his hand over her hair, and tucked a strand behind her ear. 'To be murdered in the middle of nowhere in Australia will have curious journalists descending on this property within the next few days, and there's no way you will be able to keep them out.'

Bede scowled at him and tried to pull away, but he was too strong. He wasn't hurting her at all, but she was starting to recognise the determined glint in his eyes. He would not be distracted. She wasn't certain she had ever managed to distract him. She had the impression that he had allowed her to think she had turned his attention away from what had been going on in Paris. But now, looking into his eyes, she felt a frisson of anxiety. She knew he would never hurt her or Hera or Meredith.

'Was it Meredith who arrange to have George killed?' he suddenly asked.

'Christ, no, at least I don't think so.' Bede turned shocked eyes up to him. 'What makes you think anything so horrendous?'

'Because, Bede, there really is no one else.' Drawing a deep breath, he continued quietly, 'Unless it's the terrible trio from Paris.'

Bede was furious now. 'What about your former fiancée and her dubious husband?' she snarled. She wasn't jealous of Kamila, she told herself, she just instinctively didn't like the woman. She was too smarmy and far too sure of herself.

Gabriel grinned down at her. 'Are you jealous of Kamila by any chance? You keep trying to make her responsible for more than stealing two books. Believe me when I say that neither she nor Jakub are bright enough or involved enough, for that matter, to kill George in particular. He always pays extremely well for services rendered, it would be like killing the golden goose.' He continued gently, still holding her shoulders, 'Bede, I knew in Paris that Marina and Josephine had some other reason for being in Paris. They would never stay with Laurent unless they'd been invited, which means that Laurent invited them along with my mother. I also know that Laurent had finally acknowledged how completely untrustworthy and Machiavellian George had become. He'd always hoped that somehow, George would finally prove himself worthy of his father.'

Bede was thoughtful, as she moved away from Gabriel briefly, and pulled on a pale blue camisole and knickers, then moved back to sit beside him on the bed.

'That's only marginally better,' Gabriel quipped.

'Concentrate,' she nudged him in the side. 'Are you saying that Laurent called the women to Paris to warn them about George?'

'I think it's a decided possibility, but Laurent wouldn't have ordered his execution. There would have been no need, he would simply have quietly notified everyone that George was no longer considered trustworthy.' He smiled down at her. 'Bede, that's almost like a banishment. George would no longer be invited to participate in any financial deals going down within the family. He would no longer be kept up to date with family matters.' He gazed into the distance. 'It would be worse, much worse for George than being killed. You met Laurent, spent time with him. He's always subtle in his dealings. Nothing overt if at all possible, and if there is a finite decision to be made, it will be executed quietly, so there are no disturbances anywhere. Shooting George and Edmondo in the middle of the desert smacks of revenge to me.' He wrapped one arm around Bede's shoulders, pulled her hard against his chest, and kissed the top of her head. 'Bede, I need you to trust me. I will do whatever needs to be done to protect you all, but I do need to know everything the women in Paris were planning.' He nuzzled her neck and whispered, 'And there is nothing you could tell me about the three of them that would shock me.'

Turning into his arms, Bede wanted to burrow into his chest. She had always been able to make her own decisions. She would never allow anyone to influence what she thought was right, but there was

something about Gabriel that made her want to lean. 'Gabe, I don't
know what they were up to, you have to believe me. But you're right,
they were planning something. They were on the phone to Meredith
every day, and although I've since asked her what it was all about, she
would only say that it was to do with the past and no business of mine.'

Gabe and Bede continued to sit quietly side by side now, staring out
the window, watching the soft breeze play with the curtains.

'Tell me what you suspect, Gabe, I'm starting to be really worried.'

'I think Meredith, with my mother and aunts, had a contract taken
out on George. I think that Edmondo, being with George, was just bad
luck, and he had to be disposed of as well. I also think that its roots are
in the past, back when they, Meredith and my mother, were young. The
aunts are much older, and they are also much more ruthless.'

'You're suggesting that Meredith arranged for George to be killed?'

'Yes.'

'That's insane, why would she do that? I know about what happened
all those years ago with George, but I think she felt much more bitter
about what Justin did.'

'I agree, but what if they, I mean Mother and the aunts, uncovered
proof that George was involved with James's death? How do you think
Meredith would react then?'

Bede caught her breath, and silently considered the implications
of what Gabriel had just said. 'You're right, of course, she would be
more than furious. But when she was explaining the workings within
the family, she stated that she doesn't approve of the Family's way of
dealing with problems. She wouldn't have arranged for George to be
killed, it's just not her.' Still leaning against his shoulder and feeling the
tensions building in her stomach, 'So you think George arranged for
James's death?'

'No, in fact, I'm sure he didn't. I'm fairly certain that George
had been trying to involve James in some drug smuggling using your
established freight deals. And I'm fairly certain it was George behind
Damian's problems in Perth. George actually needed James alive to
finally be able to pay him back for the Turner thing. Involving him
in drug smuggling would have been the perfect retribution. He's been

planning it for years. George was brilliant, incredibly patient, and he never forgave James for that debacle. He lost a huge amount of money and status. It took him years to re-establish his credibility.

'Bede', he took her hands in his, and turned her to face him saying carefully, 'Bede, Martin and I are now fairly certain it was Justin who arranged for James to be killed, but at the moment, we can't prove it. I need to clear up what happened to George, just in case I'm wrong.' He touched her cheek gently. 'I need you to be very careful for the next few days, and I really need you to think carefully back to Paris, and tell me everything that you heard and any impressions you have from the week we stayed there.' He looked into her eyes and kissed her softly. 'But it's really late now, I think we need to get some sleep even if it's only a couple of hours.'

Bede rested her head on his shoulder. 'Christ', was all she could think of to say, then, 'stay with me for the rest of the night, please?'

With a slow grin, 'It will be my pleasure, my pet.'

# Chapter Thirty-Two

## Justin is Very Worried

Very early the next morning, with the sky still showing the deep indigo of night, but with golden light just seeping across the horizon, Justin groaned and pulled himself to a sitting position. He sat back against the headboard of the bed and gazed out the window. He could see for miles it was so flat. He was desperate and felt trapped. What had made him think he could come here to this outlandish place with impunity? He quietly left his bedroom, moving silently down the hallway, making his way to what he knew was Meredith's room. He hadn't been in there before, but assumed it was the same layout as all the bedrooms on this floor. He opened the door quietly. It was dark, of course, but there was a little light from the dawn, just showing through the open window. Did no one in this house bother to shut the windows or pull the curtains? He wondered.

Looking around, he saw this was actually not a bedroom, but a sort of sitting room. In the low light, he could make out a desk under the window. There was a settee and a high backed armchair grouped around a low table. Another door across the room probably led to the bedroom. He moved across the room on silent feet, and started to turn the handle.

A voice spoke from behind. He turned quickly to see Meredith rising from the armchair. She was holding a rifle in her hands. Bloody hell, he thought, these bloody women and their rifles.

'Meredith, what are you doing with that?' He indicated the firearm held casually, but competently in her hands.

'Justin, I've been waiting for you. You had to approach me tonight. It's all got out of hand, hasn't it? And you're feeling a little trapped.' Her lips lifted into a cold smile. 'I wondered when you'd finally work it all out?'

'What do you mean? Meredith, put the gun down. This is me, you don't really believe I would cause you or the girls any harm?'

'No, you thought that by having James murdered, you could just move in, or at least persuade me to go back to Prague with you. But unfortunately for you, I've been talking to Marina and Josephine daily for the last few weeks. It'd been years since I spoke to them in depth. I always thought they had been involved in that swindle all those years ago. But in fact, it wasn't even George really, although you did manage to implicate him along with James.'

He held his hands out to her. 'Meredith, I don't know what you're talking about. I did not have James killed. You know I've always loved you, but over the years, James poisoned your mind against me.'

'No, Justin, you did that when you tried to seduce Mette all those years ago with such a cheap trick. I know Dominik forgave you, but James and I never did. I found your behaviour insulting.' Meredith shrugged her shoulders. 'We'd been engaged for only four weeks, and you had declared undying love for me. You seduced me, and persuaded me that you were sincere, but in fact, it was a ploy. Mette was more beautiful and incredibly wealthy in her own right, but obviously preferred your brother. You thought to upstage him by becoming engaged first. You had already planned to entice Mette into bed by pretending to be Dominik.' Meredith snorted, 'At the time, I was too stunned and hurt to enquire about details, but eventually, I spoke to everyone who had been in the house at the time, including Mette, Marina, and Josephine plus all the servants.' She paused briefly, and looked at him with contempt read clearly on her face. 'You hadn't really expected Mette to be able to tell you apart so easily, not many people could.'

Justin was white around the mouth. 'Meredith, all that happened years ago, and please, would you put the rifle down and talk to me rationally.'

'No, Justin, you see, I don't trust you. I don't think you've changed at all over the years, although you seem to have convinced most of the family that it had been a moment of madness never to be repeated. You've convinced them that you are now a paragon of virtue. That you really did regret what happened, and would spend the rest of your life making it up to Dominik! Piffle, you hate him and envy him as much now as you did all those years ago, and you've tried to seduce the two boys away subtly. It hasn't worked, you know, they are both extremely bright, and you and Dominik have both trained them well. Dominik made sure they evaluate everything and everyone. They take nothing on trust and check all their facts. It hasn't made life particularly easy for them.'

Justin spoke harshly into the small silence following this statement. 'Meredith, believe me, I did not have James killed. Why do you think I'm here? Do you seriously imagine I am trying to resurrect our relationship from all those years ago?' He was gazing at her with cold eyes now. 'Believe me, you are the lonely spinster here, I have no need to come crawling. I am here just to help solve the mystery of James's death, then I plan to leave.' He was very pale under his tan, his shoulders back, and he was standing proudly. His beautiful silver hair a halo around his head in the dawning light. But Meredith saw the hint of perspiration on his forehead, and he hadn't taken his eyes off the rifle. He held his hand out to her. 'Please Meredith, can we sit down and discuss this in a civilised manner?'

———————◆———————

Martin walked quietly across the room and put his hand gently onto Gabriel's shoulder. He really didn't want to wake Bede, and he knew any movement too fast would have Gabe throwing him to the ground with his knee in his windpipe.

'This had better be important. I had plans for this morning,' Gabriel's quiet murmur came out of the darkness.

Martin grinned to himself, and crouching down by the bed, spoke directly into Gabriel's ear, 'Justin has just gone into Meredith's room very, very quietly.'

'Umm, interesting, I'd put my money on Meredith. But okay, just give me a moment.' He untangled his legs and arms gently from around Bede and kissed her on the cheek. She grumbled sleepily, but turned over and settled deeper into the sheets. Gabriel pulled on jeans quickly and quietly left the room. 'Okay, what's he up to, do you think?'

'I think he's finally making his move, but we need to hear this.' They moved quickly down the corridor and slipped into the room next to Meredith's. 'This actually abuts Meredith sitting room, but there's no way we can listen in on the bedroom, so I hope these devices are sensitive enough to pick up what's being said.' He handed Gabriel earphones with a small listening device attached, and together, they moved across the room. Placing the head of the devices against the wall and the small buds into their ears, they concentrated on what was happening in the next room.

Gabriel, chuckling softly, spoke quietly, 'Well done, Meredith, I knew you were on the ball.'

There were the sounds of someone waking behind them, much groaning and coughing, and both turned to see Damian struggling to a sitting position. 'What the hell are you two doing here?' he muttered while rubbing at the stubble on his chin.

'Quiet,' Martin whispered with a smile curving his lips. 'I thought you hit the bottle a little too hard last night.'

Another deep groan, 'What?' Damian peered blearily across at them

Gabriel held his finger up to his lips, while keeping the device still pressed firmly against the wall. 'We'll explain later, just stay quiet.' Damian sank back down into the bedclothes with a groan and pulled the sheet firmly over his head.

———•———

'You think I'm the lonely spinster? You know nothing about my life, nothing about the girls' lives. James made sure they were independent and clear thinking. He also made sure they evaluated every situation. It's a hard lesson to learn, but in this family, it's essential, wouldn't you say?'

'Meredith, I think you're being cynical and bitter. You never did get over our relationship, I think you're still in love with me.' He smiled charmingly at her and started to move across the room. 'Put the gun down, you're not going to shoot me.'

Meredith snapped, 'Stay put, Justin, while I tell you a story, and I'll tell you why I think you had James killed. I suggest you sit down. This is going to be a shock I'm afraid.'

'What are you talking about now?'

'When you left me all those years ago, you left me pregnant.'

Justin fell back into the chair in astonishment. He was pale now and shaking. 'What? Good God, Meredith, I had no idea, believe me.'

She smiled at the expression on his face. 'You really didn't care as you blithely manipulate everyone around you. James helped me. Over the next year, I was quite young you might remember, and James wasn't that much older. Our experience of the family was a shock, and for the first time, we realised exactly why we had been brought up as far away from Europe as possible. Several members of the family did suspect something and offered to help, but you definitely weren't one of them.'

There was a heavy silence in the room.

'I have something else to tell you, Justin.'

'What else are you accusing me of now?'

# Chapter Thirty-Three

## Meredith Shocks Justin

'You have a son, Justin, a very clever and talented son.'

Justin now started out of his chair. 'For God's sake, Meredith, what are you saying?'

'Just that we brought him up mostly in the Czech Republic, and as for being a lonely spinster, I met a wonderful man whom I loved with every part of my being. Between us, we kept your son safe for years, but then Josef died, was killed in a car bomb explosion in Prague. We were with him that day, your son and I. He had literally just left us to continue with our shopping. I was in hospital unconscious, in a coma for weeks. When I finally recovered consciousness, my son was missing. The authorities didn't know what had happened to him. In the confusion he had simply disappeared, been spirited away. He was 4 years old.'

Justin was white-faced and gripping the arms of the chair, as if he wanted to launch himself across the room. 'Why did you never tell me? I had a right to know I had a son.'

'No, Justin, by that time, I'd heard enough about you to realise that I didn't want anything to do with you nor did I want my son to have anything to do with you. We'd made a life well away from the family and you. James vowed never to let you know what had happened. It took me a long time to recover physically and emotionally, and by that time, it was too late. There was no information about that small boy. I didn't know if he was alive or dead.'

Justin was on his feet, his arms flailing around him. 'That was my son?' his skin was white, and his hands shaking.

'Yes, Justin, that was your son that you managed to disappear into an orphanage under another name.'

'But, but', Justin was pacing now around the room, he held his head in his hands as he paced, 'no, no, no, I had nothing to do with any of that. I heard Josef had been killed, but believe me, I had no idea you were involved with him. You must have been using another name. I remember that the child disappeared, but we, the Family had nothing to do with it.'

'The authorities never did solve it. No one accepted responsibility for the bomb, and the police finally wrote it off as an unfortunate accident. But I always thought the Family had been behind it. I really wanted to kill you, I wanted to make you suffer, but James would never allow it. He was never convinced the Family was behind it. It wasn't their style, he said. He didn't believe in revenge per se, he had an insane notion of universal justice, but even so, he took every opportunity to undermine any of your financial schemes he was aware of.'

———— •• ————

In the next room, both Gabriel and Martin were reeling from these revelations. Gabriel turned around and looked at Damian still sleeping with the sheet pulled over his head. He turned to Martin, astonishment written clearly on his face, and that connection that is so strong between twins meant that they arrived at the same conclusion at the same moment. They both now turned back to the bed, and contemplated Damian's sleeping form.

'Christ, what next?' Martin suddenly grinned, and spoke very quietly, 'I knew I liked him more than I normally would. He's the ultimate revenge even if James didn't believe in revenge. What do we tell him?'

'Martin, we don't know anything for sure yet, so we tell him nothing until Meredith decides, presuming she has proof.' Gabriel turned back.

'We need to keep listening. This is fascinating, but we can't really let Meredith shoot him, can we?'

Martin grinned. 'No, but this does explain why James threw Damian off the property. He's their first cousin.'

---

Justin was talking again. 'Where is my son, Meredith, you malicious, cruel, spiteful bitch.' He lunged toward her.

Meredith calmly brought the rifle into play. 'Remember the rifle, Justin, I would love to put a bullet in your leg, or somewhere more painful now.'

Justin pulled up abruptly. 'Okay, Meredith, what exactly do you want?'

'Information, the truth, if you are capable of speaking it, did you have James killed? We know someone within the family did. It's the only explanation that makes any sense. We know that George was trying to use James to smuggle drugs into Europe along with our flowers, and we know that James discovered the plans and put a stop to them. But George didn't take that contract out on him. He needed him alive. Was it you?' Meredith almost spat the words with the rifle still held steady pointed at his midriff.

Justin looked at the furious woman in front of him. Had he really imagined he wanted to marry this virago? Kill James, yes, he'd imagined it many times over the years. But in his imagination, he'd been the one to push a knife into his heart. 'No, I did not have James killed. I actually needed him alive. I also needed George alive, I certainly wouldn't have had him or even Edmondo killed for that matter.' He sank slowly down into the big comfortable chair and let his head fall back. The silence was almost deafening.

Meredith spoke calmly now, 'What are you doing in my room, Justin, what do you want?'

---

'Gabe, I think we have to go in and take the rifle away from Meredith. And although I hate the idea, I think we do have to rescue Justin.'

Gabriel looked at his brother for a moment, and with a grin, shrugged, 'Okay, let's go.'

As they started to leave the room, Damian stirred and raised his head. 'What's going on, what are you doing in my bedroom, and what's the joke?' He looked at his friends who were doubled over with the silent laughter they were valiantly trying to stifle. It was hard to see in the low light, but there was a disturbing energy emanating from both of them. He sat up suddenly. 'Stop it, you two, I need to know what's going on here.'

Gabriel straightened up. 'Damian, yes, you do need to know what's happening, but for the moment, we have to rescue Justin.' And with a grin, he turned and quietly left the room.

Martin suddenly sat down on the side of the bed. 'Ahhh, Damian, Gabe and I have just heard a rather startling conversation between Justin and Meredith.' He paused as if wanting to go on, but unsure how to go about it.

Damian had never seen Martin stuck for words before. He was intrigued.

'It's not something I, or we, can repeat . . . ahhh . . . until we speak to Meredith that is, I think. I think, yes, I think, you should get up and get dressed.'

'Martin, what's going on? My head is still pounding, and my stomach is not good.' He surged out of the bed and made a dash for the bathroom.

He really had tied one on last night, but they needed him alert, so Martin wandered across to the bathroom. 'Damian, you're going to need your wits about you, so take some aspirin and have a cold shower.'

Martin left to join Gabriel in the hallway.

Meredith turned as the door opened. 'Oh, do come in, who else should I expect? Bede and Hera perhaps.' She looked furious as well she should. Justin was now sitting in the high backed armchair, very pale with a slight sheen of perspiration on his face.

He, too, turned toward the opening door. 'God in hell, Gabriel and Martin, get out of here. This does not concern you.'

'Sorry, Meredith', Gabriel answered her first, 'no, it's only me, Martin, and I hope Damian. Ahhh, we've been eavesdropping.' He held up the very sophisticated equipment he was still holding. 'And it's been enlightening, ahm', he turned to Justin, 'I take it this has all been a bit of a surprise for you as well?'

Justin scowled at him. 'A shock, to say the least, you supercilious twit, you can't suggest to me that it's not a complete surprise to you.'

Looking apologetically across at Meredith. 'Ahhh, well, in fact, I have to say that I did know most of it some time ago. James, you know, he did keep in touch with both me and Martin.'

'Just what gave you the right to eavesdrop on me in my rooms, and what right had James to discuss my personal affairs?' Meredith was very pale and was still holding the rifle firmly with her finger on the trigger, although it was pointing at the ground.

Gabriel surveyed the combatants eyeing each other with hostility from across the space of the very beautiful Turkish carpet covering the polished boards of the floor. 'I'm sorry, Meredith, we thought it would not be a good idea if you shot Justin just yet, although I can understand why you might want to.'

Martin had entered the room by then, and Damian, a few moments later. His hair still wet from the very quick shower. He halted on the threshold. 'Wow, you can cut the silence with a knife.' And not having any idea what was going on, was agog with curiosity. 'What have I missed?' he asked cheerfully. 'Are we about to have a revelation?'

They all turned to him and stared.

## Chapter Thirty-Four

# World War Three

The inspector and his sergeant arrived very early that morning, driving up in the police Toyota 4WD to find Pete sitting on the front steps, calmly smoking a cigarette. He climbed slowly to his feet, and with a grin, greeted them.

'Good morning, chaps, welcome to World War Three.'

They could hear the shouting as they approached, 'What's going on?'

'Good question, are you sure this is a good time, Inspector?' Pete was grinning. 'I'd take it easy if I were you,' he said, as they all mounted the steps and banged on the door.

To their surprise, it was Gabriel who answered. 'Come in to the madhouse.' He glanced at Pete with raised brows, and then the inspector, 'I hope you have some positive information? Anything at this point might be helpful. We actually need a distraction.' Pete saluted briefly and went back outside to sit again on the front steps.

They all moved through into the dining room, and Inspector Campbell looked around. No one was actually sitting at the table. They were ranged around the room in attitudes of aggression and rage. He could almost feel the energy zapping out of control around the room.

Gabriel drifted across, and put his arm gently around Bede's shoulder. He spoke calmly, but firmly not really raising his voice, while addressing the whole room. 'I think we all need to calm down and leave this pointless discussion, while we hear what Inspector Campbell has to say. With any luck, he'll have some information more relevant than what we've been shouting about.'

All eyes turned to him, and then the inspector. The tension in the room slowly lowered, and dissipated.

Meredith came forward. 'Inspector, and Sergeant, please come in.' She turned to Mrs Robinson who, looking stunned, was standing quietly in the background with a coffee pot in her hands. 'Robby, please, I think we need some fresh coffee. That must be cold by now.' Turning around, continued in a steely voice, 'And we'll all sit down quietly and listen.'

'I do have some interesting news folks that I think may answer a few questions, but I need some answers first.' He turned to Damian and fixed him with a steely gaze. 'Those two thugs at the club the other night, where did you actually first see them?'

Damian looked startled. 'Christ, I'd forgotten about those two. There's been so much else going on here. Give me a minute to let me think. I became aware of the Pom following me around at Curtin, a couple of days before they attacked me the first time. I can't remember an exact date, if that's what you want.' He was thoughtful. 'It was quite a while before Gabe and Martin arrived, but I can't remember exactly. I did report the attack to the police. Why?'

'Well, it seems they have a strong connection to George and Edmondo both. At the moment, neither of them is saying much, but we've been on to Interpol, and they both have records and outstanding warrants in France and the Czech Republic with no record of them actually arriving in this country. We've been able to trace their connection to George through an international group of drug smugglers working between Europe and Australia. Apparently, there is an ongoing investigation at the moment, which we seem to have stumbled into. It seems most of the hard drugs come in through Perth', he now looked toward Bede, 'and are distributed, we think, through your freight services both overseas and to the east. It's a roundabout route, but safe apparently, and this has been happening for several years.'

There was a startled silence at this pronouncement. Bede, white-faced, turned to Gabriel, 'That can't be right, James would never countenance such a thing.'

'No', he said firmly, 'I agree.' He turned to the inspector. 'There's more to the story, isn't there?'

'Yes, and we need to move very quietly because the person actually in charge of this end of the operation is someone most of you know very well.'

All eyes immediately turned to Justin. 'It's not me', he shouted jumping to his feet, 'this has gone on long enough, I'm guilty of a little manipulation, greed, and of course, debatable ethics, but I would never be involved in drug smuggling.' He sat suddenly, his face very red with his white hair uncharacteristically disordered, and muttered almost under his breath, 'Drug smuggling has got to be so passé.'

Bede and Hera dissolved into cleansing laughter. Meredith smiled, and both Gabe and Martin tried desperately to keep a straight face, while Damian seemingly was the only one adversely affected by this statement. He turned toward Justin and snarled, 'Way to go, *Dad*.'

The inspector looked startled, and the sergeant grinned. 'I guess that's what World War Three was about?'

'A little support from you two would be helpful.' Justin glared at Gabriel and Martin.

'Justin, we have more important things going on here right now, if you are not the leader of a drug smuggling gang.' Gabriel still seemed to be having trouble keeping all expression from his face.

Bede elbowed him in the ribs, and turning to her, he finally relaxed enough for his grin to show. He pulled her hard against him, and bending, buried his head in her neck. They could all see his shoulders shaking with laughter, as he tried desperately to control it.

Martin finally sat down. 'Justin, I'm sorry it's what you deserve after all the machinations over the last few years, but I agree with Gabe. When he can finally control himself, we have other issues here now.' He turned to the inspector. 'Please continue.'

'I seem to have walked into a family argument, but we will have to leave the implications of that until later.' He looked pointedly at

Damian. 'As I said, there is an ongoing investigation into the drug smuggling that's outside my province. But as it impacts onto the ongoing investigation of James's death, I intend to continue making enquiries. The person we think is very involved, but with no actual proof, is Mikael', he looked directly at Bede, 'your manager in Perth.'

There was a stunned silence in the room.

'Mikael?' Bede looked startled. 'Good God, he's been with us for the last twenty years. James knew him in France, he's part of the family connections. That's how he came to be working with us. He's been helping to manage the Perth office for over ten years.' Bede turned to Gabriel in confusion. 'Did you suspect any of this?'

'I knew there had to be someone either working here or in the Perth office, so although we didn't suspect him in particular', he shrugged, 'I admit he was on our list, and I could make a case against him, but it's all circumstantial. There's absolutely no proof.'

The inspector looked toward his sergeant who shrugged. 'I agree, there is no proof, and even with what we have managed to drag out of your two assailants, there are still questions unanswered. Neither have actually met the man they were working for, and although they're not stupid and did try for their own protection, he managed to avoid meeting or even speaking directly to either of them. I suspect he's behind James's death, or at least his activities contributed. He's very cagy. If we're to prove anything at all, we're going to have to be very careful.' He looked around at the stunned faces around him and continued, 'Which brings me to the reason I'm here. I have a plan and I'll need all of your help.'

Mrs Robinson came back into the room at that moment with a fresh pot of coffee, and moving to the table, spoke for the first time, 'Meredith, I heard what the inspector said. I may be able to help a little.'

The inspector became instantly alert, and turning to her with a look of fierce concentration on his face, 'I thought you might, Mrs Robinson, you knew him rather well at one time.'

Robby felt herself flush and with a diffident shrug nodded. 'Yes, in fact I almost married him years ago after my husband was killed.'

Hera got up and crossed to her. She gently took the pot of coffee from her and directed her to a chair. 'Sit down, Robby, and tell us all what you know.'

'Well, I didn't marry him eventually because there was something about him that never seemed quite right. He was secretive, but more than that', she paused thoughtfully, and then continued, 'I've worked for the family for a long time in various houses, and secrecy is really part of your mystique, but it was more than that. He was always asking questions about you girls and James and Meredith as well. He seemed to want to know how this property worked. It was more than being polite and making conversation. He wanted to know specifics. There were times', she paused for a moment again, then taking a deep breath, continued, 'in fact, I became very suspicious about what he was doing and why he wanted to know so many details. It was before I came to work here permanently. I was living in Perth at the time, and I started to follow him at night to see where he went. He had a number of places and people he met regularly. I had never seen any of them before. I became quite worried and even frightened in the end.' She paused to look around. 'I'm not proud of what I did, it's hard to explain, but then I decided to confront him. I thought he was having an affair. One of the people he met often was a very beautiful woman. I told him I had seen him with her when he had told me he was tired and needed to get an early night. I demanded an explanation, he denied the affair, but it developed into a violet argument.

'He became very abusive, so I ended the relationship. But he would never explain why he was so interested in the private details about James and everyone here. Then after James was killed, I became anxious and frightened again, and you all started thinking James has been murdered. I felt it had to be someone from the Family, but I really can't believe he had anything to do with it. There have been times when I thought I should mention some of this to someone. But it's just suspicions, and we were very close for a long time.' She looked at the inspector. 'If you really believe Mikael has something to do with all of this, maybe I can be of some help. I remember all the places I followed him to and the

people he met. Even though it was several years ago, it might be helpful.'
She looked expectantly around the room.

The Inspector was standing quietly. There was an aura of stillness
around him. Then finally he blinked, took a long breath, and stirred,
'This could be very helpful, Mrs Robinson, but you say you don't know
their names?'

'No, but I could identify them if you have photos or something.'

There was another stunned silence in the room. Meredith rose from
her chair and went to take her hand and squeezed it gently. 'Robby, I
had no idea. I always wondered what had happened between the two
of you, but I felt I couldn't ask. I'm sorry you felt so threatened. You
should have said something to me. I appreciate your loyalty as does
everyone here, I'm sure.'

Almost as one, they turned toward Inspector Campbell. He, in turn,
turned toward Gabriel first then Martin, 'Can you two add anything to
what Mrs Robinson has said?'

Gabriel turned to Martin briefly, and then turned back to the
inspector. 'If I could speak to you in private, Inspector?'

There was a general outcry from all present, and Justin jumped to
his feet, furiously shouting louder than anyone. 'No, you don't, my boy.
Anything you have to say, you say in front of everyone in this room.
There has been too much secrecy in this affair on all levels. Now, we
keep everything in the open.

Meredith broke in, 'Much as I hate to agree with anything you say,
Justin, in this instance, you're right. There has been too much secrecy
for years. If we're ever to get through this, there has to be total honesty.'
She took a breath. 'That means no more secrecy!' she almost shouted
the words.

There was a general murmur of agreement, and they turned as one
to Gabriel.

'Okay, Okay.' Gabriel held up his hands. 'Okay, no more secrets.'
Frowning, he looked around the room and studied each face carefully
then spoke quietly. 'Ahhh', turning to Bede, 'I need to say this before we
go any further into what Martin and I suspect, or rather, the possibilities
that need to be aired.'

'Gabriel you're starting to worry me, what are you trying to say?'

'I adore you, you know that, and I would never do anything to harm you or anyone here. You've got to know me over the last couple of weeks, so please will you trust me with this? Things could get a little sticky.'

'I reserve judgement, get on with it.'

He sighed then turned to the inspector.

# Chapter Thirty-Five

## Inspector Campbell is Pissed

Inspector Campbell was frowning. 'Okay, now can we get down to some serious business, you two? You know more than you've been saying, and now it's time to come clean. I'm becoming exasperated by all this family business, this is Australia, and we do things a certain way here. Straightforward, in fact, so start talking.' He pointed a finger at Gabriel, 'You first.'

Gabriel took Bede's hands in his, kissed her knuckles gently, then turned back to the inspector. 'I think I need to recap on how and why we arrived here, so I'll start from the beginning. Some of you know all of this, but I think it's important. We've suspected for a while that someone, perhaps Mikael, has been using the freight business from here to transport drugs, but have never been able to prove anything. We contacted James about three months ago and alerted him to what we suspected. He started making discrete enquiries, then to our astonishment, or maybe not, he was murdered. It didn't fit, for the smuggling to continue, they needed James alive. Before we could make the trip here to see what had happened, we were directed by the council to investigate Justin for theft and fraud', he looked briefly across at Justin, 'involving antique family books and jewellery. James had contacted Laurent about the books he had been offered just before he was murdered.

'We needed to see the *Book of Letters* to confirm it was one that had been stolen from the archives.' He paused to collect his thoughts. 'It wasn't, so then we needed to know where the two books had come from, as they seemed to be connected. We also needed to know and who had offered them to James and how he came to acquire them. Hence, the trip to Paris.'

Bede interrupted, 'So you knew all along that James had been murdered, and that it had something to do with those bloody books?' She looked at him accusingly.

'No, of course not, initially, it didn't occur to us that James's death was anything other than a dreadful accident, but the fact that no one from the family came to the funeral was suspicious.' He sighed. 'You don't understand, at that point, it was all conjecture. There were a few people within the family we had been directed to investigate, Justin was only one of them.' Drawing a long breath he continued, 'That was in Prague, then the full council intervened, and we were directed to come here to finally investigate James's death. Laurent wanted to keep everything quiet. He didn't know at that point where the books had come from, and if from the archives, who the thief could be. There were a number of people who had access to the archives, and to his personal library. Laurent directed us to examine the books carefully. He told us what to look for and about his conversations with James.

'After examining them, I realised that neither of them were the ones missing from the collection. It posed another mystery, which meant that we', he looked down at Bede, still nestled in his arms, 'needed to head to Paris. I needed to talk to Laurent in person, and I needed to find out where those two books came from. They were a puzzle because they should have been part of the family collection, but obviously never had been. There was also the suggestion posed by the book that Laurent may not be the legitimate patriarch.' He got up and started to pace. 'Then to our astonishment, Martin ran into Damian who was being pursued by those idiots trying to blackmail him into creating ice for them.' He paused, looked across at Martin. 'Then George and Edmondo arrived with Kamila and Jakub in tow, trying to steal James's books.' He turned to Justin. 'I have to say, your arrival was a surprise too, especially Meredith's revelations, so I think we should start with you. We need to know exactly what you know about any of the incidents that have happened.'

Martin continued the story. 'On the surface, it looks like a whole lot of unrelated events, but in Gabe and my experience, it's more likely to be connected to one thing. And in this case, the smuggling racket. On the surface though, it didn't make any sense for James to be killed.' He looked across at Gabe. 'We think James made a few too many waves, but we haven't been able to make any headway. We've had all the phone lines and James's mobile checked for phone calls around that time.'

Gabe now took up the tale again. 'We know where he travelled to the months before, and everyone he talked to. The last phone call he took, that Hera said he was so angry about, we couldn't trace. It was an overseas call, but had been rerouted a couple of times, and the mobile it originated from was one of those cheap phones from America. We've been able to trace the call to America, which could have been innocent as your freight company ships there, but why use one of those disposable, phones and why reroute it trying to disguise the caller? Obviously, it was someone James was used to dealing with. We've had our people in the US checking alibis of all James's contacts and haven't been able to spot any anomalies. There you have it, we're at a standstill unless', he took a long breath then continued, 'James was involved in the smuggling operation from the start, and there had been a falling out,' he said this last quickly in a flat, cold voice.

Bede erupted in anger and Hera bounced to her feet, shouting in outrage, 'How dare you suggest anything so terrible, of course James wasn't involved in anything like that.' Hera was standing with her hands on her hips, and her chin stuck out aggressively.

Bede was red-faced and trembling with outrage. She swung around to Gabe. 'So this is what you meant when you said that things could get a little sticky. Well, for your information, James wouldn't have been involved, so you can think again. Just because you think you're so good at solving crime.'

'Calm down, Bede.' Gabe was on his feet and moved to take her hands. 'It is possible, but we think highly unlikely. But we do need to keep an open mind.'

'No we don't, I tell you it's not possible.'

The inspector stepped into the fray. 'Calm down everyone, we're going to look at all the incidents separately and together, and try to see some connection between them all. For a start, your friends, Kamila and Jakub, have a strong connection with George and Edmondo, who have a strong connection to the two thugs hassling Damian, who were trying to blackmail him into producing drugs, not necessarily the drugs that are being shipped from this location. I think we must assume that the whole thing revolves around the drug smuggling, which also I think involves Mikael who organised the initial contact for your overseas freight contract. It's also more than feasible that the drugs are being shipped to the eastern states using your freight company. The way I see it, we just need to follow the links slowly and carefully without causing any ripples.'

Martin spoke again. 'We', indicating Gabriel, 'have been speculating that all this will eventually lead back to someone within the board of directors for the Family. There has to be some one person we think that has been able to hold all the disparate groups together and make a concerted whole. It has to be one of the directors, Damian's background is known to only a few, for instance. And although James had cut a lot of his connections with the family, he's been involved with me and Gabe for instance in a number of investments for a few years now. He didn't have any financial interests with anyone else within the family.'

Bede raised her eyebrows at the last statement, and scowled across at Gabe, 'And you could suggest that James had something to do with it all.'

'Bede, please leave it for now, we can talk about it all later, and I will explain in detail exactly what I meant. And I did not mean that I actually believed James had anything to do with this.' Gabriel was scowling now, and she could almost feel the hostility directed at her. Bede humphed, but sat down again in an armchair across the room from him.

The inspector intervened, 'Tell me how you Martin and James entered into business together? Is that common knowledge?'

'No,' Gabriel replied with a frown, while still looking at Bede. 'We deliberately kept our connection quiet, not exactly secret, we just didn't see any need to advertise it. James contacted me about three years ago. He had a proposal that really required information on a number of investments that both George and Lucien were involved in. We had a number of meetings, and gradually became quite friendly. I liked him, and admired his ethics. James was always secretive, and he didn't trust many within the family. He has always trusted and liked Laurent and our father.' He turned to Bede and continued quietly, 'But he wasn't being completely honest about something. That I knew even then. Over the years, I've become quite adapt at recognising when someone is being less than honest about his or her motives, and I was aware that James had a hidden agenda. But I was certain that it wasn't something that would affect our arrangements. I am almost completely certain he was not involved with the smuggling. In fact, at that time, I don't think he was aware of any of it. It was obvious to me though that something was worrying him.'

Gabriel now turned to the inspector. 'I think you should tell us exactly what you suspect, and what you expect us to do about this.' The inspector turned now to Mrs Robinson sitting quietly with a mug of coffee in her hands. 'I think, Mrs Robinson, that you can help me clarify a few things, and I think we can solve at least the mystery of James's death without jeopardising the ongoing investigation in smuggling currently being conducted by the joint police forces of several states.'

She looked at him with wide startled eyes, the colour draining from her face. 'What do you want me to do?'

## Chapter Thirty-Six

# *Mrs Robinson*

Adeline Robinson sat quietly nursing her mug of coffee, while the family raged at each other. They had always been like this. Saying the first thing that occurred to them—even the girls when they were young—lashing out verbally, but never physically, she had to admit. There was something not quite Australian about them, and it wasn't just the accent. She put it down to their constant travelling to Europe and other outlandish places. No stillness, no quiet contemplation in any of them. That vibrancy was very foreign, but she kept that observation to herself. Mikael hadn't liked her comments, he'd seen it as criticism. In his own way, he was very loyal. They ignored her now, as they commonly did; she had become invisible again. They were always polite of course, and their manners impeccable. But none of them, not even Meredith, had tried to know her personally.

She sat watching and listening, collecting information. It's what she did. The inspector was intelligent and determined. He was someone to be very careful around. He stood there quietly letting them pick at each other, his light, grey eyes were everywhere at once. She didn't trust those eyes, they saw too much. She must be very careful, as she went over in her mind what she had actually said about Mikael.

He turned around and spoke suddenly, 'Now, Mrs Robinson, we need your help.'

She looked up at him with wide, startled eyes, the colour draining from her face. 'What do you want me to do?'

'Nothing too onerous, Mrs Robinson, just talk to me about the last time you saw or spoke to Mikael and where that was.'

She saw the trap immediately, and took a moment to think back to what she had said. 'It was a few years ago when I was in Perth last.' She paused for a moment, then turned toward Meredith. 'I tend not to go to Perth on my days off, I prefer to go to the club or the coast here, it's quieter. So I haven't actually spoken to Mikael for a long time. I can't remember exactly, but it would have been in Perth at the office, I think.'

The inspector finally moved from where he had been standing, and picking up a straight-backed chair, sat it in front of her. He turned the chair around and sat with his legs straddled and his arms crossed on the back. 'Now, Mrs Robinson, what I have to ask you is very important and could get Mikael into serious trouble depending on your answers.' He looked into her eyes calmly, and his expression was bland, almost mask-like.

She smiled smugly to herself while keeping her expression calm. He didn't really see her either. 'Yes, of course, I'll tell you anything you want to know, anything to help catch this despicable murderer. If it turns out to be Mikael, then he should pay for his crime.'

The inspector leaned over and took both of her hands in his. 'Now, Robby, may I call you Robby?'

She responded with a small movement of her head, and looking around, saw concerned expressions on Gabriel and Martin's faces. Why were they frowning?

She turned back and looked again into the inspector's pale eyes. 'You're starting to make me nervous, what do you want from me?'

'I want a bit of honesty, Robby. You see, we know that you speak to Mikael every few days by phone.' She jerked her hands trying to get free, but he kept a strong hold while continuing, 'We know you have a satphone that Mikael gave you years ago. It's an old model but works beautifully. You've kept him informed on everything that's been happening here for years.' His voice had taken on a chilly note. 'We've been listening in, you see.'

There was a stunned silence, then Meredith spoke, 'What are you talking about, Inspector? Why are you trying to bully Robby?'

He ignored her, and just kept his eyes on Adeline Robinson. He still had her hands caught tight in his. 'Do you want to change your statement, Robby? You see, we know everything or just about everything.'

Adeline finally managed to drag her hands free, and jumping to her feet, took several steps back and swung to Meredith. 'I don't know what he's talking about. He can't speak to me like that. I was trying to help you all.' Her voice was a loud whine, and while wringing her hands, she moved quickly toward Bede, standing closest to her.

She was a large woman, tall, and heavyset with big shoulders and large hands; and yet, she moved very quickly for so large a woman. Gabriel was suddenly there, pulling Bede up out of the chair and pushing her behind him, while moving to intercept Robby. She spun toward him, while pulling a small revolver from her pocket and snarled, 'You, you arrogant little snot. Mikael warned me about you and your brother. He said you wouldn't stop digging until you came up with answers. Well, you can have your answers, but it won't do any of you any good.' She swung the gun around keeping them all covered, as she backed toward the open French doors. 'You are all so arrogant', she snarled at Inspector Campbell, 'you come here with your little sergeant with not even a gun between you, thinking you can just get me to confess by holding my hands for a moment. Mikael will be here any minute now with some friends in the helicopter, so stay where you are, all of you, or I'll shoot someone, and you'll never know which one I'll shoot until I do it.' She was calm now. She had known this would probably happen, so she rang Mikael as soon as she had seen the inspector and his sergeant arrive.

She kept backing carefully, making sure she didn't bump into any furniture. She knew this room and every bit of furniture in it. She cleaned it every day. She was watching them, swinging the gun to point at each one in turn, and backed straight into Pete's arms. He reached around and calmly took the gun from her. She reeled around swinging wildly and managed to land a stinging blow to his jaw and another to his solar plexus before Gabriel and Martin managed to throw her to the ground and subdue her. She was still struggling, hissing, and cursing fluently much to Meredith's astonishment and shock.

## Chapter Thirty-Seven

*Resolution*

It was some hours later, and again, they were in the living room. The inspector and his sergeant had left taking Adeline Robinson with them in a police helicopter. She had said enough in her fury and panic, while struggling to implicate both herself and Mikael in James's death. Inspector Campbell was hopeful of obtaining more details on how they had arranged the assassination. Gabriel expressed his hopes just before they left that the inspector would manage to get a name from her that would point to the committee member involved. Mikael, they knew, was having his own problems at the moment. The arrests by the joint task force into the smuggling operation had finally come together at about the same time as Adeline was being taken away. The message she left for Mikael had been intercepted and precipitated the arrest.

---

Bede was sitting on the lounge with Gabriel's arm around her shoulders. She spoke quietly as she jabbed him in the chest with a very sharp finger. 'Okay, so start from the beginning. When did you first suspect Robby? I want details, none of this seeming to pull it out of the air stuff.'

Gabriel clutched his chest with one hand. 'Ow, that hurt,' then grinned and tightened his arm briefly, and leaning in, kissed her unselfconsciously full on the mouth. 'You're right, you all need to know exactly what happened, or what we think happened. For a start, it was Adeline Robinson who arranged with Mikael's help to take out a contract on James. He was getting far too close to all the details on the smuggling racket. The smuggling was her idea from the start, you know, and it was Mikael's contacts from Europe that arranged most of the details. There is a connection to someone within the executive committee. We know that there are some who would like to take the Family back to the old ways. That's another reason we needed to confirm Laurent's status. These men, and they are all men, enjoyed a great deal of power years ago. Laurent will not countenance drug smuggling or murder. That's one of the reasons we've been so slow to confront her or Mikael. We were hoping that either Mikael or one of the others would slip and make a mistake. Mention a name. And make it easier for the police.'

'When you say one of the others, who exactly do you mean Gabriel? George, Edmondo, Justin, Lucien, Jakub, Kamila, Josephine, Marina, or is there anyone else I've forgotten?'

Hera was pacing around the room. She was furious. The last few days had been one surprise after another, and she was fed up. She felt unconnected somehow; drifting as if everything she knew about her life was a chimera.

Justin was on his feet immediately shouting. 'Hera, I told you I had nothing to do with the smuggling. I had nothing to do with James's death, will you stop insinuating that I did?' Taking a calming breath, he continued more quietly, but still obviously very angry. 'You would probably like to make me the scapegoat, make me responsible for everything that's happened, but you can't. We have all been duped in one way or another. I still don't know how George was involved with this, or why he was killed.' He took her hands gently and led her back to a comfortable chair. 'Sit down, Hera, and let Gabriel and Martin try to explain what's probably been happening, although I suspect even they don't really know everything.'

Hera looked up at him, frowning, and looking slightly embarrassed. She let her head droop to her breast. 'I'm sorry everyone', she mumbled, then looked across at Gabe and shrugged, 'please continue, I'll try not to interrupt.'

Gabriel grinned at her, 'Hera, both Martin and I need to apologise as well. We've suspected Mikael for some time, but there were so many other things going on it's been like an octopus with waving arms going in all directions. There was the personal aspect involving Meredith, Justin, and Damian. There were the two books that George was trying to steal. We still don't know how James came to have them. Then there were the drugs involving perhaps Damian again, but definitely Mikael, and possibly James.' He held up his hand. 'Just wait everyone.' He moved across the room to stare out of the window then turned back and continued, 'Then there is the still unanswered question about George's death, and Josephine, and Marina.' He looked pointedly at Meredith. 'I believe, Meredith, you can shine some light on their involvement?'

Meredith contemplated him in silence for several moments. 'No, Gabriel, I can't comment at all. I have no idea what you're talking about.'

Both Bede and Hera snorted in unison.

'Meredith, I think it's time that you stopped playing games. We're all aware', he indicated the room around him, 'that you've been doing some manipulating of your own for quite some time. Josephine and Marina have been feeding you information for years, I suspect, about George's movements. I'm not sure why, unless it's that old business from years ago when he tried to seduce you?' He raised his left eyebrow in what Bede privately thought an arrogant expression.

Meredith predictably reacted angrily, 'How dare you refer to something that is none of your business something that happened before you were even born.'

'I agree, it's not really my business, except where it impacts on what's been happening here. Those two books, valuable as they are, are still a mystery. As I said before, they should have been part of the family archives, but they're not and never have been. They both relate to a period in the family history. That's a little obscure, so we', he indicated

Martin with a sweep of his hand, 'believe there is another player. We don't know when or how they came into James's possession, and if they have anything to do with the smuggling. I suspect not. We do know how and why James was killed, but we don't know yet who ordered it. Hopefully, Mikael will supply some of the details about that contract.'

He looked across at Martin who took up the tale. 'George and Edmondo knew about those two antique books, and Gabe and I suspect that's why they were here in Australia, and why they hired Kamila and her lethal husband to steal them. But we don't have any concrete evidence. All we have are suspicions. Gabriel has to put some more pressure on Kamila. We're convinced she knows more than she's saying, as usual. The Family have ruthless rivals, some dating back centuries, and the rivalry is not restricted to financial matters. Our family have secrets that must be kept, but at the same time, we will continue to work with Inspector Campbell to discover who murdered George. Those deaths were on Australian soil, so Campbell won't let it go. I don't think he's entirely happy with either of us at the moment.'

Gabriel resumed, 'There are some interesting side issues with the drug smuggling that Campbell is still worrying about. Those two thugs of Damian's are not part of the Mikael smuggling racket, they're part of an entirely separate entity. They're more interested in producing designer drugs, while Mikael and company are strictly involved with heroin.' He looked around the room. 'Your set up here supplying flowers all over the world has been recognised as a perfect opportunity for smuggling, which we now know about. Damian, being on hand to manufacture drugs, is something else entirely.' He settled deeper into the couch and pulled Bede closer against his side.

Damian snarled, 'It seems I've been targeted as a baddy who can be persuaded to sink to any depth of depravity with a little strong arm stuff or blackmail.'

Hera grinned across at him, 'Welcome to the family, cuz.'

A thoughtful silence fell on the room as they all individually contemplated that last statement.

# Chapter Thirty-Eight

## *Gabriel Muses*

The next evening, Gabriel was again sitting in the library, idly turning the pages of the *Book of Letters*. There was a mystery here, and he had missed something. Having Kamila and Jakub actually steal the books spoke of desperation. George would never allow himself to appear desperate. He was the ultimate sophisticated debonair thief. He grinned to himself. Yes, thief was the defining word to describe George, but he wasn't a fool, he was clever and devious. There must be a connection between the books other than what he had already observed.

Turning to the beautiful *Book of Illustrations*, he allowed his mind to drift, to just appreciate the illustrations themselves. The colours were so vibrant even though the book was so very old. He fingered the paper, handmade stiff, almost like cardboard heavier than the 300 grams of watercolour paper Meredith had been painting on.

Meredith explained to him the basics of botanical illustration. Why, in those early years, it had been important to have an understanding of plant morphology and access to specimens and detailed references. The family had taken their gypsy heritage and understanding of the medicinal properties of various plants, and turned themselves into herbalists, healers, and finally, magicians, so the legend went.

By the eighteenth century, the printing processes had improved immensely, and it was possible to buy illustrated books on herbs. But this book was a personal reference book. The illustrations were not of beautiful roses, although there were a couple. The plants depicted were mainly herbs, medicinal herbs, detailed in every aspect from seeds through to flowering, making recognition easy. This book was an invaluable and specific reference book for someone and probably painted by the herbalist herself. Continuing to carefully turn the pages, he mused. The value of the book probably wasn't the age itself, but the illustrations and what they represented.

But how and why did James have these books, and how had he acquired them? Both Christies and Sotheby's in London had confirmed the books had not been auctioned there. He was now waiting for a response from Christies in Paris where James was also well known. It had been an expensive undertaking on George's part to try to steal them. Maybe he should try talking to Jakub again. He had no hope of getting any sense out of Kamila, it seemed.

Leaning back in the chair, he mused. Maybe he was looking in the wrong place. Perhaps it was Edmondo who had been the initial target, and George had just been in the wrong place at the wrong time. Edmondo was a small time crook, mostly. Perhaps, he should have more intensive investigations started into his background. What did he personally know about Edmondo? He was younger than George by about fifteen years, so it was a mystery why they spent so much time together. He appeared to be Italian, but he would confirm that with Campbell tomorrow. He and George had a strong connection to Lucien, as had Justin; they'd been partners in various schemes for years. Lucien was a bit of a mystery and always had been. His origins obscure and his source of income debatable.

Pushing back in the chair, he glanced at his watch. It was almost 1.30 a.m., so a couple of quick phone calls to his agents in London and Paris and he could join Bede in bed, while he waited for replies. He flowed to his feet, and stretched his arms above his head, then leaned back stretching the muscles in his back. With his lips curving in a slow smile, he contemplated the thought of her lying warm and relaxed, while he woke her gently. That was one very positive outcome of the last few weeks.

# Chapter Thirty-Nine

## Bloody Dreams Again

He woke suddenly. The dream had been vivid, George running from an unseen pursuer, fear etched clearly across his face, and himself chasing the two fleeing figures. He wiped the perspiration from his face and tried to calm his racing heart. Had they both been fleeing from him, or had he been trying to save George from the one following him? He shook his head trying to recapture the essence of the dream.

Beside him, Bede stirred, mumbling in that delightful way she had when woken suddenly from sleep. He leaned down and nuzzling her neck, murmured, 'It's okay, just a dream. Go back to sleep.'

'No such thing as just a dream in my book, want to talk about it?' Her voice was still slurred from sleep.

'No, I'll wait. It's probably an extension of my trying to sort out why someone would want to murder George. In fact, why someone would actually arrange a contract on him, and why neither Martin nor I heard about it? Damn, it's what we do. Collect lots of miscellaneous information about anything to do with anyone connected to the family. That bit of information should have come to either of us immediately.'

Bede sat up, pulling the sheet up around her shoulders. 'George was a crook, right? He had to have people pissed at him. I can't see how you could possibly be aware of everyone that had a major grudge against him.'

'Right, but he's gone to the trouble of arranging for the theft of those two books. It has to be connected to family somehow.'

'Okay, so who else would be interested? We've proved there is no way they can destabilise Laurent's position, so what else could they prove? It would be interesting to know who actually sold them, or even who owned them. That might explain a few things. Over the years, Laurent had managed to collect a huge number of books detailing the family's beginnings. I'm surprised he wasn't aware of them.'

'Yes, that's the most intriguing part about the books.' A slow smile curved his lips, as he reached for her, drawing her into his arms. 'My pet, you are the perfect partner. Who else would wake at 3 a.m. happy to be involved in a discussion of murder and possible blackmail?'

She grinned. 'Um, can't answer that one, but is it possible James bought the books privately? Why he would do that, I have no idea, but it seems feasible.'

'Yes, but that makes tracing them even more difficult. I'll wait to hear from Paris before starting down that path. In the meantime, seeing that we're awake, I can suggest a way we could pass the time.'

Raising her eyebrows slightly, she slid back down in the bed and grinned up at him. 'What did you have in mind?'

# Chapter Forty

## *Surprise*

'Well, well, well,' all eyes turned to Gabriel, sitting comfortably in a chair at the end of the breakfast table. He had his laptop open, checking e-mails while drinking yet another cup of coffee.

'Don't keep it to yourself, we're all here.'

Gabriel grinned across at Martin, 'An e-mail from Harvey in Paris. It seems that Christie's has no record of the books being sold to James or anyone else, but there is a record of a valuation done on an eighteenth century book styled *A Collection of Letters*, and another done at the same time styled *Illustrated Collection of Botanical Drawings* the valuation was done twenty-five years ago. The books were valued for insurance purposes by one Lucien Bubna-Litic. According to the records, the books were part of a very valuable inheritance he received on his father's death. There was also a lot of antique furniture, paintings, and jewellery. Apparently, he also inherited several properties.' He looked up from the computer and said, with raised eyebrows, 'We have another suspect it seems.'

Martin scowled. 'Bloody George, he stole the books from Lucien, but when and just how did James come to have them?'

Gabriel pulled at his hair in frustration, as he reread the report. Christ, he thought, could George possibly have stolen them from Lucien and then sold them to James? What a thought, but he doubted that James would have bought anything from George.

They needed to contact Lucien, but maybe he should ring Bede's friend, Alain, first. Was there a link between the Caruso-Kern and Bubna-Litic families?

Martin now grinned. 'You realise what this means. If there is a legitimate link between the two families going back hundreds of years?'

Meredith spoke crisply, 'Yes, but it doesn't seem to get us any nearer to knowing who killed George, does it?' She turned to Justin. 'You knew Lucien better than I did, and the three of you were inseparable at one time. Did you ever suspect any connection?'

'No, I didn't. Lucien never suggested such a thing at any time, and if George stole the books, which is starting to look as if he did, how did he find out?'

'Well', Martin thoughtful again, 'the most obvious is that Lucien himself told him. But the not so obvious is that George, being George, liked the look of the books while browsing and helped himself. Lucien may not even be aware that they're missing.'

'Lucien would not have shown the books to George without showing me first. And as you pointed out, Gabriel, if the connection is legitimate, there's the possibility for a huge amount of money involved.' Justin got up from the table and stormed around the room. 'Someone should have done something about George years ago.'

Hera glanced across at Bede, shrugged, then turned to Meredith. 'I don't understand what the problem is, and I thought we decided the books weren't nearly valuable enough.'

Meredith was leaning tiredly back in her chair and looked at Hera, Bede, and Damian's puzzled faces. 'The books themselves don't matter really. It's the implication.' She raised her eyebrows at Justin, still pacing. 'Perhaps you would like to explain to these three.'

Justin snarled.

Bede's face broke into a grin. 'Was that a snarl I heard? Surely the very controlled Justin would never snarl.'

Justin pulled his shoulders back, straightened his back, and took several deep breaths to control his rage. He finally moved quietly across to the table and sat back down. 'The implication of a legitimate claim on the Family dating back for so long has the potential to bankrupt the family depending on where exactly the connection started, and in which branch of the family.'

Justin held up his hand to stop the immediate flood of questions from the three cousins. 'The way the financials were set up in the early days, and have never been substantially changed, is this. Each family has a pro rata percentage share in the profits of the company or companies, depending on which branch of the family they belong to. For instance, the original founding family gets a much larger percentage than one of the smaller offshoots.'

Martin and Gabriel were sitting quietly, both very serious and pale.

Justin's quiet statement had stunned Bede. She gasped, and turning to Meredith, blurted, 'This would explain everything even James's death could be seen in this light.'

Gabe interrupted quietly. 'Let's not jump to conclusions just yet. I admit that's what it looks like at the moment, but we need more information. I won't make the mistake of assuming anything based on insufficient evidence. I did that once before, never again.' He continued. 'Firstly, we need the information about how James got hold of the books and when. He obviously didn't buy them in his usual manner, so we need to check his credit card statements, bank transfers, etc. Secondly, someone needs to talk to Lucien, probably you Justin.' He looked intensely at each person in the room. 'And thirdly, we need to be very careful about what we say and do in the next few days. Take care with phone calls, particularly on mobiles, and even your e-mails. Martin and I will arrange to talk to Alain and get him to continue with his very discreet investigation.'

Bede grabbed Gabriel's hand and gazed intently into his eyes. He simply nodded, while giving her hand a gentle squeeze. 'I'll check his credit card statements. Thankfully, they tediously go back over several years.' Then swinging around, Bede walked purposely out of the room.

Hera grabbed Damian's hand, and pulling him to his feet, said, 'Come on, I'll explain it to you, as you're looking confused. We can look carefully through the last couple of years' tax invoices. James always kept everything.'

'Meredith', Gabriel said, 'I suggest you speak to those three witches in Paris carefully. Justin, you ring Lucien, and Martin, you come with me while I talk to Alain.'

All was silent in the room after everyone left. Pete stepped quietly into the room through the French doors. 'Well, well, well. Gabriel's a clever bugger.'

———— •———

Much later that day, Bede rushed excitedly into the room where Gabriel was again on the phone. 'I think I've found it,' she shouted, skipping across the room, and throwing herself onto Gabe's lap. 'Look,' she thrust an American Express statement under his nose.

'I'll call you back,' Gabe said into the phone, while his arms shot around her. 'What have you found?'

They both looked at the two entries Bede had highlighted. 'This is a small, but exclusive. Meaning, expensive antique bookshop in London. I've been there with Dad. See, these could be the books and he bought them twelve months ago in separate transactions, three days apart. It's still a mystery, but we can phone and get the details.'

Gabriel took the statements from her, holding her tightly across his lap. 'Bede, we're finally getting somewhere.'

Her shout had alerted everyone in the house, and they all crowded into the room.

'Reports, please.' Gabe looked first at Justin.

'Okay, I'll go first. Lucien not only remembers the books, but was aware that George had stolen them.' He held up his hands for silence, and then continued. 'James contacted him about three weeks before his death, told him he had the books, but asked him not to confront George because this time, George had gone too far, and the Family would deal with him. That's all he knew. But he also assured me, I might add with much laughter, there is no connection between the two families. His grandfather told him the story behind the books, which are valuable, but not enough to cause a murder.'

Hera snorted, 'Well, continue. What's the story?'

'It seems the books were stolen centuries ago, but Lucien's ancestor, who he admits was a larcenous sot, stole the books then kept them because he liked them. Simple. They've been in Lucien's family ever since. A sort of in-family joke against the very wealthy Caruso-Kerns,' he shrugged.

# Chapter Forty-One

## Meredith Drops a Bombshell

'Now, I'll continue,' Meredith spoke quietly. 'There's something you should all know. I thought that we could keep it quiet, but Gabriel, you've suspected for a long time.' She gazed at him thoughtfully. 'This must stay in this room because it does affect all of us. The contract for George's death was arrange by Marina and me with help from Josephine and Mette.'

There was a collective gasp, and Pete once again stepped through the French doors. 'I know you're aware I was listening, Gabe, I have a confession to make as well. Josephine is my aunt, and I actually arranged the contract, but I arranged it here. We didn't want the family to be implicated at all. George was desperate to recover the books because I let him think that he had Lucien after him and Laurent as well. Laurent had given him a final warning a while ago, and he thought he was about to be cut off from the family totally. That's what brought him to Australia, and why he contracted the Czech couple. I won't go into specifics, but George was blackmailing both Josephine and Marina. It was something that happened many years ago, and had nothing to do with the family. You knew they were spying for France for years. They knew it had to be George, and I confirmed it quite recently.

'He had really gone too far this time, but I used the books as a way to get him to Australia. I'm sorry about Edmondo, he shouldn't have been touched. He was simply in the wrong place at the wrong time. I don't think Inspector Campbell will ever be able to prove anything definite.'

Meredith looked around the room, her long lost son, two nieces, Gabriel, Martin, Justin, and finally, Pete who spoke, 'James knew about the scheme. I might add that I think the contract you were all looking for had something to do with George. I think somehow George found out about the smuggling, and was probably blackmailing Mikael as well. I was hoping this wouldn't all have to come out, but I should have known you wouldn't give up, Gabriel. What do you want to do?'

Suddenly, they were all shouting at Gabe.

He held up his hand in protest. 'Stop, stop, stop, let me talk. Meredith, I'm not going to do anything, as Justin said earlier, something should have been done about George years ago, and it should have been one of the executives who had the courage to give the order. It shouldn't have been allowed to get to the point where you four women were forced to deal with him.' He turned to Pete and held out his hand. 'Thank you.' There was a collective sigh of relief from everyone.

There was a thoughtful silence in the room, and finally, Gabriel broke the silence. 'If anything comes of it, the Family will deal with it. Meredith, you and Pete will never be in any danger of exposure. We can manufacture evidence if necessary.'

Bede jumped to her feet. 'Do you think this calls for champagne?'

Hera threw a cushion at her, and they all laughed.

## The End

Ps If you are interesting in hearing what happens to Damian, look for the next book in the trilogy.